# The SONGS You've NEVER Heard

## BECKY JERAMS & ELLIE WYATT

CLOCK TOWER

Clock Tower Publishing, an imprint of
Sweet Cherry Publishing Limited
Unit 36, Vulcan House,
Vulcan Road,
Leicester, LE5 3EF
United Kingdom

Small Press of the Year 2021

First published in the UK in 2022
2022 edition

2 4 6 8 10 9 7 5 3 1

ISBN: 978-1-78226-675-4

The Songs You've Never Heard

Cover design and illustration
by Sophie Jones

www.clocktowerpublishing.com

Printed and bound in Turkey
T.40619

# MUSIC ALBUM
# ALSO AVAILABLE

And What?
Didn't I?
Domino Effect
Fireworks Display
Invisible Monsters
Make Friends with the Dark
Maximoo
My Shadow
Next Best Thing
One Day at a Time
Scripts
Second First Impression
The Songs You've Never Heard

**AVAILABLE ON ALL DIGITAL MUSIC STREAMING PLATFORMS**

www.thesongsyouveneverheard.com

# CHAPTER ONE

'Oh my God, that's Meg McCarthy!'

'Who?'

'Caspar McCarthy's sister.'

They think I can't hear them because I've got my headphones on. Annoyingly, my music doesn't drown out their cheery, chirpy voices.

'How do you know that?'

'Every Caspar fan knows that. He's got loads of photos and interviews with her online.'

I turn the music up louder. Lana Del Rey is pouring dreamily into my ears, but even her luscious voice can't distract me from their chatter. They seem about my age or maybe a bit younger. I can't tell anymore. All the fangirls look the same to me these days.

'Are you sure it's her? She doesn't look much like Caspar.'

'I'm positive. He's from Brighton so it makes sense that she'd be hanging around here.'

The waiter hands me my bill on a plate covered with tempting chocolate mints. I push them away to the other end of the table. If there's one habit I've learned growing up with Caspar, it's to never indulge too much. Because someone is always watching.

As I reach for my purse, I feel an unwanted presence over my shoulder. The girls have picked up their drinks and are honing in on me. They are a cloud of blonde hair, sticky lip-gloss and flowery perfume, wrapped up in two beaming smiles. They seem nice.

They always *seem* nice.

'Meg, hi!' says the leader of the duo as though I'm someone in her class or a cousin she's grown up with. 'Do you mind if we sit with you?'

All I can summon up is a non-verbal grunt. I don't bother taking my headphones off, hoping that they'll get the hint.

'I LOVE your eyeliner!' the second girl says, or rather yells right in my face. 'It looks amazing on you. What brand is it? Your whole style is, like, serious goals.'

When I get these kinds of questions on Twitter it's easier to deal with. I can ignore them. Or block them. Unfortunately, there's no way to block human tweets when they turn up at your table.

'Hey, can you hear us?' the first girl asks, waving her hand in front of my face. I am genuinely not real to them. I'm just a 3D version of the photos on my brother's Instagram. 'Can you turn your music down a second?'

'Sorry, I don't have time to chat right now,' I say, getting up to go and pay.

'Rude!' she squeaks indignantly as I brush past her. 'You could at least talk to us for two seconds. We were just trying to be nice!'

Like I said, they're always nice ... at the start.

I make an ungraceful exit, getting my bag tangled up on my chair as I try to escape. I can still hear the girls over my music.

'What the hell is her problem?'

'Probably just jealous of her brother ...'

'Stupid, stuck-up bitch!'

Strangers insult me so often, both in real life and on the Internet, that I guess I should be used to it by now. But the fact is, it still stings me every time.

♫

**Top 5 Friends Who Weren't Really My Friend:**

1. Ruby McNeil, Year 7

My best friend for the whole first year of Senior School, or so I thought. On the final day of term, she begged me to give her Caspar's number but didn't ask for mine. I moved away and she didn't keep in touch.

2. Jessica Brown, Year 8

Sat next to me in every class and came over for sleepovers. After a few stays at mine, she realised Caspar was barely ever home and made excuses to stop seeing me.

### 3. Richard Willbury, Year 9

Asked me out to the movies. Spent the whole date trying to convince me to give his demo to Caspar. He was also a crap kisser.

### 4. Melissa Hunter, Year 10

I probably should have learned my lesson about trusting people by this point, but she seemed so sweet. We were partnered on a music project and for a few weeks we shared ideas without any mention of the C word. However, as soon as our song was finished, she asked me if I could pitch it to Caspar. When I told her that was out of my hands, our newfound friendship fizzled out quicker than a sparkler dropped in a puddle.

### 5. Ness Hawkins, Years 10 to 12

You know the story by now. She was all over me like a rash until she realised Caspar didn't live with us anymore. Then, for some reason, I was public enemy number one. And I still am.

♫

I like lists. Unlike people, lists never let you down. Lists are sturdy and accurate. They bring order into the world when everything else is a swirling vortex of chaos. This is why I list everything. Favourite songs. Revision notes. Facts. Feelings. If I were to write a list of things that keep me sane, lists would be at the top of my list. And the sea would be number two. I took it for granted before we moved away, but now I'm back here I vow never to underappreciate that churning, grey expanse again.

London was totally devoid of horizon. All smog and noisy madness – like a depressing, grotty version of Disneyland where you end up spending all your time standing in a queue while your soul leaves your body one atom at a time. Not that anyone in my family cared much about my disintegrating soul during The London Years™. Why would they? My soul was not the thing getting playlisted on Radio 1. Therefore, I was given no choice but to fulfil my sisterly duty, i.e. silently putting up with being nothing more than a bit part in The Caspar Show.

My time in London was an endless, nauseating carousel of people, parties and prying eyes at every window. I didn't think it was ever going to stop. Until one day … it just did. The minute Cass turned eighteen he insisted we all get the hell out of his hair. So that was it – bye-bye Big Smoke and hello Brighton, once again. Mum and Dad had a million excuses for moving back. Their favourite was claiming that Caspar was out on tour so much that it didn't make sense to rent an expensive place in Putney.

They even started pretending it was about me. *It's the perfect year for you to change schools, Meggy, before all the important coursework starts.* Blah, blah, blah. Whatever. More like: Little Lord Cass says jump and my parents put on their gym shoes.

Usually the beach is heaving in July, but today the weather looks like the start of some kind of disaster movie involving

**9**

shipwrecks. There are still a couple of Mountain Warehouse families down here, valiantly pretending to enjoy their houmous sandwiches in the wind. And the odd dog-walker. And a miserable, hungover-looking hen party dressed as bedraggled Playboy bunnies. And me.

I always come here when I don't want to be interrupted. The pebbles might be uncomfortable, but it's the perfect place to get my thoughts together and write song lyrics. Today I don't have a pen or paper though, only my phone. I scroll through my playlist of artists until I reach my own name. Then I hit play.

*Looks like I told*
*Too many lies*
*You've fallen for my disguise*

*If I knew*
*How to tell the truth*
*You'd have seen it in my eyes*

Closing my eyes, I let the song wash over me. The person I wrote it for comes crashing into my mind like a wave. I remember the way I felt when I wrote it. The intense blast of emotion that demanded to be unleashed. At the time, I didn't question a single line because every word was true and raw and necessary.

Now I only have questions. Does the melody move in the right way? Do the lyrics sound clumsy? Are my chords boring? Does the recording do justice to the orchestra I heard in my head when I first started writing it?

The answer is no. Of course it doesn't. After all, there's only so much I can do with a laptop and a basic microphone in the corner of my bedroom. Dad has taught me bits and pieces of music production, but I'm nowhere near his or Caspar's level. I'll need to watch a few thousand more YouTube tutorials before I get that good.

I guess this is one more song that will exist forever in digital purgatory, along with all my other unheard demos. And I guess I'll never have the guts to send it to him ...

*Will your heart wait while*
*My heart's breaking?*
*Is it too late*
*To make a second first impression?*

I sigh and pause the music for a moment. The sounds that surround me clear my head a little. The wind and the squawking seagulls. Taking a deep breath, I scroll to a new song and press play.

My brother's chiselled face appears on the screen, brooding with a hint of a smile. His dark eyes stare out with complete confidence from under a mess of dirty blonde hair. It's the cover from his first single 'Next Best Thing', released when he was just sixteen – a whole year younger than I am now.

The music hits my ears, a cool mix of dance and acoustic that still sounds cutting-edge four years on. Caspar's voice is smooth honey, filled with emotion. It's beautiful and intimidating at the same time.

*Full stop, listen up I've got a question*
*Tell me now am I wasting feelings?*
*Telling stories you don't believe in …*

There's a reason people noticed his early demos. Sure, they got tweaked and polished by high-level producers, but the seeds of what made the songs so special were all sown by Caspar himself. He always has a concept and a vision when he's writing. He writes the kind of songs you feel like you've known forever, even if you've only heard them once. He writes songs that make sense.

*I don't wanna be your next best thing*
*I don't wanna be another five-minute wonder*
*More than just a catchy song you sing*
*Not the kind you throw away*
*Want you to hit replay*
*Over and over I'm gonna show ya*
*That I really wanna get to know know know ya …*

The irony of the lyrics isn't lost on me. Caspar has never been anybody's 'next best thing'. He's number one on everyone's list. And yet he still had to claim the sentiment for his own song concept. He couldn't even let me have my own misery to wallow in without taking a piece of it too.

*I'm not gonna be your next best thing*
*Coz I'm everlasting …*

I rip my headphones off and toss them onto the pebbles. I think I've had enough music for one day.

Sometimes I wish I could be more like my brother was at my age. He was always so bloody sure of his own talent.

This is why he has millions of listeners, whereas I only have two. And one of them is me.

# CHAPTER TWO

So, in case you hadn't guessed, I'm totally procrastinating right now. The whole reason I came into town today was to job hunt, not sulk on the beach comparing myself to Caspar. But for some reason he manages to infiltrate everything I do, even when it's got nothing to do with him.

I stuff my phone back in my bag and head into The Lanes. Obviously my dream job would be well-paid and creative, but as my CV has a grand total of nine GCSEs, one commendation for my achievements in the Year 10 debating society and zero hours of actual work experience, it's looking unlikely.

Mum is insisting on me getting 'a taste of the real world' this summer, but as far as I can tell the real world pretty much sucks for teenagers. In order to get a job, you need a reference ... which you needed a job to get ... which you needed a reference for ... Urgh, the endless hamster wheel of unemployability. Oh well, maybe there's a charitable owner of an indie clothes store who will see my potential. Or take pity on me.

I feel a familiar buzz of excitement as I weave my way through the Saturday shoppers. (Hello Mr Moustachioed Victorian Steampunk bar-tender-slash-magician-looking guy. Where did you get that waistcoat?) Rainbow flags hang from the buildings and the trademark Brighton smells of fish and chips and Small Batch Coffee hang in the air. It's a beautiful assault on the senses and, as usual, I get distracted.

The sound of a piano catches my ear and I follow the delicious melody, looking for the Ryan Gosling jazz pianist of my dreams, only to discover the piano is actually being played by a dog. Yep, you heard me. A busking dog. Only in Brighton can you find a) such a talented musician, b) playing an ACTUAL real piano in the street, c) dressed as Rowlf the dog from The Muppets. Before I realise what I'm doing, I've listened to four songs in a row.

I'm getting nowhere fast so I reluctantly pull myself away from the music and push on through a massive crowd of lost-looking fourteen-year-old students who have collectively lost the ability to choose a direction and walk in it.

I thought the swearing was only in my head, but a few choice expletives must have slipped out because a sweet olive-skinned girl looks up at me and says, 'There's no need to be so rude. We're only trying to find our way to the Pavilion.' Oops. I decide the most mature response is to pretend I can't speak English and hurry on ahead of her.

It seems to take me twice as long as usual to make it to my favourite three-storey Victorian terraced shop at the end of Kensington Street. I stop outside, like I do every Saturday. It's some perverse form of self-torture. I spend the whole week psyching myself up and telling myself this weekend will be different. But when I get there, it never is.

I mean, how hard can it be to just talk to him? What's the matter with me?

The shop bell rings as I enter Aladdin's Cave. Unoriginal name, granted, but very apt because there is junky, second-hand treasure bursting from every available space. Rails heave with 1970s flares and vintage coats still smelling of their original owner's perfume, Trilby hats, platform boots, fifty-year-old Chanel handbags, Japanese patterned parasols ... It goes on and on like some kind of retro optical illusion. And the best thing about this optical illusion is I can blend in, so no one knows I'm here.

My heart rate shifts up a gear as I look around. He's not here. I head to the first floor, which is as overcrowded as the ground floor. There's no sign of him. Maybe he's on his lunch break? I'm poised between the velvet curtain of a changing room and a cabinet of Game Boy cartridges, about to give up hope, when I finally catch sight of him.

Matty Chester.

I know it sounds like a total cliché, but the effect is physical. Dry mouth, blurry eyes and that rollercoaster feeling in my stomach. Every clear thought leaves my mind and I realise I've forgotten to breathe.

He's explaining one of the old, chunky cameras to a middle-aged woman. Of course he is. What else would he be doing? Explaining tedious camera functions is one of his favourite pastimes. That's why he loves this job. I watch the enthusiasm spilling out of him, in the adorable curve of his mouth as he chatters excitedly with his usual excessive detail.

Matty loves *things*. He finds meaning in what other people find pointless. His energy for life is totally infectious.

Losing my nerve, I step back behind a stack of old suitcases like some kind of deranged stalker. The woman he's assisting smiles politely, but she's clearly not interested in a sale. He takes it on the chin. 'Alright then, Madam. If you need any more help, give me a shout!'

Adrenaline courses through my veins at the sound of his voice.

He puts the camera back in the display cabinet and I watch the way he moves. He is gentle. Careful. He has to stand on tiptoes to reach the back of the cabinet, causing his David Bowie T-shirt to ride up just above his waist. I can't help imagining what it would be like to put my hands there, just above his belt.

At school people make fun of him. They think he's weird and geeky. But they don't see what I see. When I look at Matty, I see hope. I see proof that the world can be a better place.

There's no point trying to talk to him. I know these feelings could never be mutual, so it's probably best if I creep back downstairs before he sees me. Anyway, this painful, ridiculous process is necessary if I want to improve my songwriting. Isn't unrequited love what so many great songs are about? With one last longing gaze in his direction, I turn to leave.

Suddenly, I'm face-to-face with my ex-friend Ness Hawkins, who pops up like an evil meerkat from behind a rail of denim jackets. She yells my name so loudly that everyone in the shop turns to look at me. Including Matty.

'Meg! Oi, Earth to Meg!'

You know when dogs pretend to play dead? Well, that's what I'm doing. Keeping completely still, eyes fixed on the floor, hoping that she'll disappear back into her burrow.

'Hey, did you hear me?' Ness bellows. Melissa snorts with laughter behind her. 'God Meg, you're always in your own little dream world.'

There was a time when both of these girls were my friends, but now ... not so much. They might talk to me in syrupy voices, but the words always have a bitter, nasty taste. To make things worse, Matty is looking right at me. There's nothing I can do. I'm cornered.

'Hi Ness,' I say flatly. 'Sorry, I didn't see you guys there.'

'You're such a space-case,' Ness giggles, tossing her immaculate waves of caramel-blonde hair behind her shoulder. 'What are you doing in here anyway? Surely you don't need smelly old vintage clothes when you get tons of new stuff for free? Or is this all part of your try-hard rock-chick aesthetic?'

I flick awkwardly through the jackets in front of me, scraping the hangers as loudly as I can to drown out Ness's passive-aggressive comments. 'You'd be surprised how much free can actually cost ...'

It's true that brands do send me freebies, but in return they want me to wear what they want, when they want. They give me exact instructions on how to pose for Instagram and what caption to write like I'm their real-life dress-up doll. That's why I would send it all back if my parents would let me. It's anything but free.

'I seriously don't get you, Meg,' Ness exclaims, still in her fake, sugary tone. 'You must be the only girl in the entire world who can find a reason to moan about people giving you stuff!' She turns to Melissa, laughing. 'Right, Liss?'

'Definitely,' Melissa nods. 'I'd literally die to have your life, Meg.'

That's right Ness, get your little minion to back you up. Right on cue. I wouldn't expect anything less. I feel my cheeks burning with embarrassment because I know Matty is watching this whole excruciating scene play out. I have to get out of here. Now.

'I've got to go,' I mutter, but Ness employs her usual selective hearing.

'So I'm having a huge party for my birthday next week and I'm trying to get some outfit inspiration. I'm not exactly loving these old Grandma dresses though.'

'I'm sure you'll find something.' I turn to leave.

'Ooh, totally random idea,' Ness squeals, blocking my path. 'Do you think Caspar would come along on the night? Maybe play a little set or something?'

'YES!' Melissa shouts, nodding her head like a demented dashboard-dog. 'That would be amazing!'

I can't believe the nerve of these girls. We're not friends. We don't even pretend to be anymore. For the last few months of the school year neither of them has had a single nice word to say to me or about me, and now they want me to do them a favour for a party I'm not even invited to? WT actual F?!

As if reading my mind, Ness keeps talking manically at me. 'You can come too if you want. I just didn't think it would be your scene, since you're a loner goth or whatever now. But I'm sure everyone would want to talk to you if you convinced Caspar to come. You'd be a hero to the whole year group.'

'He's not actually here right now,' I reply, my eyes darting to anywhere but Ness's face. I feel my neck heating up like it always does when I'm lying. 'So, you know ... It would be pretty pointless to ask him.'

'Oh really?' Ness counters, her tone a disbelieving sneer. 'If he's not here then how come I read on *MuzikHype* that he was working on his new album in Brighton?'

Melissa jumps in right behind her. 'Yeah, I read that too! There were photos of him on the pier from like a week ago.'

I don't answer. I badly need to get out of here, but they're both still in my way, like a couple of bitchy bouncers.

Ness folds her arms and tuts. 'Why do you always have to lie about Caspar? Are you jealous of him or something?' She shoots Melissa a conspiring look, then shakes her head like she feels sorry for me. 'Seriously, it would make everyone's life if Caspar came to the party. I mean, even if it was for ten minutes. Why can't you just get over yourself and ask him?'

'And why can't you just get out of my face?'

Oh no. That came out a lot more aggressively than I intended. And of course, God's brother Sod decides this is the exact moment Matty walks over to us.

'Is everything alright over here?' he asks, blinking in bemusement behind his black-rimmed glasses. 'I thought I recognised you all from over there. Can I help you guys?'

He's so polite. We've all been at the same school for years, but he speaks to us tentatively, as if he's not yet earned any real level of familiarity. Why is he so damn cute?! And WHY did I just lose my cool in front of the one person whose opinion I care about?

'Oh, hey Matty,' Ness says in her oh-so-casual-nothing-bothers-me voice. 'We're great, thanks. I'm shopping around for a new party dress. It's majorly stressful. Especially when you bump into certain people who think they're better than everyone else. Know what I mean?'

Melissa bursts into spiteful giggles at Ness's dig. I want the clothes rails to swallow me up.

'No, I'm not sure I do know what you mean.' Matty scans their faces, uncertain of what to make of the situation. Then his eyes land on me. His gaze is so bright and sincere that I can't bear to meet it. It's too much. 'Meg? Are you alright?'

When he says my name, it's enough to make me self-destruct.

'Can everyone stop harassing me?' My voice comes out harsh and hard and ugly. For some unknown reason a dark force takes over my vocal cords whenever Matty tries to speak to me. 'Look, I've got to go. Get out of my way ...'

I push roughly past the three of them and run down the stairs. I can feel them all gaping in horror and I know they'll all talk about how awful I am the second I'm out of their sight.

Matty's bound to tell them that I'm always like this to him – a total cow. And the worst of it is that he doesn't know why or what the hell he's ever done to me. And let's be honest, he hasn't done anything. This is all on me.

Fighting back tears I take a deep breath and leave the shop. I've had enough now. I just want to go home, where I can cry without anyone seeing me.

# CHAPTER THREE

'MEG!' Mum yells from behind a camera lens. 'What have I told you about knocking before coming in? It took me twenty minutes to get him in that God-forsaken outfit and now you've ruined the shot.'

Maximillian, our portly, Persian Blue cat has some sort of apron around his middle and a doll-sized chef's hat tied to his head.

'What the hell is she doing to you?' I ask, picking him up. He's a heavy, fluffy sack of potatoes.

'I'm keeping on top of our social media,' Mum huffs as she gets up from the floor. 'He's only a few hundred away from 90,000 followers!'

This is probably the point where I should mention that my Mum is insane. She runs the official Instagram for our cat and takes the role of making kitty-costumes and backdrops *very* seriously. Her latest creation is a cardboard kitchen with 'Great Kittish Bake-off' painted on the side.

'And dressing him up like a chef is going to get him more fans, is it?' I ask sarcastically.

'We've got to think outside the box if we want to catch people's attention,' Mum answers, still looking at the camera. 'It's proven in the stats that the costume photos perform five times better than all other posts.' She flicks through her shots, frowning at the screen. 'Oh, these aren't right. The light's no good. Why did you have to come in and distract him?'

I put Maximillian down and he plods forlornly back to his baking station. 'I'm so sorry. I thought I actually lived here or something.'

Mum tuts at me. 'I know this is a big joke to you, but keeping the fans happy is a serious business. They absolutely love our Maximoo and doing this keeps the McCarthy brand in their minds while Caspar's working on the album.'

Wow. It's been, what? All of two minutes since I walked in the door? And already the two main key words in this family have been checked off. Caspar, tick. McCarthy brand, tick. OK, technically that's three words, but the amount Mum says them they may as well all run together in one big long super-word, *CasparMcCarthyBrand*.

'By the way, have you done your Squeezy Culture promo thing yet? That package has been sitting there unopened for nearly a month now.'

'I'm getting to it,' I grumble, glancing towards the mountainous pile of branded boxes in the corner of our living room. 'But you know I hate their stuff. It isn't my style.'

'Jazz it up with one of your jackets or something,' Mum suggests, waving vaguely. 'You'll make it work, my little fashionista.'

'I'll get to it later,' I sigh.

Mum finally puts down the camera and looks at me. 'Oh, how did I get such talented babies? A musical genius son and a fashionable daughter. A fashionable, *smart* daughter.'

I hate it when she does this. Trying to make out that taking a few selfies in ridiculous outfits is even remotely comparable to writing an album. Caspar is creating and working on his own ideas, whereas I'm just wearing someone else's.

'Ooh, how did the job hunt go?' she suddenly asks, the thought popping into her brain like a big, empty bubble. 'Any luck?'

'Kind of,' I say, edging my way to the door. 'One of the hotels was looking and I tried a few shops too. I guess I'll have to wait and see.'

I decide not to mention the humiliating frenemy incident that played out in front of my crush. That's one memory that will haunt me long enough without my mother knowing about it too.

'A job will be so good for you,' Mum says with a smile. 'Keep you grounded, you know?'

Yeah right! Because what with my super-famous brother and my mum who is obsessed with getting followers for our cat on Instagram, *I'm* the one who needs grounding. Oh, and then there's Dad. Don't get me started on him. He never grew out of being a raver, but tries to compensate for all his years of clubbing with daily yoga and juicing. Not that his current hippy health routine can rid him of his cringeworthy acid-house smiley tattoo. (Drunken mistake in Ibiza, so we're told.)

'It's difficult though,' I say. 'No one wants to hire a teenager with no work experience and most places pay a pittance. It's basically like signing up for slave labour.'

'Oh, nonsense!' Mum exclaims. 'Plenty of your friends have

weekend jobs. And it's not always about the money, Meggy. Working teaches you valuable life skills.'

I have to stop myself from pointing out the irony of this lecture. Mum hasn't worked a single day since Caspar signed his big deal. Not unless you count making cat props as a job, which I most definitely don't.

'Whatever ...' I mumble under my breath.

Mum's pretty features darken into a scowl. 'I know you don't think helping Caspar is a real job, but I can assure you it is. There's no way he would keep on top of everything without me. Who would organise his emails and sort out all of his promo?'

'Err, possibly his manager?' I reply, unable to keep the sarcasm out of my voice. 'The guy he's actually paying to do all that stuff?'

'Yes, yes,' Mum dismisses. 'But TJ's only got one pair of hands and Caspar is a bloody handful and a half – we both know that. His whole career would fall apart without me. I'm the invisible glue that holds everything together!'

Invisible is not the word I'd use to describe my mum. Maybe she's got confused with *visible*. Or *loud*. Or perhaps *totally overdramatic*. Those are all much, much better descriptions of her.

'Maximillian McCarthy! Stop destroying your cattenberg cake! I haven't got the shot yet, you great big, ungrateful animal.'

Evidently, I have now used up my sixty-second allowance of Mum's attention so I decide to escape to my room. I'm so over thinking about job-hunting and posing for photos, and the bloody *McCarthyBrand*. I'm done with rehashing the shittiest moments of today. It's time to block it all out, plug in to my music and disappear into my own little world.

At the top of the stairs, I'm bombarded by the sound of a heated argument between the two men in my family.

'Just give it a chance. You can't write it off when we haven't even finished it yet.'

'NO! This was a terrible idea. What the hell was I thinking?'

'It's not terrible. Honestly, I think we've got something here. It needs decent production of course, but it's a brilliant starting point, it's a good shape.'

'It's shaped like a turd, Dad! That's what bloody shape it is.'

Footsteps thunder along the hall and a second later I'm face-to-face with two glaring, dark eyes under a grey hoodie.

'Jesus, Meg,' Caspar shouts in my face. 'Where the hell did you come from?'

I shake my head at my vain, spoiled, famous pop star big brother.

'Hello Caspar,' I say, dryly. 'Nice to see you too.'

# CHAPTER FOUR

**Top 5 Things I Can't Believe About My Family:**

1. That there are girls and boys across the UK and beyond who have posters of Caspar on their bedroom walls. Why would anyone in their right mind willingly look at his sulky face?

2. That my dad still hasn't given up his dreams of being a famous music producer, despite the fact he's super old now and has no idea what's current. He thinks he does, but he almost always gets it wrong. I don't want to sound mean. He does have a lot of talent and he taught me everything I know about music. However, I don't think he should quit his day job any time soon, which, by the way, is the very rock-and-roll profession of 'digital architect'.

3. That Mum *did* quit her day job. She was a receptionist at a dance studio before Caspar got signed. Now she spends her life

running around after him, driving him to interviews, talking to companies on his behalf, and sticking her nose into everything his manager TJ should be doing. (3a. Caspar pays her for this!)

4. That, believe it or not, Caspar and I were close once upon a time and loved playing silly games and singing together. These days, not so much. Now we argue more than we get along.

5. That anyone would see our family and actually want to be like us. I always see photos of the four of us being shared online with #FamilyGoals alongside them. If only people knew the truth behind those pictures. We are as disappointingly dysfunctional as every other flawed family out there.

♫

Caspar looks abnormally tired and his hair is a scruffy mess. I don't think he's been sleeping much lately, what with the stress of making the new album and the even more stressful business of staying out all night being a player.

'Oh hi, Meggy!' Dad calls down. 'You're back! Come and take a listen to what me and Cass have been working on this morning. It's brilliant.'

'No! It's not,' Caspar shouts up the stairs. 'God, Dad … just accept that it's not working. I don't know what possessed me to even try this in the first place.'

'You're not giving it a chance. I know I'm not as up-to-date as all these cool London producers, but we could get someone else to polish it up afterwards. This is about laying down foundations and getting back to your roots.'

Caspar rolls his eyes to the ceiling and shoves past me.

'I thought you wanted to capture the good old days?' Dad squashes me against the hallway bookcase as he runs after Prince Caspar. I am just an annoying obstacle in his way. 'Remember all those brilliant jam sessions we had when you were a kid? There was magic in that, Cass! I think our track really captures your original vibe.'

'It's not right,' Caspar growls, grabbing for his jacket by the front door. 'It sounds old-fashioned and forgettable. Have you heard Shawn Mendes' latest record, Dad? He wouldn't be caught dead releasing this kind of insipid shit.'

'But you're not Shawn Mendes, you're Caspar McCarthy. It's not a bad thing to be trying something different. We could change the chords on the chorus, add a post-hook on the end?'

It always makes me cringe when Dad uses songwriting terminology. He's picked up loads of it from watching Caspar work and now he thinks he's part of the 'biz' himself. I'm sure he and Mum were born to be celebrity luvvies. They can't get enough of all the buzzwords and name-dropping that comes with having a famous son.

'I'm sorry, OK? I told you not to get your hopes up. Things have moved on way too much since our old stuff. It's not gonna cut it anymore. Just stick with designing websites, eh Dad?'

I watch with pity as Dad's shoulders droop. He looks like a Labrador that's been hit on the nose with a rolled-up newspaper. I know how proud he is of all the songs they created together.

They used to put them on YouTube and get thousands of views and enthusiastic fan comments.

But that was a long time ago. The moment TJ discovered Caspar and signed him, my brother never really needed Dad again.

As if to emphasise this point, Caspar pulls a packet of cigarettes out of the back pocket of his jeans. Wow. Awesome move bro. Because nothing says 'I'm-all-grown-up-and-independent' like wrecking your own lungs. If this is his latest way of upsetting everyone it's definitely going to work.

'Mate, mate ...' Oh no. Here we go with Dad's feeble attempt at playing the bad cop. 'What are you doing? You shouldn't be doing that.'

Caspar stares at Dad without answering and deliberately lights his cigarette.

I prepare for the fallout in three ... two ....

'CASPAR! What the hell do you think you're doing?' Mum throws open the living room door. 'You are not allowed to smoke in this house! I thought you'd given up. You're going to ruin your voice ... and my soft furnishings!'

'My voice isn't the problem here, Mum,' Caspar replies sharply, yanking open the front door. 'It's the totally uninspired material that's messing everything up.'

'But the songs are wonderful!' Mum sighs. 'You're overthinking this album far too much, sweetheart. You've got to start getting it out there.'

Dad nods in wild agreement. 'Exactly. You can't give up on our song before it's finished. People are dying to hear the real, raw Caspar McCarthy and together we can give them that!'

Caspar exhales once more in a taunting, languid kind of way. 'Whatever. I'm outta here.'

He slams out of the house, donning his trademark, overpriced sunglasses. He assures us they stop fans from recognising him, but I highly doubt it. Despite moaning about signing autographs in public, I know how much he loves the attention.

Dad's feeble bad cop has become pathetic sad cop. He turns to Mum. 'I don't understand why he's being like this. I thought we'd made something really magic today. Come up and have a listen.'

'I think it's wonderful that you're trying to push him,' Mum says, following him upstairs. 'It's been months now and he's got absolutely nowhere with this bloody album! I'm honestly worried the fans will move on to someone else, and we're still recouping the last tour.'

'Maybe I'm an embarrassing old fart and I shouldn't have interfered, but people loved those old demos, didn't they?'

I trail behind them, wishing I could be uninterested. But really, I'm desperately curious to hear what they've written.

*When did it stop being easy?*
*When did the power go out?*
*My answers always felt certain*
*And never left me space for doubt*

*But now I'm tripping up and stumbling*
*The walls around me crumbling*

*When the lights all blow out, one by one*
*Can't see clearly anymore*
*Oh, I've been here before*
*And the fight inside me is never done*
*So until I find a spark*
*Better make friends with the dark*

The song is actually really good. Sure, the production is basic, but Dad is right. It has the same melodic magic as Caspar's early material. I dunno what my brother's problem is. It's like he wants to hate every idea before he's even given it a chance.

Mum and Dad replay the song and become engrossed in the same old 'how-to-please-Caspar' conversation that's been going on in this house for weeks now. *Oh no! Poor baby Cass-Cass has lost his artistic inspiration! What will we do? How many stupid cat pictures can we take to keep the fans interested while he shags his way around Brighton?*

Meanwhile, I hover, unnoticed in the doorway to Dad's studio. I can hear so much potential in the song. I want to suggest a harmony that would lift the chorus and an obvious place where an instrumental hook could go. But what would be the point? No one has asked for my opinion so I don't say a word.

In this family, I'm completely invisible.

# CHAPTER FIVE

My phone pings in my bag twenty-four hours a day, but the only time I enter the online world is here, at my computer in the sanctuary of my bedroom. I try and limit the amount of doomscrolling I do. I know all too well it's as destructive as it is addictive. I'd never be able to keep up with the endless stream of inane tweets and emails that flood my inbox anyway.

Both my followers and my parents criticise me for it all the time. They want me online and available for their entertainment every second of my existence. It's exhausting. I'd rather be in the moment by myself without a whole cyber-entourage tagging along behind me.

Since Caspar has gone silent on his fans, it's apparently up to the rest of us to oil the cogs of the *McCarthy* machine. Oh yeah, did I mention that it's OK for golden balls to take a break from social media? That's because he's the artist and he's 'creating, darling' and it's mysterious and it causes hype, and Ed Sheeran did the same thing, and it builds suspense for the album and blah, blah, blah.

OK then, let's give the people what they want. I open Twitter and type the first thing that comes into my head. This feels so pointless, but it's honestly not worth having yet another fight with Mum over it.

 **@MegMcCarthy** Love living in Brighton! Is there anything more relaxing than listening to music on the beach? What's on your playlist right now?

Mum always tells me I should ask questions to get the fans involved. I actually don't mind getting discussions going, but I always find the responses somewhat soul-destroying.

Sure enough, within ten minutes, my five classic types of followers have left their predictable comments. Since I love lists so much, let's go through them shall we?

**Top 5 Annoying Tweeters:**

1. The Wannabe BFF

OMG MEG!!!! When were you on the beach?! I was just there today! Would LOVE to meet up and hang out! You're my idol – DM me!!! <3 <3 <3

How can you idolise someone just for the clothes they wear? These girls don't know me. They never answer my questions or engage in a proper conversation. I'm just their fantasy best friend in a deluded dream where getting to know me equals getting one step closer to Caspar.

2. The Caspar-Questioner

> ENOUGH TEASING! JUST TELL US WHEN CASPAR'S ALBUM IS GONNA BE FINISHED ALREADY?!!!

In some ways, I admire the 'fans' who get straight to the point. There are no hidden motives or trying to pretend they care about me. I'm simply an extra channel of information. But the thing is, I can't give them any answers. Caspar never tells me anything. The only exclusive I've got is that my brother is a colossal pain in the arse.

3. The Self-Promoter

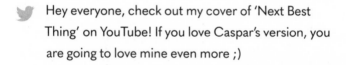

> Hey everyone, check out my cover of 'Next Best Thing' on YouTube! If you love Caspar's version, you are going to love mine even more ;)

The music industry is tough. I know you have to stand out if you want to survive. Otherwise you end up like me, getting nowhere because nobody knows your music even exists. However, it's so rude to try to get an instant, ready-made fan base by hijacking someone else's Twitter. There's no shortcut to fame and fortune, whatever the reality shows would have you believe.

## 4. The Pervert

🐦 U r soooo hot, got any new pics?? Do u have a bf? I
could show u a REALLY good time ;) ;)

OK, this one is self-explanatory.

## 5. The Hater

🐦 No offence, but you are such a try-hard. Who gives
a shit if you're at the beach? NO ONE CARES!!!

I've saved the worst for last. A lot of the comments I get on a
daily basis are 100% toxic. It doesn't matter how many positive
ones I get alongside them, it's always the nasty, bitter and most
hateful words that jump out at me from the screen.

🐦 Not you trying to be a celeb. You're not Caspar FFS.
Sorry but you are pointless & have no talent. 💀💀💀

🐦 Why does everyone call **@MegMcCarthy** pretty?
I don't get it. She looks like a miserable ugly cow
most of the time!!!

🐦 Don't act like you're soooo nice! My friend goes to
your school and says you are rude and horrible to
everyone! Bitch, go die.

Caspar hires PR people to run his social media and focuses all his energy on music instead. I guess he couldn't survive without them. God knows he's neurotic enough about reviews and chart positions without having to deal with the poisonous hellscape of online comment sections as well.

I know I should ignore this kind of stuff, but stepping away from it is far easier said than done. Sometimes I'm compelled to go back and revisit the worst messages again and again, and I have no idea why. It's like I have to keep checking they're real and that they're as bad as I remember them.

*No talent. Ugly. Pointless. Rude. Bitch.*

It feels like these words will leave their scars on my heart forever.

*Go die.*

I force myself to look away. That's more than enough 'feedback' for tonight. This is why I don't share my music. The thought of all these strangers ripping apart my heartfelt creations is too much to bear. I can't do it. If people make fun of my fashion or my personality, I can deal with it. I'm not trying to be a model or anyone's best friend. But music is different. Music is personal.

That's why there is only one person who I trust enough to send my songs to. He's the only living human who has ever heard my questionable production skills, my unfiltered lyrics and my slightly nervous voice.

He is my biggest supporter. He knows my darkest secret.

And he has no idea who I am.

I switch tabs and load up the Discord server I've grown to know and love: *Music Hunger – Support group for music addicts across the world!*

I know he won't be online yet to chat to in real time, but I'm craving his healing words right now, especially after today's rotten batch of evil tweets.

Sure enough, there is one new message waiting in my inbox. From BandSnapper. The very sight of his username releases a thousand frantic butterflies in my stomach.

I click *open*, exhilarated at the thought of whatever's waiting. At least I know this message will be one worth reading.

# CHAPTER SIX

I have a little list-based game that I like to play with BandSnapper. It's how I first got his attention on the server and we've been playing it ever since we met. At the start of every DM we set each other a category: top 5 songs that dot dot dot. The category could be anything: top 5 songs that I listened to when I was ten; top 5 songs that make me want to smash my laptop; top 5 Songs with (insert word here) in the title. That one is a favourite of ours. In fact, it's today's category. As I read BandSnapper's answers, the stress of this evening's cyber-harassment melts away.

> **BandSnapper:** Hey LostGirl.
>
> I've got to say, this round was a tricky one.
>
> I had way more than five on my list, but here goes ...
>
> Top 5 Songs With 'Girl' In The Title:
>
> 1. Girls Go Wild – LP
>
> 2. Bad Girls – M.I.A

3. Girls Chase Boys – Ingrid Michaelson

4. Are You Gonna Be My Girl – Jet

5. Girls – The 1975

Now, for you – top 5 songs that inspired you to start songwriting?

This is a hard one. I'm sure you have billions of songs that inspire you, but just type the first five that pop into your brain, even if you think of something better a second later. (I know, I'm evil!)

I'd love to know more about your influences. Your songs are so beautiful and unique. I can hear hints of other artists in the melodies, but there is always something specifically 'you' about them.

Not that I know who 'you' are. Can you believe it's been over two years since we started chatting? Surely it's time for some more real life details – you know loads about me ... How about if I send you a puppy-dog eyes selfie? No? Not attractive?

How's the new recording going btw? No rush, but can I hear it when it's ready?

Yours impatiently,

BandSnapper x

**BandSnapper:** PS. Damnit, I just remembered another song with 'Girl' in the title!

Can I have six and add 'Girls/Girls/Boys' by Panic! at the Disco too?!

As soon as I've read BandSnapper's song choices I add them to the Spotify playlist where I keep all of his recommendations. He has the most eclectic music taste of anyone I've ever met – everything from rock, indie and EDM to classical, country and cheesy pop. Often the songs are obscure and I've never heard them. But one thing is for sure: if he likes them I will too.

This is why his opinion means so much to me. He seriously knows his stuff, so I must be doing something right.

> **LostGirl:** Hey BandSnapper.
> Yes, you are TOTALLY cheating by adding an extra song! And your category choice is impossible. How am I supposed to choose? I'm going to shut my eyes and type whatever comes into my mind. OK, here goes. Songs that made me want to write music myself ...
> 1. Next Best Thing – Caspar McCarthy

As soon as it appears on the screen, I hit backspace even though it is undoubtedly true. Hearing Caspar and Dad constantly writing songs naturally made me want to write my own. But I can't tell BandSnapper that. It's too close to home. It might be the one clue that gives away who I am. Plus, he doesn't even like Caspar's music as far as I can tell. It's not like he's ever mentioned it. So I start again from scratch.

> 1. Happier Than Ever – Billie Eilish
> 2. Homesick – Dua Lipa
> 3. Royals – Lorde

4. Symphony – Clean Bandit feat. Zara Larsson

5. Moral of the Story – Ashe

Arrrgggh! I'm already thinking of five different songs ... and another five ... and another! I've been inspired by so many artists from so many decades. My whole family loves music and we play it constantly. If you ask me this question again next week, the answers will be completely different.

**LostGirl:** Shit, I forgot to add a musical theatre song! OK, that gives me an idea for your round ...

Top 5 songs from a musical. (Yes. They are my guilty pleasures and I need you to embrace them.)

In answer to your questions. No, I'm sorry but puppy-dog eyes won't work. As for real life details ... Music Hunger is the one place I can be myself. I love the fact we talk so openly here and I don't want to ruin it ...

I promise I'm not a catfish, I'm just a normal 17-year-old girl. Although, sometimes my life feels anything but normal. Sorry, I know I'm not making much sense, but please don't give up on me.

**LostGirl:** And yes, my new track is nearly finished. I'll send it over as soon as it's done.

LostGirl xxx

I open up Logic, the program I use to record my music. There are labelled rows of coloured blocks on my screen. Vocals. Guitar. Piano.

Drums. Strings. I'm no virtuoso, but I can play any instrument into my laptop, one keyboard note at a time. It's all you need.

I hit play and listen back. Within the first few bars I'm frustrated by my recording limitations. My mic seems dull and fuzzy, my speakers are way too bassy, and my plug-ins sound amateur. Let's face it, I'm nowhere near Caspar's level.

But maybe there's something ...

It might not be glossy or polished, but there is a feeling there – a real, heartfelt emotion. I have to trust it.

*I've got hidden waters running underneath*
*I've got buried treasure you wanna see*

It's so hard for me to explain my life to BandSnapper. If he knew the truth about my crazy world, our virtual sanctuary would be shattered. But at least I can trust him with my feelings in the form of lyrics and melodies. That's where he'll find the real me.

*Feels like I'm giving my all in an empty space*
*Nobody watching the firework display*
*Giving my all as you walk away*
*Nobody watching the firework display*
*If you just turn around then maybe you'll discover*
*I am right behind you, filling up the sky with colour*

The sudden pinging noise of an incoming message interrupts the song. My stomach does an Olympic triple back flip. He's online. Right now.

> **BandSnapper:** Are you there? Or are you working?

I hurriedly type back my reply, my heart beating a syncopated rhythm.

> **LostGirl:** I loaded up the files just now. It sounds OK. I only need to make a few more tweaks.

> **BandSnapper:** Send, send, send!!! (Please?)

> **LostGirl:** OK, give me half an hour. How was work today?

The moment I ask the question I regret it. Memories of my outburst come flooding back to me. I feel sick.

> **BandSnapper:** Yeah, not too bad thanks! Nothing much to report.

Phew. That's a relief. Guess I had nothing to worry about after all. Wait, he's typing again ...

> **BandSnapper:** Well, some girls from my school came in, including that Meg girl I told you about. They were causing a bit of a scene in the shop, and when I tried to help Meg shouted at me. So rude! I don't know why she's so vile to me, but for some reason she seems to hate me.

Even though I knew this was coming, it crushes me.

Because, in case you hadn't already figured it out, (drum roll please) BandSnapper is none other than Matty Chester.

My muse. The boy I can't stop thinking about. The boy I'm in love with.

And the worst part of it all, the part that makes me want to vomit my guts up with worry, is he has no idea that LostGirl is actually me.

The rude, vile girl at school who hates him for no reason.

Because nothing says true love like being a total bitch, right?

# CHAPTER SEVEN

**Top 5 Times I've Been Mean to Matty Chester:**

1. Shoving past him in Aladdin's Cave today. I'd like to say it was the one and only time I've pushed him out of my way, but that would be a lie.

2. In Year 10 P.E. my class played American dodgeball against Matty's. His magnetic pull on me was such that a ball flew out of my hands straight into his face. Have you ever seen someone get sent home from school for a nosebleed? I have.

3. In Year 11 Matty caught me looking at one of his band photos in a school coursework display. The passion he'd captured on the singer's face nearly made me cry, but I shrugged and walked away like I hated it.

4. Every single time I pass him in the corridors at school. He's so

used to my death glares by now that he looks down whenever he sees me approaching.

5. The day we met, around the middle of Year 10. I'd just moved back to Brighton and Bitch Meg was at the steering wheel …

♫

Back then, I wasn't as much of a loner as I am now. Coming into a new school as the sibling of a pop star definitely earns you instant peer group approval. I had friends in all my classes and I'd been on a couple of dates with boys in my year, but despite the attention I still preferred to be by myself.

I was alone in the library writing an essay on *Lord of The Flies*. The book confirmed my solid theory that boys left unattended are a bunch of idiots. If a group of girls had crashed onto the island, they would have formed a commune, organised a rota and started knitting each other leg-warmers out of coconut hair.

Out of nowhere, a camera flashed right in my face, jolting me out of my concentration and making my vision blur.

'What are you doing?' I shouted, pushing my chair back.

And then I saw him.

Before that moment, I didn't believe in love at first sight. But there is no other way to describe the feelings that flooded me when I looked into his earnest blue eyes. I loved him, all at once. And I know it sounds ridiculous, but I *knew* him all at once too.

I knew he was kind and gentle. I knew he loved music and valued creativity. I was pretty sure he'd be funny and I was certain he was smart and eloquent. It was in his movements, his whole aura, in the way he held his camera and the shy smile that flickered across his face as our eyes met.

So naturally, being me, I had to go and sabotage our relationship before it even had a chance to begin.

'Why are you taking my photo without permission?' The barbed words shot out before I could stop them. 'Let me guess, you're planning to send it to some crappy blog for money?' The communication channels between my heart and my mouth had clearly broken down.

Matty jolted at my harsh reaction and started fumbling with his camera. 'Oh, erm, yes, sorry, I mean, no I'm not going to send it to a blog. I mean, I didn't mean to startle you is what I mean.'

The awkward way he was standing and his self-conscious babbling made my insides melt like one of those posh chocolate desserts you have to pop with a fork. He was the sort of guy who didn't need the bullshit of celebrity parties and flawless selfies. He had his own thing going on. He was looking out on the world, not in on himself.

Which is why, from that very first moment, I knew. Matty Chester was everything I'd ever wanted. He'd turned my heart into a Gü pot.

'Delete it!' I demanded, furiously.

Other kids in the library were peering over their homework, trying to hear the drama unfolding.

'I'm s-so sorry,' Matty stuttered, his cheeks burning. 'I honestly didn't mean to upset you. Look, I'm deleting it, I'm deleting it!'

As he pressed some buttons on the back of his camera, a sixth former called out from a table in the corner. 'Don't delete them, mate! Caspar McCarthy's sister is a mini-celeb. You could get some cash for that picture!'

His eyes widened with surprise at the revelation. 'But I didn't know about the Caspar thing, honestly! It's not the reason I took your picture, I just ...'

'You just *what*?' I interrupted, slamming my book shut on the table. 'What makes you think you can stick your stupid camera in my face?'

'I just thought that, I mean, I don't know how to explain it, it's just that you ... you looked so fascinating,' Matty blurted out. 'And I couldn't *not* take your photo.'

Silence fell as his words penetrated my heart. They knocked me off balance, leaving my world spinning so fast I completely lost my sense of gravity.

'Ooooo!' teased a Year 8 girl from behind a bookcase, before bursting into giggles with her friend. Embarrassment, adrenaline and panic hit me like a punch. The holy trinity of teenage mortification. I had no idea how to react.

'Shh,' hissed the librarian from the back desk. 'Pack it in right now before I chuck you all out.' She was a miserable old dragon, but in that moment I could have kissed her for giving me a reason to escape.

'I'm sorry, that came out all wrong,' said Matty, stepping towards me. 'It's just that I love taking pictures. It's what I want to do with my life. I'm always looking out for interesting shots and there was something about you, reading your book. You looked so intense, but kind of ... vulnerable as well. I had to capture it.'

Giving him a withering, ice-queen glare I grabbed my bag and stormed straight past him.

'Wait, please don't be angry,' he said. 'I swear I didn't mean to upset you. It's gone now – I've deleted it. Look, it's gone!'

'Good,' I snapped, spinning around to face him. 'You don't know anything about me, so stop pretending you do.'

OK so he totally shouldn't have taken my photo without permission, but why was I being so horrible? It seemed like the kinder he was the more I retaliated. It was my stupid, go-to defence mechanism.

He blinked at me in shock. 'I ... I wasn't pretending. I see moments, that's all. Moments that are open to interpretation.'

'Yeah?' I replied. 'Well, interpret this.'

Then I stuck my middle finger up at him and left.

# CHAPTER EIGHT

Caspar's third single was at number one. Three out of three. He was high on the fumes of fame. Meanwhile, I was finding it hard to be nice to anyone. It seemed like everyone who spoke to me just wanted a little piece of my brother. I felt more and more like an outsider in my supposedly perfect life.

At school, Matty was also an outsider, but he handled it so differently. He was always buzzing with creative energy, drumming tabletops with his headphones on or enthusing wildly about bands and photographers. Our classmates' eyes tended to glaze over when Matty spoke. But I would cling to any tiny fragment of conversation I overheard, yearning to join in.

For some tragic reason, the more I liked him the more incapable I was of actually speaking to him. I thought about Matty constantly. I knew every single band T-shirt in his collection and which days he stayed late in the ICT suite to edit his beautiful, story-telling photographs. But I still couldn't be the slightest bit civil to him. What was I so scared of? Maybe I just couldn't bear to expose someone so sincere and honest to the insane Caspar-centric tornado of my life.

During my months of 'silent appreciation', I noticed that whenever Matty wasn't taking photos he was engaged in another obsession. I would catch sight of a red logo on a dark grey background on his phone or when he used the school computers. One day my curiosity got the better of me and after running a search I discovered the *Music Hunger* discord server.

I felt my heart pound with anticipation. Was Matty a secret songwriter too? That would be seriously weird and cool at the same time. I picked the username LostGirl so that I could investigate the server. It became clear that most users were music lovers rather than creators.

There were dozens of threads dedicated to musical debates, discussions, weird facts and sharing of playlists. In almost every thread, there was one user who always left their opinion. BandSnapper.

I knew instantly it was *him*. His avatar was the iconic image of The Beatles striding across the Abbey Road zebra crossing. I'd caught sight of the picture on his screen a hundred times. *BandSnapper was Matty Chester* and I had instant access to everything he was writing!

For a few days, I was a lurker. I read as many of his posts as I could find, laughing at his jokes and learning more about his love of music. Everything he said meant something to me. It was like finding the perfect chords to a melody. He inspired me.

I found myself picking up my guitar more and more in the solace of my room. The ideas I'd been holding back started to flow.

I knew I wasn't a prodigy like Caspar, but I felt compelled to start writing lyrics of my own. Matty's passion was giving me a strange sense of confidence.

Eventually, I built up the courage to join the conversations. I felt free for the first time since Caspar got signed. Tailoring my opinions to fit the *McCarthyBrand* had become suffocating, but here I could finally be myself – an anonymous music lover. Not @MegMcCarthy, the Instagram model or celebrity sibling, but a normal teenage girl. For once!

I was addicted from the start, posting my opinions on all the artists in the charts. I had met a fair few of them at parties and at Caspar's gigs and I knew which starlets were bitchy or total egomaniacs, which clean-cut performers had hidden addictions, and which award winners used heavy auto-tune to disguise pitchy vocals. I could've spilled so many secrets and perhaps I should have stopped and deleted my account, but I was having way too much fun. With reckless abandon I sent BandSnapper a direct message.

> **LostGirl:** Hey! Thought I'd say hi since I've been posting on some of your threads. I've got my own music game if you want to play? It's called Top 5 (dot dot dot) ... I'll start. What are the top 5 songs you can't help dancing to? Go 😊

I could see little green dots next to his name, and to my delight he replied straight away.

**BandSnapper:** Hi! Thanks for inventing the best game ever! You should know I am never, under any circumstances, seen dancing. However, if I were to occasionally, sometimes, dance on my own, in my room, it would be to:

1. Get Up Offa That Thing – James Brown
2. Juice – Lizzo
3. Jump Around – House of Pain
4. Runaway Baby – Bruno Mars
5. It's Like That – Run-D.M.C., Jason Nevins

Now it's my turn. Top 5 best album covers of all time. (Sorry, I have to ask. I'm a photographer!) How old are you btw and where are you from? I'm 15 and I live in Brighton.

I immediately panicked. This whole scenario didn't seem like such a brilliant idea anymore. What if he found out I was the awful girl from the library? He couldn't find out, not if I was going to share any real connection with him.

**LostGirl:** Wow, that's a really hard question. I'm going to choose five album covers from my parents' collection. They're big into their vinyl!

1. Around The World In A Day – Prince
2. Tragic Kingdom – No Doubt
3. Odelay – Beck
4. Boys for Pele – Tori Amos
5. Nevermind – Nirvana

> **LostGirl:** I've grown up with these albums so they mean a lot to me. I'm 15 too.

I paused at the keyboard, thinking about leaving my message at that. However, it didn't feel like much of an explanation. Could I reveal a little more? Just a little. It's not like he'd ever know it was me …

> **LostGirl:** I write songs of my own. I've been thinking of posting some on the server but I'm not sure if I'm ready to share them with the world. Does that seem ridiculous?!

> **BandSnapper:** No, it's not ridiculous. I get how hard it is to put yourself out there. What kind of songs do you write? I'm intrigued …

> **LostGirl:** I guess they're pop songs, but they're organic. I play a bit of guitar and piano, and I've been messing around with my own production too. My Dad has shown me the basics and I'm teaching myself the rest as I go along.

> **BandSnapper:** Wow, it sounds like you're from a very musical family! Do you have anything you could send me? I'd love to hear it. 😊

I froze, unsure of what to do. I'd never shared my songs with anyone. But this was different. This was Matty Chester, the world's most passionate music fan. And I wasn't Meg. I was LostGirl.

> **LostGirl:** Well I just wrote a very silly song about my cat. 😊 It's definitely not my deepest and most meaningful work, but I could send it to you ...?

There were so many reasons I shouldn't send it, but I was getting sick of hiding such an important part of myself away. After all, songs aren't supposed to be locked up in dark cupboards. They're written to be heard.

> **BandSnapper:** I'd love to hear it! Sounds hilarious. I promise I won't say anything that isn't constructive. Please?

My remaining defences collapsed faster than a last-go Jenga tower. I had to know what Matty thought.

> **LostGirl:** OK. But PROMISE you won't share this with anyone?

I attached the MP3 and hit send. There was no going back.

Although it was a light-hearted song I was kind of proud of it. The *La La Land* vibes in the melody always made me smile so I played it out loud on my laptop and listened to my voice over the ukulele. Sometimes the simplest arrangements are the most effective.

*Oh-oh-oh-oh-oh, Maximillian*
*You're o-o-o-o-one in a billion*
*When all I've got is no one to talk to*
*Not been smiling like I ought to*
*Feeling like the sky is caving down on me ... ow!*
*You'll be there when I am hurting*
*I'm safe when I hear you purring*
*Rescue me when I'm stuck up a tree*
*Now you might have stinky breath but I don't care,*
*My whole bed is covered in cat hair*
*You're the fuzzball I adore*
*Might bring back a dead mouse or two*
*You know that I will always forgive you*
*Maximoo ... My heart is in your paws*

As the song played, I had a low-level panic attack. I'm not talking hyperventilation, but there were definite stomach bubbles. What if Matty knew about Maxi's ridiculous Instagram account? What if this song gave away my true identity?

For endless minutes I refreshed the screen, wondering what he was thinking. Did he hate it? Or had he guessed my secret? There was nothing I could do now, even if I wanted to.

Then, at last, a response pinged up in front of my eyes.

> **BandSnapper:** Oh. My. GOD. It's so cute and hilarious I had to listen to it three times in a row. How are you SHY?! Your voice and songwriting are incredible! Please tell me you have more?!

My panic gave way to relief. He liked it. He actually liked it!

The rest is history. BandSnapper and LostGirl's virtual friendship was born. I don't think we've gone a single day without speaking since.

Just not in real life. Obviously.

♫

> **BandSnapper:** ... Are you still there?

Matty's message flashes up at me and I realise I've been lost in my memories. All I can think about is the stupid, horrible stuff I've done to him over the past few years, let alone today. What am I supposed to say? How can I support him when *I'm* the reason he's upset in the first place?

I'm trapped in a lie. A double life. An inescapable Jekyll and Hyde situation. 'School Meg' is the evil Voldemort on the back of LostGirl's head. I don't know what to do.

> **LostGirl:** Sorry, I'm still working on the song. OMG, that Meg girl sounds nasty. Is it post-exam stress or something?

Matty doesn't talk about 'School Meg' very often. Only on the days when she's particularly annoyed him.

> **BandSnapper:** Maybe ... but I think she's like that all year round. Apparently her famous brother has moved back home. Must be freaking her out or something.

> **LostGirl:** Oh yeah, Caspar McCarthy? He's pretty well known. I guess it must be weird having your family in the public eye when you just want things to be normal.

Oops, that sounds a bit defensive. I have to remember Meg isn't me. Not when I'm LostGirl. I don't know the first thing about her. She's nobody.

> **BandSnapper:** Meg is anything BUT normal. She does all these Instagram brand deals and is always going to celebrity parties. She's not properly famous like her brother, but people still recognise her. It's like she gets all the fun parts of fame while still keeping her regular life. It's the perfect balance. So WHY is she so horrible?! You'd think she would be happy with all those amazing opportunities thrown her way.

His words are like bullets. I have to remember he's not talking about me. At least not the 'me' he knows. But the lines between the two versions of myself are getting hazier with every conversation.

> **LostGirl:** How do you know those parts of fame are actually fun? She might hate parties and people recognising her? It might be harder than you think having a famous relation.

> **BandSnapper:** Who knows. She's obviously unhappy even though her family seem to have a dream life.

> **BandSnapper:** I can't wait for sixth form to be over. Only one more year, then I'll be at uni and I'll never have to see her again.

Bang. Final shot fired. He literally can't wait to see the back of me. And who can blame him?

*No talent. Ugly. Pointless. Rude. Bitch.*

> **LostGirl:** Ah, I'm sorry, I've got to go ... Mum is calling me. I totally forgot I promised to watch a movie with her.

Usually I love spending hours chatting with Matty, but tonight I can't do it. I don't know if it's Caspar stomping around the house or the stress of seeing Ness and Melissa today, but I'm feeling way too fragile to deal with any more home truths. The haters are one thing, but criticism from Matty is more than I can handle.

> **BandSnapper:** Oh no! I didn't get to tell you my Top 5 musical songs yet. And what about your new song? Please don't make me wait another day. I have to hear it!

> **LostGirl:** Send your Top 5 later – I'll upload the song for you now. I can't wait to hear what you think, and please be honest. Speak soon x

I shut down *Music Hunger* before Matty can reply. For a while, I try to distract myself by noodling around on Logic, but I'm not in the mood to start anything new. All creativity has left my body.

As I flop onto my bed, Matty's messages jump and skip in my mind like a disappointing scratched record brought home from a car boot sale.

When I'm not making music, the noise inside my head is deafening.

# CHAPTER NINE

The kitchen is in chaos. Caspar has already broken his promise to lay low and last night's partying has left him with a foul-tempered hangover.

'It's pointless TJ,' he barks into his phone. 'I don't have anything to show you yet ... No, we tried that guy. I'm not dragging myself back up to London to work with him again ... Yeah, well, I'll have something soon ... NO, not yet ...'

Mum is also on her phone, doing the hands-free head-and-shoulder hold as she simultaneously fries some bacon. 'So that's 11.30 on Thursday? Should we bring our own wardrobe or will outfits be provided? Ah right, not for filler pieces ... OK, fine, what kind of look do you want?'

I edge past her to grab some juice from the fridge, but Maximillian gets under my feet almost tripping me up. Meanwhile, Dad begins blending one of his disgusting green super-food breakfast smoothies. The whizzing noise causes Mum to shout louder on the phone. '... JUST CHECKING – THIS WILL BE IN

TIME FOR THE AUGUST ISSUE, RIGHT?'

Not to be outdone by Mum or a blender, Caspar also raises the decibels. 'HANG ON, I CAN'T HEAR YOU NOW. DAD'S BEING AN ARSE!'

Welcome to breakfast at the McCarthys. May as well kiss goodbye to any peace and quiet until Caspar's gone back to London.

'OK, see you then.' Mum wiggles her shoulder in my direction. 'Darling, could you put my phone somewhere safe?'

I untangle the phone from her voluminous blonde hair and chuck it on the dining table. Caspar is finally finishing his call, too. 'Yeah, fine, but it's seriously not going to be worth your time,' he grunts. 'Yeah, whatever. Bye.'

'TJ?' I question, daring to sit down opposite him.

Caspar slumps across the table with a groan. 'He's insisting on coming down to check up on me. Like that's going to help anything.' He sits back up and snaps at Dad. 'Will you quiet down with the bloody blending already?!'

'It's good for me, son,' Dad shouts back cheerily. 'You should start your own regime instead of going out drinking all night.'

'Had a late one then?' I cut in. 'So much for keeping out of the public eye while you're down here.'

'It was one night,' Caspar mutters, running a hand through his messy bedhead. 'I just wanted a bit of fun. I'm stressed, OK? It's not like I can sleep right now so what does it even matter?'

'Actually, it does matter,' I reply resentfully. 'The last thing I need is a ton of journalists hounding me for sound bites.'

Mum plonks down two plates of scrambled egg and bacon on toast. 'Cass, that was Girl-Time on the phone, I've arranged an interview for Thursday morning. It's not the main article, but every little helps.'

'I don't want to do a stupid interview,' Caspar moans. 'I've got nothing to talk about.'

Dad joins us at the table with his green glass of grossness. 'You can tell them about our song! Father and son bonding. It's a great story even if it doesn't end up on the album.'

'It won't end up on the album. I've already told you that.'

'But TJ hasn't even heard it yet. Let him take a listen before making any decisions.'

'Jesus, Dad! Give it up already. It's not good enough, OK?'

I start eating my breakfast. Morning Meg, how did you sleep? What are you up to today? How is anything in your life going? What are you up to at any point in your entire existence?

'Girl-Time don't care what you say,' Mum chimes in. 'They just want a nice picture of you. It's important to talk to local magazines while you've got the chance. Remind people of your roots.'

'Exactly,' Dad agrees. 'Roots! Family duo! From your rise to fame to coming back home for album number two. You've come full circle. It's a heart-warming story.'

'I'm not saying anything about the album,' Caspar responds scathingly. 'We're nowhere near a release date so I'm not whipping people up about it.' With that, he scrapes his bacon onto the floor and whistles Maximillian over, as if he were a dog.

'What are you doing?' Mum exclaims. 'That's not for the bloody cat.'

'It's too fattening. You know I can't eat this stuff. Not when you're booking pointless photoshoots.'

'They're not pointless, not if you have any intention of keeping your fanbase.' Mum takes a huffy bite of her breakfast. 'And it's veggie bacon, for your information: "fake-on"! It's low-fat.'

As if to confirm this fact, Maximillian sniffs at the rashers then plods away unimpressed. I guess he's not planning on going vegan any time soon.

'I'm having one of Dad's smoothies,' Caspar announces. 'Meg can eat mine. She likes being the fat one in the family.'

That's it. I've had enough of him this morning. 'Why do you have to be so goddamn rude to everyone? I wish you'd just piss off back to London. You've been a total pig since you came home.'

'I think the only pig here is you. It's not me, Meggy, and it's certainly not the bacon!'

'Come on, Cass,' Dad intervenes. 'Leave your sister alone.'

'Just being honest,' Caspar shrugs. 'She's the one doing all the modelling stuff. I'm only trying to help.'

'Don't listen to him darling,' Mum says. 'You're perfect. He's just under a lot of pressure right now.'

My parents never tell Caspar off. He can say and do whatever he likes and they continuously make excuses for him. Sometimes I think they are literally starstruck by their own son. It's pathetic.

'By the way,' Caspar continues, locking eyes with me from the kitchen counter. 'Can you stop telling your sad little schoolmates about me being here? They were stalking me outside the club last night.'

'I haven't told anyone,' I answer defensively. 'If people know you're in town, it's your own fault for drawing attention to yourself.'

'I do actually have a life, Meg,' Caspar yells over the noise of the blender. 'I can't stay cooped up in the studio, I'll go crazy. I need to get out and find inspiration. Meet people. Do things. You know, normal, young people stuff that you don't do.'

'I do meet people and do things. And at least ...'

At least I actually write songs, is what I almost say, only I stop myself at the last second. My family doesn't know I make music. Not serious music at any rate. And I intend to keep it that way.

Caspar sneers. 'At least what? At least you have all your little Internet followers? How many is it again, a few hundred thousand? Really cute, Meg. I remember the days before my first million. Keep tweeting and maybe you'll finally catch up with me.'

'That's enough now,' Dad interrupts. 'Can't we just have one civilised family breakfast without you two sniping at each other? You'll give your mother one of her migraines.'

Mum is oblivious on her phone, ignoring everyone. Yup, she's clearly distressed.

'I haven't done anything,' I mutter through gritted teeth. 'He's picking on me for no reason.'

'You were winding him up,' Dad scolds. 'And Cass, I know you're feeling stressed, but stop taking it out on your sister. Can we please just be a happy family for once? Think of the McCarthy brand! Honesty. Communication. Support. Remember?'

Wow, I think I'm going to throw this fake-on bacon straight back up, all over the dining table.

'Dad. There won't be any McCarthy brand if I don't write this next damn album ... And so much for Brighton being less distracting – you lot haven't shut up since I got here.'

Caspar abruptly leaves the room, taking his rancid-looking smoothie, his phone, and his bad attitude with him.

'Well, thanks for breakfast Mum.' As much as I'd love to sit here in the wake of Hurricane Caspar, I think I'd rather find somewhere else to be. Like, literally anywhere else. But as I stand up, Mum reaches out and grips my arm.

'Wait, Meggy, I've got something to tell you.'

I freeze. She sounds so serious I wonder what on Earth she's going to say next. Maybe it's about money or the house. Maybe something is terribly wrong. Is she ill? Is she ... pregnant?! Oh dear God, no. It can't be that. She's, like, old.

'What is it?' I ask, preparing for the worst.

She finally looks up from her screen, smiling brightly. 'I've found you a job! Ta-da! Isn't it wonderful?'

OK. That wasn't what I was expecting. 'Job? What job?'

'Dodo Yoyo,' Mum beams. 'It's a frozen yoghurt shop in The Lanes.'

'Dodo Yoyo?' I repeat, saying the words slowly so I'll understand them. 'You mean that place on the corner with the weird cross-eyed parrot on the window?'

'It's a Dodo, darling. Obviously.'

I stare at Mum in disbelief. 'Whatever kind of bird it is, I never applied for a yoghurt job.'

'I know you didn't,' Mum laughs. 'I put in a good word for you. I remembered my old school friend Laura runs the place, so I gave her a tinkle last night and she said there's a job available for you. Twenty hours a week over the holidays. It's perfect!'

Oh. Twenty hours a week. At a ... yoghurt shop. Without

sounding ungrateful, it's not exactly the sort of place I imagined myself working this summer.

'Right ...' I say, treading carefully. 'Err, thanks. That sounds fab and everything, but I think I'd rather hang on for some of the other places I applied to.'

Mum ploughs on. 'Why wait when you've got something here and now? You've got to grab opportunities when they fall out of the sky like this!'

Dodo opportunities? I can see the gossip headlines now. *Caspar McCarthy's sister needs extinct bird mascot to survive. Click here for EMBARRASSING photos!*

'Yeah, but I was after something a bit ... different,' I say. By different, I mean less shit. 'Somewhere I won't be out in public, you know?'

I look pleadingly towards Dad for some kind of back-up, but he doesn't help me. 'I think working in retail will be good for you, babygirl! You can be sociable, meet some new people.'

'Yes, make some friends for goodness' sake, Meg.' Mum shakes me like I'm a giant maraca. 'You never have anyone over anymore, I'm getting worried about you. There's a lovely girl around your age at the shop. Laura has assured me you'll get on brilliantly.'

Oh yay, my very own Rent-A-Friend. Just what I always wanted.

'I don't need you to make friends for me, Mum,' I say, squirming away from her. 'I know what's gonna happen at a place like that. I'll be trapped behind the counter with loads of little Caspar fangirls taking my photo.'

'Exactly. It will look great on social media. Working in a shop shows how down-to-earth we are, just like any other family.'

I repress the urge to scream. It's not that I don't want a job, but I was hoping for one that won't brand me as a total loser forever.

'Seriously Mum? It's not like I'm desperate for the cash ...'

'It's not all about money Megster,' Dad says. 'It's about getting out there and experiencing things!'

'And this house is going to be a chaotic mess over the summer ...' Mum adds.

The penny drops. The fog clears. The puzzle piece clicks. A lightbulb materialises above my head and I want to lob it at my parents. 'So basically what you're saying is you want me out of here?'

Mum and Dad exchange an awkward glance, then Dad clears his throat. 'No, no, not at all.' He pauses. 'Well, I mean, it would be easier for Caspar to have a bit of quiet to sort this album out once and for all. But that's not the reason we want you to go for the job ...'

I get up and chuck my plate carelessly in the sink. 'Sooooo sorry Dad, I momentarily forgot the universe orbits around Caspar. Don't worry I'll give him allllll the space he needs to flounce around playing the tortured artist. How about I move into a beach hut for the summer?'

Dad flounders, speechless in the face of my melodrama, before Mum swoops in. 'Look Meg, I know you're feeling frustrated about Cass being here. It's been very disruptive and difficult for all of us. But it would make things so much easier if you could just help us out a teeny, tiny bit.'

Of course, this isn't about me and the yoghurt job. It's never about me. It's about tiptoeing around The Earl of Cassbridge yet again. And the irony is they are the ones suffocating him with their over-spilling, over-involved, overbearing love and attention.

I stand in sullen silence, debating the pros and cons in my mind. Pros: My own money. Something to do over summer. Not being in this madhouse. Cons: Serving pots of yoghurt ... to giggling girls ... all trying to take my photo ... while dressed in a repulsive, highly flammable, polyester uniform.

'Come on, it'll be a laugh!' Mum continues, persistently. 'And Laura could do with the extra business. You get a fun little job and Cass can get on with his music. It's a win-win-win situation!'

Sure, win-win-win for everyone but me.

We are interrupted by Caspar's thunderous stomping and yelling upstairs. 'I'VE ATTACHED IT. YOU SHOULD HAVE IT BY NOW ... NO, I SENT IT TO THE OTHER EMAIL ... SERIOUSLY, TJ, WHAT IS UP WITH YOUR INTERNET CONNECTION?'

Maybe it's not such a tough choice after all. The yoghurt job may well be hideous, but being stuck here with my spoiled, diva brother is guaranteed to be a hundred times worse.

'OK, fine,' I sigh. 'I guess I'll check it out then.'

'Perfect!' Mum trills. 'I'll ring Laura back and tell her you're heading over right now.'

'What? Right now?!'

I've got so much to do. Twitter. Instagram. Promo stuff. And more importantly, my music. Plus, I haven't even looked at my Discord messages yet to find out what BandSnapper thought of my new song.

'There's no time like the present.' Mum pushes me towards the door. 'Go on, I'll tell her you're coming. She'll be so thrilled.'

And there was me looking forward to summer.

# CHAPTER TEN

Long ago, back in the days before Caspar signed his deal and my family were still innocent and naive, I used to think there were only two types of musician: famous and unfamous.

Famous musicians had songs on the radio and photos in magazines. They had lots of money, played shows to thousands of people, and never had to work boring, regular day jobs.

Unfamous musicians made recordings in their bedrooms with crappy equipment, took any possible gigging opportunity (even unpaid gigs in shopping centres), and never needed to worry about being recognised in public.

You were either somebody or you were nobody. It all seemed so simple.

But when Caspar started gaining attention on YouTube, the lines between these two definitions began to blur. He was an ordinary fifteen-year-old, going to school and making videos with Dad in his spare time. He wasn't living a celebrity life of luxury – he was worrying about revision just like everyone else in Year 10.

Despite our ordinary family life, extraordinary things were beginning to bubble under the surface. Caspar's views were getting higher every day, ranging from the hundreds to the thousands, to the hundreds of thousands. Before long, people were stopping him in town, asking for photos. Companies were emailing with brand sponsorship deals. Not only for him, but for Dad, Mum and me too.

Everything was changing. We weren't famous, not in the way I understood the word. But we were getting loads of opportunities as though we were.

Now I realise there are many levels to this insane fame game. You can be bumped up and down the ladder in the space of a single news article. Today's headlines are tomorrow's fish and chip paper, and all that.

At the start of his career, Caspar was a solid B-lister. He wasn't selling out huge arenas like Ariana Grande or Ed Sheeran, but 'Next Best Thing' was a huge number one hit and was constantly playing on UK radio. After that, his success grew really quickly. He toured across Europe and America, stopping off for zillions of interviews and TV appearances along the way. He won various Best Newcomer awards and even cameoed on a couple of sitcoms.

Those hectic few years feel like a blur to me now. The paparazzi, the VIP passes, the famous friends, the endless glitz and glamour that all of us had no choice but to get totally swept up in.

Then one day it all sort of died down. Caspar's album fell off the charts and fell off the playlists. The gigs became smaller and the interviews less frequent. It wasn't that the fans loved him any less, it was just that the material was old. Dated. They had moved on to other artists who were taking their turn on the rollercoaster.

Suddenly, the days of mingling with American film stars and having songs featured on Radio 1 were over. Which leads us to the present moment where our whole family is wandering aimlessly in the no-man's-land of fame.

Caspar still has plenty of hardcore, dedicated fans, which is more than most people ever dream of. He could make a massive comeback if he wanted to and he *says* he wants to. It's all he ever talks about. But the comeback hasn't yet materialised so I have trouble actually believing him these days.

As for where I fit in on the slippery, slidey scale of fame ... I have a lot of fans online who follow my fashion or who know me through Caspar. But most people in the street wouldn't recognise me. I do get invited to events like movie premieres and theme parks, but I'm the unpaid Polyfilla kind of celeb right at the back of the red carpet. An M-lister you could say. And M-listers aren't allowed to mix with As and Bs unless, of course, they're related.

♪

When I open the door to Dodo Yoyo, I instantly feel claustrophobic. Neon-pink tables and chairs are crammed together in the bay window and lining the back wall is a counter filled with tubs of frozen yoghurt, sprinkles and syrupy toppings. This place is a dentist's worst nightmare.

Standing behind the till is Mum's friend Laura, wearing a glowing fuchsia polo shirt. It's hideous, but what really sends chills of horror down my spine is what's on her head. A baseball cap with a beak. I knew it would be bad, but seriously? A beak?

As I'm considering faking my own death, Laura catches my eye and waves enthusiastically at me. 'Meg, it's so good to see you! Joanna said you were coming down. I'm so pleased she told you about the job.'

I force a smile as the reality of this bird-based headwear situation sinks in. I'm going to kill Mum when I get home.

'Alana!' Laura yells. 'Meg's here, are you changed yet?'

'Sorry L-Dog, just coming!' a voice calls from the back room.

'Alana came in early so she could watch the till while you have your induction.'

Wait. What? No one said anything about an induction!

'She's really into her music, by the way,' Laura adds, like music isn't something that everyone on the planet is into. 'I'm sure she'd love to hear all the exciting news about your brother. I still can't believe he's Joanna's boy! Who would have thought it? Mind you, back in school we always knew she'd lead a glamorous life.'

Her face is glowing with exhilaration. She's obviously a *McCarthyBrand* fan. She probably couldn't believe her luck when Mum offered to sacrifice me to her giant Dodo of doom.

'Yeah, I guess it's kind of crazy,' I say, on autopilot, reciting the standard response I use for friends and family. 'He's done so well.' Blah, blah, blahhhhh.

The back door bursts open. This must be the Rent-A-Friend. She locks eyes with me and smiles a huge, radiant, red-lipped smile.

The main word I can use to describe Alana is big. She has a big body – definitely bigger than most of the bodies I know. Her hair is big and beautiful, falling right down to her waist in long brown waves. She has big boobs too, a vision of big, curvy lines taking up all the space in the room. She's nothing like I imagined.

'Hey!' she grins confidently. 'So you're the mysterious Meg then?'

'Um, yeah,' I reply, feeling stupidly small in comparison to someone so mighty. 'Hey.'

She makes a high-pitched, inquisitive noise, which cuts through the air. 'Aaaaaaah! I'm excited to meet you. Laura got me to drop everything when she heard you were coming down. And by "everything", I mean sleeping.'

I watch her closely as she talks, trying to work out how old she is. She seems young and old at the same time. Physically I wouldn't put her as much older than me, but her confidence feels light-years ahead.

'Alana,' Laura snaps, pointing to the top of her head.

'Sorry, boss-lady,' Alana replies in the breezy kind of way that suggests a telling off never bothers her. She whips her hair into a high ponytail and completes the look with one of those heinous Dodo hats. The pink polo shirt is definitely doing nothing for her, but she doesn't seem to care.

'We take health and safety very seriously here,' Laura says to me firmly. 'No hat, no serving. And hair up at all times.'

Self-consciously, I pull my own long hair back and make one of those awkward I'm-laughing-but-it's-not-really-funny noises.

'Right then, let's get on.' Laura shoulder steers me through to the 'office'. 'We'll probably be a couple of hours, but Alana can cope.'

A couple of hours? What the hell is she going to make me do?

Alana grins at me as I'm ushered out. She is so engaging I can't help smiling back even though I know from experience how this whole 'friend' thing goes. Better to keep my distance. My life is complicated enough without adding random, weird yoghurt-girls into the mix.

♪

As the hours tick by, I can see my entire summer disappearing before my eyes. All the songs I won't get to write. All the day-long conversations with BandSnapper I won't get to have. All the ranting from Caspar I won't get to witness. OK, that last one's valid ...

Laura seems disproportionately delighted about me being here and keeps unsubtly hinting that I should post about my new job. I didn't think dodos could fly, let alone tweet!

It's mid-afternoon by the time I escape. I've been forced to sign my soul away to numerous contracts and disclaimers, as well as being made to watch a laughable food hygiene movie which must've been filmed in the 1980s on a budget camcorder. Alana is politely listening to a lone customer who is telling a mind-numbing anecdote about returning a faulty suitcase to John Lewis. I slip past her without saying goodbye. Better to set the boundaries early before she starts expecting stuff from me. Friendship stuff.

Two hours and forty-seven minutes feels like a very long time not to have checked *Music Hunger*. My heart races when I see there's a new message waiting.

**BandSnapper:** Hi. First things first, my top 5 musical songs are as follows.

1. Wait for It – Hamilton
2. Waving Through A Window – Dear Evan Hansen
3. Jet Song – West Side Story
4. You Give a Little Love – Bugsy Malone
5. The Other Side – Greatest Showman

**BandSnapper:** WOW! That sent me through a musical wormhole I've not been down in a while!
Now for you: top 5 songs that always make you cry. Because I have a confession to make. Your new song actually brought a tear to my eye, especially as I know what those lyrics mean to you. I love the whole concept of 'Firework Display.' 'How much longer will I be invisible? Lost girls never find their way home.' That hit me hard.

**BandSnapper:** Your voice gets better with every new recording. No lie, it gives me chills, especially when you let go and belt out the high notes. You have to get your music out there, LG. You've got talent and people need to hear it. Do you know how many wannabes release their rubbish music without a second thought? Your songs are a million times better than theirs. I know one day you'll get over your shyness and do it. And I hope it's one day soon.

> **BandSnapper:** OK, I'm going to listen to your song for the 54th time …
>
> And if you ever feel invisible again, please remember that I see you. xxx

I sit down on the grass in the Pavilion gardens so I can try and make sense of all the feelings that are swirling inside me after reading Matty's message. Elation that he loves my song. Fear that I'll never be brave enough to share my music and he'll lose faith in me. Guilt at how much I've lied and how hard it is to explain my stupid headspace to him. And most of all a sad kind of disappointment.

Because BandSnapper might see me, but Matty Chester doesn't. And I'm not sure that he ever will.

# CHAPTER ELEVEN

When I get back home Mum is still at the kitchen table, glued to her laptop. More Caspar-related admin to do, no doubt.

'Oh, you're back.' She barely looks up from the screen as she types. 'How did it all go?'

I give a half-hearted shrug. 'Alright, I s'pose.'

The only response I get is the arrhythmic sound of her manicured nails incessantly jabbing at the keys.

'Sorry Meggy, I am listening,' Mum says, her words spaced too far apart for me to believe her. 'I've been chasing up some producers for Cass. I know he's being all sulky about co-writes, but I think he *really* needs the right tracks to inspire him.'

I hate the way Mum talks about music like she's some kind of expert. She might know a bit of the terminology, but she couldn't write a tune to save her life. She can't even sing, although being tone-deaf doesn't stop her trying. Whenever she's had a few too many glasses of Chardonnay she always belts out 'Total Eclipse Of The Heart' by Bonnie Tyler at the top of her lungs. So cringe.

Suddenly I feel like throwing stuff. Mum pulls the laptop sharply away from my incoming bag fling. 'Hey, mind the lappy! Goodness Meg, I thought you'd be pleased about this job, not coming home a stroppy moo.'

'I'm not being stroppy!' I snap … stroppily. 'But you could have at least told me I was going in for a whole induction. I wasn't psychologically prepared.'

'McCarthys are born prepared. Anyway darling, think of all the nice things you can buy with the extra cash.'

Hmm, she's got a point. I picture the beautiful electro-acoustic Ibanez guitar that I had a go on in GAK last week. Or maybe a new microphone? … Or an iMac? Maybe even all three? Well, not likely on minimum wage, but surely I can get *something*? At least I'll be earning it myself rather than having to ask Mum and Dad for handouts courtesy of the bank of Caspar.

'Yeah, I guess there are a few things I need,' I admit.

At long last, Mum looks up from her oh-so-important email and smiles. 'That's the spirit Meggy. Laura's so lovely, I'm sure you'll get on with her. And did you get to meet the singer girl she told me about?'

I do a double take. For some reason, I'm surprised Alana is a singer. Without sounding snobbish, she doesn't really look like a stereotypical performer.

'Well, we said hello but we're not exactly Thelma and Louise yet.'

Mum makes a half-listening noise of acknowledgement as the sound of clacking keys fills the space where our conversation should be.

'Right then,' I say, grabbing a Babybel cheese from the fridge.

'I'm off to my room.'

'OK honeybee, have fun. And make sure you do that Instagram post this afternoon.'

'Yes, Mother.'

'I'd also highly recommend keeping out of Cass's way. He's ... well, he's emitting somewhat of a negative energy today.'

Awesome. What the hell else is new? 'What's wrong with him now?'

Mum sighs with exasperation. 'A certain guest turned up on the doorstep not long after you left ...'

'Oh right. So he means business this time then?'

'Apparently,' Mum replies. 'Caspar's not a happy bunny, though. They've been arguing all bloody morning. Your father's upstairs with them now, trying to smooth things over. Making everything worse, no doubt.'

OK, this is one war zone I definitely don't want to walk into. I head upstairs, carefully avoiding the squeaky floorboard outside Caspar's door. But just when I think I've got away with it, I'm stopped in my tracks by a familiar, booming voice.

'MEGGY MOO MOO!'

Ah shit.

'I was wondering where you'd got to. You weren't sneaking past without saying hi to your most favourite Londoner, were you? Come on, bring it in! I've got a squishy cuddle with your name on it.'

I can't help but smile as I turn to face those mischievous brown eyes and the grin that could persuade Prince Charles to go on The Voice.

'Hey TJ,' I say, hugging my brother's manager. 'How's it going?'

Flying under the radar rarely ever works with TJ. He's the one person I never feel invisible to. He's far too perceptive to let anything get past him.

♫

The day we met TJ was a day of firsts for me and Caspar. It was the first time either of us had been in a chauffeur driven car, the first time we'd eaten at a Michelin star restaurant, and it was the first time we'd ever met anybody quite like the man who paid for it all.

Tall and striking with dark skin and model-like features, TJ seemed to be constantly in motion, telling stories and cracking jokes. His suit was cut and his energy was boundless. With an anecdote for everything, he charmed everyone he met. You couldn't help but be in awe of him.

'Your songwriting is *incredible*,' TJ was praising Caspar, arms waving. 'I mean *incredible* – so ahead of your years. *Wow*. The minute I heard your voice I knew I had to meet you.' More enthusiastic hand gestures and slamming the table. 'The stuff with your Dad? Genius. And the piano covers? Haunting. And the *view counts*.' Slam, slam, slam! 'Seriously, I am *floored* at how far you've managed to grow this by yourself.'

Words, words, and more words. Too many complimentary adjectives to take in.

'Now without sounding too presumptuous, this is where I'm proposing I might be able to get involved. I've got the contacts and the know-how; you've got the talent. I think together we can make something really, really special.'

I watched Mum gaping like some kind of overwhelmed goldfish, attempting to jump into the conversation herself. Only there wasn't a single gap to squeeze into.

'Lara Zane has absolutely taken off since she signed with me. Three top ten singles in the past year and a sell-out tour. Devon Callow is touring Japan, *huge* following out there. He started off with acoustic covers too, but now he's hit over 2,000,000 YouTube subscribers. I know you can double that, Caspar. *Triple* it.'

All the statistics and celebrity name drops were too much for my thirteen-year-old mind to take in. It was like being in a movie. My brother had been discovered by a big-shot London manager and in the space of one meeting everything was about to change. I looked over to see if Caspar was fizzing with as much excitement as I was. Even though he was smiling, I could see a hint of panic in his eyes.

As usual Mum didn't notice anything was wrong. She was already imagining red carpets and double page spreads in Hello! magazine. 'Well, this all sounds *very* interesting, Mr Jackson ...'

'Please, call me TJ.'

'TJ, right!' Mum chirped, her face flushing. 'We were all thrilled when you contacted Caspar last week, and everything you're talking about sounds like a dream come true. But he is only sixteen years old. What about school? He's studying for his GCSEs right now so we don't want him to get too distracted.'

Back then Mum cared a lot more about things like school. These days, not so much.

'Of course, of course,' TJ replied, smoothly. 'We'd be more than happy to fit meetings and recordings around Caspar's revision schedule. Then we'll look at hiring a private tutor, depending on how much things take off.'

Mum turned to Caspar. 'Wow. How do you feel about that, darling?'

He shrugged a little. 'Yeah, it sounds ... good, I guess.'

'It's more than good, young man!' TJ pointed his finger to accentuate how pleased he was with this 'correct' answer. 'Your talent is unlike anyone else's I've come across for a very long time and we need to strike while the iron's hot. I'm thinking we get some proper demos recorded in my studio, then I can set up meetings with the labels. I've got no doubt they'll be fighting to sign you once they see your potential. Then believe me, GCSEs will be the furthest thing from your mind.'

He laughed loudly. I couldn't help but laugh along. So did Mum, albeit guiltily. The only one who wasn't laughing was Caspar.

'I'm sure that's not quite true,' Mum said finally. 'Exams are still important, even for pop stars.'

'I was never much of an academic myself,' TJ admitted. 'Didn't stop me starting up one of the most successful management companies in the UK, though. Sometimes all you need is killer instinct or, in Caspar's case, a huge amount of talent.'

The praise kept rolling in until Caspar excused himself to go to the bathroom. I watched him walk away from the table, head down and hands thrust in the front pocket of his hoodie. Other people wouldn't have noticed, but I knew my brother and I knew something was wrong.

'Actually, I might go too,' I said.

I followed him through the restaurant. 'Are you OK?' I asked.

He sighed at the sound of my voice and turned around to face me. 'Is it that obvious?'

'Not to them,' I replied. 'But it is to me. What's up?'

Caspar ran a hand through his hair, mussing it up like he always did when he got nervous. 'Nothing. It's just ... I dunno. All this sounds too good to be true. I wasn't expecting him to get straight into touring and leaving school. It's all happening really fast.'

'TJ just wants you to be excited. It probably won't happen that fast. You should be happy about it!'

'I *am* happy, but ...' Caspar didn't seem to realise he was anxiously kicking at a very expensive looking water feature. 'He keeps saying how great I am and stuff, but I'm not *that* good. Just because I've got fans on YouTube, it doesn't mean the rest of the world is going to like me.'

It was weird seeing my brother like this. Usually he was 120% confident about everything. Usually he never stopped to question himself. Usually being a famous singer was all he talked about.

But I guess this was an unusual situation.

'What do you mean Cass? You're *super* talented. It's the reason you're getting this chance in the first place. Look how many people already love your songs.'

'Oh for God's sake, Meg, what the hell do you know about it?' he hissed at me under his breath, eyes flashing with an anger I didn't recognise. 'You're just a kid. You've got no idea what any of this is really like.'

Then he turned and disappeared into the men's toilets, leaving me feeling more insignificant than the tiny drops of water that were falling from the fountain beside me.

Back then I saw the world in black and white. There was no in-between. Caspar loved music. He was insanely talented at music and someone was going to promote his music so that the whole country would hear it. What possible reason was there not to be happy? He was right. I didn't understand.

I dejectedly returned to the table, catching the end of Mum and TJ's conversation. He was dazzling her with more facts and figures, and reassuring her that he knew what he was doing where musical teenagers were concerned.

'So, what about you little miss?' he asked as I sat down. 'Does creative genius run in the family?'

'Oh, Meggy's super creative,' Mum answered on my behalf. 'She's going to be a real trendsetter one day.'

I looked down at my napkin, not wanting to meet TJ's eye. However, it was hard to resist his magnetic smile and I found myself cautiously smiling back.

'Do you like music too?' he asked me directly. 'Do you sing or play any instruments?'

Once again, Mum butted in and answered the question before I had the chance to. 'She messes about with Cass and her father all the time, you know, a little bit of guitar and backing singing. But she's far too young to be doing YouTube videos with them.'

TJ's eyes widened in surprise. 'But you won't be too young forever! I bet you'd love to be making your own music, right?'

I shrugged as if it was an ambition that had never crossed my mind.

'Maybe in another few years?' TJ asked with a conspiratorial wink. 'You're bound to have the McCarthy musical gene. I can sense it in you.'

This was the first time anyone had ever asked me about my own music. More than anything, I wanted to tell him that I constantly scribbled lyric ideas in the back of my school books; that I always seemed to have a tune in my head and hummed melodies around the house when no one was listening; that I'd been teaching myself guitar and had almost mastered my first barre chord; that one day, I wanted to be as good as Dad ... or even Caspar ...

But then, before I could voice any of these thoughts, my brother came back to the table. He'd obviously had a little chat with himself in the mirror, because he was all straightened posture, confident laughter and cocky swagger – his previous dark mood forgotten or at least very well hidden.

So, naturally, all the conversation went straight back to him.

# CHAPTER TWELVE

Hugging TJ is like hugging a Golden Retriever. I can feel his invisible tail wagging behind him as he greets me with his usual overflowing warmth and enthusiasm.

'I'm super, Meggy Megster!' he exclaims. 'Never better. I mean, I'm stressing like crazy about this whole album situation and your brother is intent on giving me a nervous breakdown. But other than that I'm just grand.'

A frustrated groan escapes from Caspar's room. I walk in to find him slumped on the sofa, rubbing his head like it's on fire. 'Look, can we focus please?' he snaps. 'I've got a thousand better things to be doing, so let's just get it over with.'

'What's going on?' I ask. Dad is at the computer wearing the tatty baseball cap he digs out whenever TJ's here. It's so embarrassing that I think I might die if I look at him for too long.

'TJ's decided to come down and hassle me in person,' Caspar growls.

'I'm not hassling you Mr M.C., I'm simply *cajoling* you.' TJ sweeps across the room and hits the space bar, nearly knocking DJ Dad off his swivel chair. Heavy, electronic music fills the air. 'Now this guy is hot. He's getting cuts with all the big UK acts and he's dying to work with you.'

'I hate it,' Caspar interrupts. 'It's not my style at all. There's no way I can write to this.'

I don't know what he's talking about. The instrumental track is incredible and already I can hear an ocean of melodies inside my head.

'I've got plenty of options,' TJ says coolly. 'There's going to be something here that you like, trust me.'

'Or how about going back to our song?' Dad suggests, valiantly. 'TJ said it had real potential when we played it to him. Maybe we could get one of those Swedish producers onto it?'

Caspar starts pacing impatiently. 'Just forget our song Dad, it's not right. None of the tracks are right. I don't feel inspired by any of them.'

'Have you ever thought that maybe *you're* the problem here, Cass? These tracks sound fine to me.' The words burst out of my mouth before I have time to tell them not to. Oops.

He glares at me with a look that could instantly turn fresh flowers into those yucky bowls of potpourri Mum insists on putting on top of the toilet. It doesn't matter how old I get, I'll always be his irritating little sister – the one who doesn't understand.

'You don't get it, Meg. *Fine* isn't good enough. If I'm making a big comeback then it can't be *fine*. It has to be a guaranteed, massive hit.' He stomps over to the computer and stops the music. 'These aren't hits ... They're SHITS!'

TJ raises an eyebrow, something he seems to do a lot when he's with Caspar. 'Wait, wait, wait. I haven't played you everything yet. Let me find some more options, I know I've got something hit-worthy in here.'

Oh no. That speaky-before-thinky thing is happening again ...

'It's not just the track that makes a hit, you know, It's what you do with it. If you can't hear potential in any of these productions then maybe you're not being inventive enough.'

Double oops. All of Caspar's pent-up artistic frustration gets dumped on my head like an ice bucket challenge.

'You think it's easy, do you? Well then, little miss Meggy Moo, why don't you write the topline yourself since you're so clever? Go on, be my guest! I'd love to see what fantastic ideas you manage to come up with.'

*OK then.* That's what I should say back. *OK then, I will. And it will be awesome. And even if it's not, I'll actually finish it without overthinking every single note a thousand times.*

But of course, I don't say anything. Because I'm nowhere near as brave as I want to be. I'm just as scared of taking chances as Caspar is.

'Yeah, didn't think you'd have an answer,' he snarls after a pause. 'Piss off and play your little dress-up games. Leave the grown-ups to deal with the music, OK Meg?'

'Woah, calm down Cass. Meg's only trying to help.' Dad gives me a half-smile. The 'oh goodness, what's your brother like, eh?' half-smile I know so well. 'It's all got a bit heated in here this afternoon. I don't think any of us mean to be quite so touchy.'

'Any of us.' Ha ha. More like one of us. The super spoiled, egomaniac, bratty one of us.

'It's alright,' I reply breezily. 'You guys carry on. I'm off to my room ... to play my little dress-up games.'

TJ selects another new instrumental, wilfully ignoring the disruption. 'Now this one will definitely get you excited. Wait for the chorus, it's a big, big sound.'

As I turn to go, I realise the Babybel I've been holding has become the innocent victim of my epic frustration. I've squished my fingernails into the red wax as if it was some sort of cheesy, executive stress ball.

'Hey, Meggy! How did the job interview go?' Dad suddenly remembers to ask. He looks so earnest in his stupid, embarrassing hat. It's difficult to get too annoyed with him, even under the circumstances.

'Fine thanks,' I reply.

Dad smiles brightly at me, then turns straight back to the The Caspar Show™

Maybe 'fine' isn't good enough for the number one son and his entourage, but it seems to be just 'fine' wherever I'm concerned.

# CHAPTER THIRTEEN

Here is a little-known fact about my brother. He's actually a very patient teacher. It was Caspar who showed me my first guitar chord. One Saturday, when I was around ten years old, I wandered into his room as he was practising a song Dad had taught him. It sounded so good that I had to get a closer listen.

'What are you playing?' I asked.

Caspar barely looked up, he was concentrating so hard. Back then his fingers moved across the strings with much more effort. He was obviously talented, but he was still learning and had to think hard about what he was doing.

'"Learn To Fly",' he answered. 'By Foo Fighters.'

I sang along. Dad loved playing that song so the first line was burned into my memory.

Caspar smiled at me and joined in.

He shifted along his bed so I could sit next to him, then we sang through the first verse and chorus together as he played. It was a little slow and clumsy in places, but by the second verse we were loving the sound of our voices blending together.

'Hey, can you teach me a chord?' I asked.

'Sure. Which one?' Caspar placed his fingers into a complicated looking shape and strummed. 'C?'

I shook my head. 'Not C. That looks hard.'

He laughed affectionately. 'You can tackle it, child genius. But OK … how about E minor? That's only on two strings.'

He gave me his guitar, but it swamped me. 'This is heavy! How do you even hold it?'

'Practice. Now give me your hand.'

He guided me, positioning my index and third fingers beside each other on the fretboard. The guitar twanged tunelessly, protesting at the sudden owner-switch.

'I can't do it,' I sighed. 'It sounds rubbish.'

'Look, press down as hard as you can and make sure you stay on the right fret.'

I did as I was told, squeezing so hard my fingers hurt. Determined, I kept on strumming until something resembling a chord started to sound.

'There you go,' Caspar laughed. 'E minor. You're a rock star now!'

I played it over and over, elated at my miniature victory. 'I'M PLAYING IT! WOOHOO!

Foo Fighters didn't sound quite as convincing when it was over one continuous, clunky chord. But Caspar sang along with me anyway.

♫

**Top 5 Half-Truths BandSnapper (aka. Matty Chester) Knows About LostGirl (aka. Me):**

1. I write love songs. (He just doesn't know they're all about him.)

2. I have a musical older brother. (But name, age, and the fact he's an internationally known pop star have been altered slightly … for obvious reasons.)

3. I live in the South of England. (Only he thinks it's some little village in Hampshire, not his home city.)

4. I'm from a 'happy and together' family of four. (But not that we are a #goals, #pictureperfect, #spon, #gifted, #instafamous, #justhit1milfollowers frickin' FAMILY BRAND!)

5. I now have a summer job. (This is where I have to start thinking carefully about which facts I need to 'adapt'.)

It's tricky talking to BandSnapper. One tiny crack in my story would unravel everything, which is why I give Matty the *half-true* version of what's going on. The white lie version, if you will. It's not like I'm full-on lying or anything. I'm merely editing the facts. Well at least that's what I try and tell myself.

> **LostGirl:** Loving your musical theatre choices! But nothing from Waitress? Come on, sort your life out. As for sad songs … OK, these are the gut-wrenchers that

always bring a tear to my eye.

1. Someone You Loved – Lewis Capaldi

2. Breathe Me – Sia

3. Sober – Demi Lovato

4. Surrender – Natalie Taylor

5. Falling – Harry Styles

I'm welling up just thinking about them, so I'm going to change category immediately.

Your next list is Top 5 songs about working/jobs. The reason for this choice is – guess who's started a new job at the library? The answer is me. (I'm assuming you guessed right.)

A library is basically the same as a frozen yoghurt shop, right?

**LostGirl:** It's not exactly rock-and-roll, but on the bright side it's a bit of extra cash.

See. Not lies. Half-truths.

**LostGirl:** I'm so happy you liked 'Firework Display'! Seriously, it means a lot. Thanks for the pep talk too. I know you're right and I shouldn't be so nervous about performing, but I'd honestly rather put my head in Dad's worm-infested compost heap than sing in front of strangers. The only person I trust with my songs is you.

Well at least that bit is true.

> **LostGirl:** Thank you for listening. You make this LostGirl feel a little less lost xxx

You might think it's odd for someone as rude and sarcastic as me to write such a sappy message, but what can I say? Matty is the tap to my maple tree ... he draws the sap out of me.

My lovesick daydream is suddenly interrupted by my message alerts bleeping at 200bpm. The same notifications appear on my laptop screen, sending my Twitter tab into overdrive. Confused, I click on the page, which is being flooded with tweets from local fans.

> OMG, YOU'RE WORKING AT DODO YOYO?! WHEN DID THIS DEVELOPMENT HAPPEN?!!

> Totally gonna drop by Dodo Yoyo to get a selfie with **@MegMcCarthy** tomorrow ...

> OK, ONE QUESTION ... WILL CASPAR BE THERE?!!

What the hell? How does everyone know? I run a search and discover, to my horror, that Laura has posted the same message all across the shop's social media.

> Great news froyo fans! Tomorrow we have a special celeb starting work with us. **@MegMcCarthy**, sister of **@CasparMcCarthy**, will be here over summer serving you all your favourite flavours! Looking forward to her joining the team.

I scroll down.

🐦 Yawn, she's not even a real celebrity.

🐦 Me watching **@MegMcCarthy** get handed
everything on a silver platter: 👁👄👁 ?

🐦 Way to stay relatable. NOT.

I was expecting this, but it's so much worse when you see it with your own eyes.

'So tomorrow is gonna be fun,' I say to Maximillian who is lolling on my bed. 'Can we switch places? You go work at the yoghurt shop and I'll stay home and be a cat.'

He turns around a couple of times then starts licking his own arsehole.

Good to know I can always rely on him for wisdom and comfort during these stressful times.

# CHAPTER FOURTEEN

'THERE SHE IS! IT'S REALLY HER!'

'NO WAY. AHH!'

'MEG! MEG, CAN I GET A SELFIE? PLEEEEASE?'

A crowd of teenagers are screeching and snapping photos as I approach the shop. I smile awkwardly as I try to get to the door. 'Wow, thanks for coming down, guys. I've just got to set up for my shift. Sorry, excuse me, err ... do you mind? Sorry, can I get past?'

It literally blows my mind that anybody would go to the trouble of getting out of bed early in the summer holidays for the sake of a selfie. I'm already stressing about the new job but now I've got to also think about looking 'camera ready' at all times.

'Meg, you're here!' beams Laura. 'Come in, come in!' Then she calls over my shoulder to the fans. 'Five minutes and we'll be open. Have a look at the menus while you're waiting. All our yoghurt is low-fat, organic, nut-free, and there are vegan options available so there should be something for everyone!'

Subtle, Laura. Real subtle.

'Goodness, this is the biggest crowd we've had here in donkey's years. Thank you so much for bringing them all, Meg.'

Self-consciously, I tuck a loose strand of hair behind my ear. 'I didn't do anything. You're the one who put the word out.'

'Well you must've done something,' a voice calls out from behind the counter. 'When she put the word out about *me*, the only person who turned up was my Nan.'

My eyes meet Alana's. She's in her bright pink uniform leaning on the till like she owns it. She's inescapable. Unavoidable. She seems so comfortable taking up all the space that it suddenly feels like there's not much space left for me.

'You didn't see a little old lady in that queue, did you? About yay high. Specs, slippers from Lidl, moans a lot ...'

Her super-charged confidence is the exact opposite of what I'm feeling right now. Come on brain. Think of a hilarious, witty reply ...

'No.'

Brilliant banter Meg. Up there with some of your finest work.

'Right, we shouldn't keep them waiting,' Laura trills. 'Meg, why don't you put your things in the back room, then we can open up?'

'OK.'

'You can shadow Alana today. She'll train you on the till and the toppings station and everything. Don't worry too much, you'll soon get to know the place.'

'OK,' I repeat. My language skills are diminishing by the second.

Alana opens the back door and beckons me over to her. She has a huge smile. I'm talking Cameron Diaz huge ... Zac Efron letterbox-mouth huge. Huge as in half her entire head is smiling at me. Or maybe it's the bold, red lipstick that makes me think that.

'Follow me, I'll show you where to put your bag.' Alana makes theatrical jazz hands in the tiny staffroom. 'OK, here's the super-quick tour. Fridge. Kettle. Lockers. Microwave. Table and chairs. Calendar. Oh, and of course, super-alluring hat in the shape of extinct bird.'

She hands me a spare Dodo cap with a flourish. I take it begrudgingly. 'Err, thanks.'

'You'll learn to love it,' she replies, deadpan.

Trying not to mess up my carefully styled Ariana ponytail, I put it on. 'Right. I'll have to take your word for that.'

Alana giggles and pats me on the shoulder. Oh no. She's a toucher. Way too soon. Waaaay too soon.

'Don't be nervous. It's super-chilled here. I'll help you out.'

I give her a smile, attempting to look grateful. 'Thanks.'

For a brief second, I wonder if maybe Mum was right about meeting new people. This girl is definitely friendly and I've got to try and keep an open mind. But just as I tell myself this, she opens that oversized, red-lipped mouth and says the one thing that causes all positive hope for the future to shrivel up and die. 'Are you actually Caspar McCarthy's sister?'

Here we go again. What are we, like four sentences into our relationship and she's already dropped the C-bomb? The familiar heavy weight of disappointment drops from my chest, down into my stomach where I know it will ferment for the rest of the morning. Ugh.

'Laura was telling me all about your family. I'm such a big

fan of his. I can't believe I'm like, one step away from him now that I've met you! What is he like? Is he as cool as he looks in his music videos?'

'Mmm, kinda. I reply in a deliberately vague way as irritation prickles under my skin. 'Anyway, we'd better get out there.'

I turn my back on her sharply and stride out of the staff room. The whole reason I'm here is to get away from Caspar, not to stand around talking about him. This job was supposed to be an escape, something for myself. I should've known that wouldn't last long.

♫

The first few hours as an official Dodo Yoyo employee go by faster than an episode of RuPaul's Drag Race. As soon as Laura opens the doors the place is packed with kids, all buying frozen yoghurt in order to get to me. Alana and Laura both rush up and down the counter, switching frantically between pouring toppings into cups and taking money at the till. I'm trying to watch what they're doing, but it's difficult when every customer stops me for a chat and a selfie.

Whenever I try to help with the orders Laura shoos me back to the mob. 'No, no, Meg, you stay there with your fans, we've got everything under control.' I'm clearly just here as human advertising.

Eventually the flurry of excitement dies down. Alana lets out a massive groan and slumps against the counter. 'Bloody hell. That was intense. I've never scooped so many sprinkles in my life.'

I grab a pair of plastic gloves from under the sink. 'I'm sorry about all the madness. Here, let me help.'

Laura laughs. 'Sorry?! There's no need to be sorry honey, this is amazing for us! We've taken more in two hours than we usually do in a whole weekend.' She furiously wipes down the counter until it's spotless. 'Why don't you two girls take a quick break while it's quiet?'

'Already?' I ask. 'Are you sure? I don't feel like I've done anything yet.'

'*Never* question the chance for a break!' Alana exclaims. 'L-Dog doesn't give them out lightly. They are a gift to be cherished!'

I follow her to the staffroom, trying to collect my thoughts, but she is already talking at me. 'Wow, that was totally insane! I've never seen anyone be mobbed by so many people. Are you famous?'

'No, I'm not famous,' I reply taking a seat. 'I just have a few fans from Instagram and stuff.'

Alana does that annoying thing where instead of sitting opposite me, she comes round the table and sits right next to me. Here we go again with the personal space issue.

'That was way more than a few fans. There were loads of them. You're a real-life celebrity! I can't believe you're working here with us. It's mad.'

'They're my local followers. They're always mega-supportive, but now they've seen me here I doubt it will get busy like that again.'

This is the thing that is so difficult to explain to people. These 'famous' moments are easy come, easy go. They can be such a buzz and feel like they will go on forever, but they never do. If the famous moments don't last for Caspar, they sure as hell won't stick around for me.

'So, these Instagram fans …' Alana is leaning way too close for my liking. 'Are they because of Caspar? Hey, can I follow you?' She is already Googling me.

Stay calm, Meg. Count to three.

'Yeah, I'm known through my brother, but …'

'Oh my God, is this you?!'

My Instagram appears on her screen. Dozens of carefully filtered pictures of me posing in different outfits. I don't usually see people looking at these. Not in the real world anyway. I don't think I like it.

'Yeah, that's me. I get sponsored. Don't judge, they're kind of embarrassing …'

'No, they're COOL,' Alana booms, flicking through image after image. 'Wow, you look gorgeous. No wonder you have all those fans, you're like a supermodel.'

I try to see myself through her eyes. 'Not sure about that. Anyone can look good with the right editing.'

'No way! Is that your cat?'

She's on a picture of me holding the fat, furry space hopper.

'Yep, that's Maxi,' I smile. 'He's got nearly as many followers as I do.'

Alana clicks on a picture of him dressed as Yoda. She laughs so much that she snorts, but that just makes her laugh even more. 'Ha! This is amazing. Your cat is utterly brilliant. I'm gonna follow him right this second. And you too, of course.'

Great. Now I have to follow her back otherwise it's rude. I'd kind of hoped we wouldn't have to do the whole swapping social media thing yet. Now all she's going to see is the flawless, *McCarthyBrand virtual MegTM*, not the me sitting right in front of her.

Oh well, who cares? She's loud and she's cocky, and I'm not even convinced that I like her, but I hit follow anyway.

*AlanaHoward*. I briefly scan her page. 'Wait, is this you?' She's singing into a microphone and playing a turquoise-blue acoustic guitar. It's a static photo, yet I can feel her in motion, brimming with so much charismatic confidence that I suddenly get goosebumps.

The real-life Alana, with the pulled-back ponytail and unflattering uniform, gives me an amused grin. 'Yes, that is indeed me. I'm a singer-songwriter. I play loads around Brighton at open mics and stuff.'

'Open mics?' I parrot back stupidly, while my brain tries desperately to reconcile the stunning singer shot with the sloppy shop girl in front of me.

'Err yeah, it's where all the singers who don't get airplay hang out,' Alana answers giving me a what-planet-have-you-been-living-on look.

'Well, I'm not eighteen yet,' I say defensively. 'I can't officially go to pubs.'

Alana laughs, dissolving the prickly atmosphere in an instant. 'Technically, I've only been old enough to drink since last year, but most pubs don't mind you performing if you're only having soft drinks.'

Her words switch on a lightbulb in my head and send my little brain-cockroaches scurrying. Open mic nights! Why have I never considered doing something like that before? They're the kind of thing Brighton is famous for.

Wait, what am I thinking? That I'm going to get up in a pub and start singing? In front of a room full of total strangers? Or, even worse, in front of fans?! Yeah right. Welcome back cockroaches.

'So, I'm guessing your brother bypassed all the local gig legwork?' Alana's leaning back in her chair, looking totally at ease. Unlike me. 'He's so lucky that his songs made it to the right people. I'd do anything to get discovered like that!'

'Actually, he's brilliant at what he does,' I find myself shooting back, a lot more sharply than I mean to. 'He's not just some bubblegum pop star. He's worked hard to hone his craft and get where he is.'

Caspar might be the biggest douche known to mankind, and the most attention-sucking sibling in the UK, but I won't have anyone telling me he's not talented or that he doesn't work hard. Correction – that he *didn't* work hard, past tense. The present is perhaps a little more questionable.

'Oh, no, no, I didn't mean that,' Alana backtracks. Her blue eyes are widening in horror as she realises she's put her foot in her mouth. 'I'm only saying that the music industry is insanely hard. It's amazing he got so far at such a young age. I've been out playing for years and going round in circles. Honestly, it's inspiring to know someone from Brighton can actually make it!'

I have to bite my tongue. I don't know much about Alana,

but I've heard this same old story a hundred times before. Oh I could have got there too, if only I'd had Caspar's luck. I could have got there too, if only I had Caspar's looks. It should have been meeeeee!

Seriously. People are completely delusional about their own abilities. Caspar made it in music with a little bit of luck and a hell of a lot of talent. Most other people couldn't measure up if they tried.

'You want a career in music then?' I ask.

'Serving froyo isn't exactly my dream vocation. My heart's on stage, not at the bottom of a yoghurt pot.'

I can't help but smile at her bonkers analogy. In fact, I can't help but smile at Alana in general, despite my reservations. She is an overflowing sprinkle tub of boldness and enthusiasm; colourful and messy and annoyingly addictive.

Suddenly I'm curious. I want to know what she listens to, where she plays, and why on Earth she's working here if she'd rather be a full-time musician. But before I can voice a single one of my thoughts I'm interrupted.

'Hey, while we're on the subject, can I send you one of my songs? I'd love to know what you think, especially considering your family's so musical and everything.'

The drawbridge inside me snaps shut before she's finished her sentence. How many times have I been here before? How many times will wide-eyed wannabes try and use me as their one-way connection to Caspar? They all leave once they short-circuit, so let's save time for us both and cut the wire right now.

'I can't pass on unsolicited demos,' I say, bluntly. 'Sorry. If you want feedback on your songs then you should send them to Caspar's management directly.'

Alana stares at me. 'O ... K. I didn't mean Caspar. I just wanted to know what *you* thought.'

Yeah, yeah. That old chestnut. As if anyone cares what the Instagram girl thinks about their songs. 'I'm not allowed to accept anything. It's all really complicated because of Caspar. Sorry.'

I'm not sure if Alana's features have changed to anger, disbelief, or amusement. Maybe a little of all three.

'Right, so you can't listen to a song because of your brother? Wow. You really do live on another planet from the rest of us regular folk, don't you?'

Where do I even start? I could try to tell her about the endless stream of demos and desperate pleas that come my way; about the conveyor belt of 'friends' who are only nice to me because they want to get signed; about the feeling of deflation I get when people pin their hopes and dreams on me. But what would be the point? Nobody ever truly believes they're using you. They always think they're the exception to the rule.

So instead we sit in awkward silence, fiddling with our phones, the table stretching out in front of us and the walls of the staffroom closing in.

Thankfully the door swings open and Laura interrupts the dead air. 'OK girls, break's over. It's getting busy again, so I could use a hand.'

We scramble out of our chairs, eager to get away from the frosty atmosphere. Alana raises an eyebrow at me as we head into the shop. 'Can't leave the fans waiting, can we?'

There is the hint of a grin on her face so I'm not sure if her comment is meant as a cheeky olive branch or some kind of attack on me.

I don't answer, choosing to believe it's the latter.

Let's face it. It's always the latter.

# CHAPTER FIFTEEN

**Top 5 Things That Are Super Awkward:**

1. Being the new girl

If I thought being new at school was bad, being new at work is worse. I can't seem to get any of the prices to stick in my head and I manage to pull the chain off the toilet on my first visit. Fail.

2. Meeting new people

Especially those who have minimum interest in you as a person, but maximum interest in what you can do for them. Now I remember why I hate making friends. They're never actually real. In general, people suck.

### 3. Posing for photos

I try to appreciate my fans, but after the fiftieth girl snaps a selfie with me my jaw starts to ache and go all wobbly. In most pictures floating around the Internet, my 'camera-ready smile' looks more Bride of Chucky than Jennifer Lawrence.

### 4. Sharing your house with someone else

When I get home, I discover that TJ has unofficially moved in and taken over. Laptops, paperwork, and to-do lists cover every surface. He seems to be in every room, talking loudly on the phone, talking loudly to my parents, or even talking loudly to himself. My house is chaotic enough without another personality added to the mix. But TJ's constant presence is still not as awkward as my fifth most super awkward thing, which is ...

### 5. Walking in on my brother mid-snogging session

I just want to unwind and watch some Netflix, but no such luck. Caspar is on the living-room sofa with some random, raven-haired girl. He's got her shirt undone and his hands in her bra. I get a sweet front-row view of her lacy red knickers, as her skirt has ridden up around her waist.

'FOR GOD'S SAKE, CASPAR!' I shout. 'Do you mind?!'
Apparently their passion is so great that they've forgotten this

is a family space. Acknowledging my presence is not high on their current to-do list. This is nearly as bad as the infamous Mum-and-Dad-anniversary-hot-tub incident, but I'm not prepared to go into that right now.

'CASPAR, PLEASE!'

More delightful slurping sounds.

'I'm just getting to know Sharla,' he finally says, coming up for air.

'Shauna,' she corrects.

'Oh right, Shauna. How about we just go for "Gorgeous" so I don't forget?'

I'm fully expecting Shauna to see sense and slap him round the face, but instead, she squeals hysterically while pulling her skirt down and making a vague attempt at looking slightly less naked. 'Caspar! You're so cheeky. But sure, I'll go by whatever name you want.'

Ugh, vomit rising! *Vomit rising!*

'I'm sorry, but who are you?' I ask the newly-appointed 'Gorgeous'. 'Caspar never mentioned he had a girlfriend.'

Caspar gets up from the sofa, pulling Shauna with him. 'Woah, woah, don't get too carried away. We only met today.' He winks at her, causing her to glow red and giggle even more. 'But who knows what could happen?'

'OH MY GOD,' Shauna squeals. 'I can't believe this. Like, who goes down to the pier and bumps into their favourite singer?! And then gets invited to *their house*. This is like a dream ...'

'Why don't we go up to my room and let the dream continue?' Caspar whispers audibly to her.

OK, this is too much. I'm going to quench their fire with my projectile puking.

'Technically, it's not your room anymore,' I say, my voice like steel. 'Sorry Shauna,' I add, shooting her a sympathetic look. 'I'm not trying to make you feel unwelcome or anything, it's just ...'

My sentence trails off. They're already halfway upstairs, hands all over each other. TJ appears out of nowhere and stops Shauna in her desperate little tracks.

'Phone, please,' he instructs, holding out his hand.

He knows the potential dangers of girls being alone with Caspar ... Let's just say that a dick-pic scandal wouldn't exactly be ideal for the *McCarthyBrand*.

Shauna rummages through her handbag and practically throws her phone at TJ so she can get upstairs quicker. 'Sure, no problem. Take it.' She beams at me, her face wild with excitement. 'It was so nice to meet you!'

There is no way I can return that particular sentiment. Instead, I call up the stairs after them, 'Is this your way of getting inspiration, Cass? Maybe you should try actually *writing a song* first?'

'Maybe you should try growing up and having some fun,' he calls back over his shoulder. 'You never know, you might actually like it.' His bedroom door slams shut.

TJ laughs, despite my embarrassment. 'He's a wild card, isn't he? I'm sure he'll feel much better once he's got all that stress out of his system.'

'Urgh GROSS, TJ. How is this fair? I've been pushed out of my own house so Caspar can have his *precious* space, but then all he does is go out on the pull. It's disgusting! I don't want to come home to random girls I don't know sprawled all over our living room.'

'She's not random. She's Sinéad!'

'It's Sharla. No, wait. Shauna. Oh, whoever she is, it's gross!'

'Oh come on, Megster. It's all part of being young and famous. Don't get all judgmental just because you've joined the working world.'

'Yeah, I am working and actually being productive with my life. And what's he doing? How is Shauna/Sharla going to help get his stupid album off the ground?'

'I'm working on the album part, don't you worry. By the end of the month, we'll have something started.'

'End of the MONTH?!' I can't handle a whole month of TJ spreading out everywhere, Mum fussing endlessly, Dad trying to be cool, and Caspar sulking. And now random strangers doing sex shows on my sofa when I get home!

'What's all the fuss out here?' Dad strides down the hallway, still wearing that bloody backward baseball cap. 'You alright, babygirl?'

'No, I'm not!' I exclaim, crossing my arms in annoyance. 'Why are you letting Caspar take over the whole house? He was all over that girl when I walked in!'

To my horror, Dad laughs. Which makes TJ laugh. Upstairs Shauna is definitely laughing. The only one not laughing in this situation is me.

'It's not funny, Dad! This is my home too.'

'Boys will be boys,' Dad answers, still chuckling. 'Isn't that right TJ, my bro?'

He holds his hand out to TJ in a limp fist bump No. No. Make it stop.

'Oh. In that case, how about I go find some bloke off the street. I'll bring him back and shag him in my room, shall I? You don't mind, right? Since there don't seem to be any rules in this house.'

Dad's laughter instantly stops and is replaced by his strict, parent voice. 'Meg, watch your language! You're seventeen and you're certainly not allowed boys in your room.'

'Don't you think that's a bit of a double standard, Dad?'

'Well, he's over eighteen so there's not much I can do, but I'll talk to him tomorrow. Anyway, he's not hurting anyone and to be perfectly honest it's easier to let him get on with it.'

Sure, Dad. Let Caspar keep being King of the House, walking over all of us and showing zero respect. He's not hurting anyone … except maybe your own daughter.

Urgh. I will be taking every possible shift available at Dodo Yoyo, because new people may be super awkward, but at least they can't disappoint you as much as your own family.

♫

**LostGirl:** Hey, are you online?

**BandSnapper:** Yeah, I was about to send you my top 5 songs about work …
1. 9 To 5 – Dolly Parton
2. Bills – LunchMoney Lewis
3. Work Song – Hozier
4. Harder, Better, Faster, Stronger – Daft Punk
5. Work Bitch – Britney Spears

**BandSnapper:** Have you finished your first day? On a scale of Dolly to Britney, how did it go?

**LostGirl:** Yep! Not as kick-ass as Dolly but not as trashy as Britney. It was OK.

**BandSnapper:** Just OK? What did you have to do? What are your co-workers like?

**LostGirl:** To be honest I was mainly standing around, trying to learn stuff. My new boss is nice enough, but I think she only gave me the job because she knows my mum.

**BandSnapper:** Ah well, I'm sure you're the coolest librarian around! Did you meet anyone new?

**LostGirl:** Only a tall, dark, handsome stranger in-between the Poetry and Biography shelves ...

**BandSnapper:** Oh ... Right.

**LostGirl:** Lol kidding! There were no hot guys. Just another girl around my age.

**BandSnapper:** Hey, don't make me worry like that! I thought someone was going to steal you away from me then ... ☺

**LostGirl:** You've got nothing to worry about ...

**BandSnapper:** Well, that's a relief! What's the other girl like?

**LostGirl:** She's OK. A bit annoying.

**BandSnapper:** How come?

**LostGirl:** Loud. Doesn't shut up. Thinks she owns the place.

**BandSnapper:** Wow, that's some first impression. Maybe she was nervous?

**LostGirl:** Maybe. I think she wants to be my bestest friend, but I can't see that we have much in common. Apart from music, I guess.

**BandSnapper:** Liking music has to be a pretty good start! Give her a chance, you might find a best friend where you least expect it. Stranger things have happened.

**LostGirl:** But I already have a best friend. I don't need another one.

**BandSnapper:** You mean ... me?

**LostGirl:** Who else?

**BandSnapper:** Awww, LG. You're mine too.

**LostGirl:** 😊

**BandSnapper:** When are you going to tell me who you really are?

**LostGirl:** Please. Don't ask.

**BandSnapper:** It's been two years now and I don't even know your real name.

**LostGirl:** Can't we just keep things the way they are?

**BandSnapper:** I don't know. I'm not sure how much longer I can keep waiting ... Next time you might really meet a tall, dark, handsome stranger ... and then what?

**LostGirl:** What do you mean? That was a joke ...

**BandSnapper:** I know.

**BandSnapper:** It's just ...

**BandSnapper:** I dunno. Never mind.

**LostGirl:** Are you trying to tell me something here?

**BandSnapper:** Yeah. I'm trying to tell you to think of your top 5 water related songs.

**LostGirl:** And what's the reason for this choice?

**BandSnapper:** I've been taking pictures by the sea all day. I'd better crack on and edit them.

**LostGirl:** OK. Adios best friend xxx

**BandSnapper:** Adios LG x

# CHAPTER SIXTEEN

Caspar is hogging the upstairs bathroom. His magazine interview is today, and apparently he needs to do his hair and make-up before the hair and make-up people arrive. Because that definitely makes sense.

I end up late for work with sweat circles showing in the armpits of my revolting pink polo shirt. A new gang of fangirls are already preserving the image for all eternity. My reputation is as crumpled as a Chinese takeaway menu that's been shoved through the letterbox by a spotty thirteen-year-old.

On top of all this, I find out that Alana is going to be my 'work mentor' for the entire summer. My fate is sealed.

**Top 5 Things I Learn About Alana During Our Shift:**

1. She is useless at taking hints

Especially when it comes to topics I DON'T want to talk about.

Seriously. Within the first hour she's already interrogated me about my school life, my love life, and my future career prospects. All of these are subjects I evade like a conversational ninja because it's literally none of her business. It doesn't stop her spilling her guts up to me though. Uninvited.

'So you're thinking of Uni then? I didn't bother with it. I was sick of all the exams and coursework. So boring. What's the point when you only want to do music?'

'No way, you're still single?! Not that I blame you. I gave up on love during sixth form too. It was even more stressful than the exams!'

'Hey, have you changed your mind about hearing my demos yet? I'd still really love to know what you think. Can't you break the industry rules, just this once?'

Talk about majorly frickin' awkward. I think she'll force me to listen through her phone at some point and then the awkwardness will get even more excruciating. I honestly can't do anything for her career, however much she hopes I can. Especially because it's obvious to me that ...

2. She is an amateur

I mean that in the musical sense. And I know it sounds horrible, but sadly it's true. She's been working at Dodo Yoyo for two years while she 'gets her career off the ground'. But in this time she's never played a single gig outside of Brighton and has only recorded in the shittiest local studios that barely know their XLRs from their arseholes.

Don't get me wrong, open mics are fun, but they aren't going to do anything life-changing for an aspiring songwriter. Does she seriously think a big record label head is going to be in the audience one day and magically discover her?

That might happen in the movies, but in real life A&R people have better things to do than trawl around little pubs in seaside towns on the off-chance that the next Rita Ora is singing through a cheap PA. Talent scouting is all online now and time is money. Alana being so clueless does not give me a lot of hope for her musical abilities. However ...

3. She is excellent at her job

If music doesn't work out for her then I'm certain there are plenty of other career routes she could take. She's effortlessly good at what she does. And yeah, I know it's just scooping yoghurt into pots, but it's about so much more than that.

Alana is a people person. I notice immediately how she puts every customer at ease, even the grumpy ones. It seems like there is no possible situation that can phase her. She's organised and thorough and she's great at explaining things. Which almost makes up for the fact that ...

4. She says the weirdest things

Here are some of the things she said to me over our few hours together – totally out of the blue.

'Did you know that in Wales they call a microwave a popty ping? A POPTY PING!'

'That guy I just served really looks like how I imagine Picasso to look. I've never seen a picture of Picasso but he had that kind of Picasso vibe, don't you think?'

'Do you ever wonder if we see the same colours as each other? Like, what if I'm looking at strawberry yoghurt and thinking it's pink, but for you strawberry is blue, but you've been taught to call blue pink even though it's actually blue ... for you? How insane would that be?'

'Who do you fancy more? Picasso ... or Van Gogh?'

It's hard to know how to react to some of the nonsense she's been coming out with. It's like she has no filter between her brain and her mouth. Which leads me to my fifth and final point ...

5. She isn't bothered what people think about her

I mean, she really, *really* isn't bothered.

She says whatever she wants without worrying if strangers get it or not. She bunches her hair into a messy ponytail and wears her ugly, stretchy top like she's rocking it down a runway. She eats stray Smarties off the counter and laughs about the fact they're making her fat. She looks every customer dead in the eye, staring them down with a beaming smile, even the hot guys.

I wish I could grab one of the serving spoons by the till and start scooping out some of her self-assuredness for myself. Because right at the end of my shift, who should walk in through the door but my delightful school frenemies, Ness and Melissa.

There is nowhere for me to hide. And unlike my new co-worker, I *am* bothered by what people think about me. I'm bothered by what *everyone* thinks.

Even those whose opinion should matter the least.

# CHAPTER SEVENTEEN

'So it's *true*! Meg McCarthy is working at Dodo Yoyo. How *random*!'

Ness glides over as though I'm a magnet pulling her to me by her dangly, metallic earrings. Melissa follows directly behind her, giggling inanely. Two smiling assassins. And I'm trapped behind a counter.

'Hey, what brings you two here?' I say, pretending like the scene in Aladdin's Cave last week never happened. When in doubt, block it out. That's a good motto for life, right?

Ness leans casually on the counter. 'I read your Twitter last night and wanted to come check the place out.' She shifts her sunglasses higher up her blonde head, scanning the room with a bemused expression. 'Is this seriously where you're working now? I'm kind of in shock.'

'Why?' I ask, trying to hide my own shock at the horrendous orange foundation she's misapplied to her face.

'Well, you know,' Ness answers vaguely. She exchanges a slithery, mocking smile with Melissa. 'I just thought you were a bit above this kind of thing, being a *McCarthy* and everything.'

Her tongue rolls around my name, drawing out every syllable in the most patronising way imaginable. Melissa snickers. Then Ness joins in. They are both outright laughing at me. I begin to deflate, agonisingly slowly. There's only one reason they've come here: to see Caspar McCarthy's snooty, bitchy sister stripped of all her power and to cackle loudly about it. Ha. Ha. Ha. There's nowhere I can go. Nothing I can say. They're the customers. And the customer is always right.

'These two friends of yours?' Alana steps into the space beside me. I snap out of my frozen trance and feel her positive energy forming some kind of fearless forcefield between us and them. I'd forgotten she was here, but suddenly I'm bloody glad she is.

Blinking rapidly, my vision comes back into focus. 'Err, yeah. This is Ness and Liss. They go to my school.' Ness smiles tightly, folding her arms. Melissa mirrors the action, tossing her long brown hair behind her like she's issuing a challenge. I can tell instantly that they hate Alana. Perhaps even more than they hate me.

I can also tell that Alana doesn't care.

'You must be over the moon to have a mini-celeb at this little place,' Ness says, throwing the first verbal punch. 'I thought she'd be far too *big* ...' (she looks Alana up and down on this particular word) '... for some minimum wage job.'

'Yeah, how come you need a job like this, Meg?' Melissa adds, unable to hide her snarky tone. 'Doesn't your family have loads of money? Your brother's like, famous!'

'I think you just answered your own question there, darling,' Alana cuts in, her sarcasm an equal match for my so-called friends.

'Meg's *brother* is the famous one. Or rather the *rich* one.' She throws me a cheeky wink like a lifeline. 'Right?'

'Exactly,' I answer, finally finding my voice. 'I don't expect hand-outs from him.' I look Ness straight in the eye. 'Unlike some people.'

Ness stares at me as though I've grown a second head. 'OK. Weird. I thought you'd be doing modelling work or something. Not this.'

How much money do people think I make from Instagram posts? Because besides all the freebies, the answer is zero. Even with the McCarthy surname.

Alana slides open the freezer cover. 'Right ladies, what are you having then?'

She's dripping with politeness, but she's totally in control. Ness and Liss are starting to morph into the two ugly sisters from a Cinderella – their badly drawn-on panto-dame eyebrows scowling in sulky furrows. I have to bite my lip to stop myself from grinning. 'Give me a scoop of vanilla,' she replies. 'Low-fat.' Then she mutters under her breath, 'If you can figure out what that is ...'

Melissa snorts with wicked laughter, her eyes fixed on Alana's body. I am furious. Alana, however, isn't phased in the slightest.

'Low-fat vanilla,' she beams. 'Wonderfully *original* choice. Now can I tempt you with any toppings?' She smiles wide, like a shark. 'Wait, let me guess. You're more than sweet enough aren't you, sweetie pie?'

I'm pretty sure a tiny laugh escapes from me this time. I try to suppress it, but it's too hard.

Ness narrows her eyes. 'I'll have some strawberries. Please.'

As Alana scoops out a tub and hands it across the counter, Ness lets out a high-pitched scream and throws it all over the floor with a squelchy splat.

'Are you trying to kill me?! There was a NUT in that. I'm allergic to nuts! One single trace can send me into anaphylactic shock.'

OK, seriously? SERIOUSLY? This is how low she's going to sink? Because I distinctly remember us scoffing peanut M&Ms together, once upon a time in another life where we actually used to be friends. Or has she forgotten about that? Just like she's forgotten how to be nice to me.

Melissa sweeps to her side, fanning Ness madly with her hands. 'Are you OK, hun? You didn't touch it did you?'

'I ... I don't know,' Ness answers, breathing deeply and gripping Melissa's arm, truly hamming up the whole panto double act now. 'Ohh, I think I'm having a reaction!' In-between croaky breaths, she addresses Alana with fury. 'I can't believe you served that to me. I'm reporting you for negligence!'

No way. This has gone too far now. I can't let Ness hurt Alana's reputation with her out-and-out lies. I clench my fists, building myself up to challenge her – to remind her that this so-called allergy is a complete fantasy and we both know it. But Alana doesn't need me. Of course not. She's got this more than covered.

'We don't store nuts on these premises. Like at all. Zero nuts.'

Ness pauses midway through a faux-wheeze, her eyes widening. 'W-well, there's got to be! I can feel my throat closing up!'

Alana is as chilled out as a Brighton yogi coming out of a hot yoga class. She points to a massive sign at the side of the counter. *No nuts stored on the premises.*

'We pride ourselves on accommodating all allergies and intolerances, and we're very thorough with the nut thing. As you can read here on this *gigantic* sign which is also in the shop window. *Gigantically*. So no one could possibly miss it.'

Ness snaps upright, her face glowing. The sign really is larger than it needs to be. Even I feel stupid for forgetting about it.

Alana pulls a clump of blue paper towels from the dispenser beside the sink and hands them to Ness. 'You look like you're over your anaphylactic shock now. So maybe you could clean up the mess you just dumped on our floor?'

There is a bubble of laughter in my stomach threatening to burst out at any second. I have to clamp a hand over my mouth to stop myself outright cracking up.

'This place is disgusting! Meg, you should be ashamed to show your face here. I'm tweeting everyone I know to tell them your fat friend nearly *killed* me.'

'Fame at last!' Alana beams. 'Brilliant. Can you link them to my Soundcloud as well while you're there?'

Every shot Ness fires rebounds like a boomerang back in her face. I'm floored. What is this power that Alana has? I want some of it too.

And I want to get to know her. Suddenly I want to get to know her more than anything.

'Let's go, Liss,' Ness fumes, dragging Melissa out by the wrist.

'Oh, but I didn't actually order a yoghurt yet ...'

'LISS, NOW!'

They storm out the shop, slamming the door as they go. To their horror, Alana waves brightly at them through the window.

And the bubble finally bursts. I laugh and laugh.

'I take it they're not actually your friends, right?' Alana asks, raising an eyebrow mischievously. 'Because otherwise, I'm gonna feel really uncomfortable right now.'

'Oh, they are *not* my friends,' I answer, still laughing so hard I can barely get the words out. 'Not anymore.' I look at the sticky mess they've left all over the floor. 'God, I'm so sorry they came in and did that. I'll clean it all up.'

Alana grabs the cleaning spray and chucks me a cloth. 'We got this. Don't worry.'

She smiles her super-confident smile at me, and so I decide to do what she says.

For once in my life, I don't worry at all.

# CHAPTER EIGHTEEN

When I get home Mum is buzzing around the kitchen. Or more specifically, she's buzzing around Caspar who is slumped at the dining table, grunting back responses in what I assume is meant to be English.

'Darling, why didn't you talk a bit more about the album? You know it's what the fans are waiting for.'

'Uh-uhm.' (Translation: *I dunno.*)

'You could at least be teasing it a little. Give out a teensy clue or two?'

'Ugghhh.' (Translation: *I don't want to talk about the album yet.*)

'There's only so long the fans will keep reading about your fashion tips, Cassy. They want exclusives! That's what will get you trending again.'

'UGGGHHH.' (Translation: *Expletive.*)

'I take it the interview went well then?' I interrupt.

'It wasn't too bad,' Mum answers, sighing a little. She's leaning against the kitchen counter with a vodka tonic. That means it was bad. 'But I wish your brother would actually talk about the new album otherwise there's not much point in doing promo.'

'Mum, it's not READY!' Caspar explodes, finally forming actual human language. 'You know it's not ready! I'm not going to talk about something that doesn't even exist yet, am I?'

Mum slams her glass onto the counter making both me and Caspar jump. 'Well, when *will* it be ready, Cass? We've given you so much time to get on with it. We've done absolutely everything to accommodate you. But you seem more interested in girls than in doing any bloody work!'

Woah ... Go Mum! I didn't expect that. I was about to head up to my room, but maybe I should stick around to watch the action.

Caspar scrapes his chair back. 'Have you ever stopped to think that maybe I'm feeling the pressure enough without you adding to it? I'm doing my best Mum, but it's not as easy as you seem to think it is. I can't just pull hit songs out of my arse.'

Mum's resolve breaks instantly. I should have known she'd crumble after two seconds.

'Oh, Cassy, wait. Don't be like that. I know you've been working so hard. I didn't mean you weren't trying, darling!'

Stomp, stomp, stomp, footsteps upstairs, followed by a house-shaking door slam.

Mum takes a large swig of her vodka, staring blankly at the toaster. I wonder if she might remember to ask me about my day, my new job, my *anything*. But she doesn't. She's got that all too familiar, far away, preoccupied-with-Caspar, sad look in her eyes. So I decide to leave her to it.

I throw off my evil uniform while my laptop fires up. For once,

I don't immediately check Twitter for the deluge of love and hate. I don't even check *Music Hunger* to talk to Matty. I type two little words into the search instead. *Alana Howard.*

To my surprise, a whole page of results appears. Facebook, Soundcloud, Twitter, local news articles and a row of YouTube thumbnails. I click on the first video in the list.

*Alana Howard – One Day At A Time (Original) LIVE at The Brunswick*

I hit play. Alana is poised at a piano, wearing the same wide-brimmed hat I saw in her Instagram profile picture.

'OK, here goes,' YouTube-Alana laughs, glowing under the spotlight. 'I apologise in advance for any dodgy notes. This is the first time I've played this one live.'

*I don't have a map, I don't have a lot inside my pocket*
*I'm making the most of the things that I've got and that's how*
*I like it*
*Maybe I should get myself together like everybody else*
*They say they've worked it out*
*But I don't think they're being honest …*

I stare at the screen in disbelief. Alana's voice is … incredible. It's strong, soaring with complete ease, but somehow vulnerable at the same time. She wraps so much emotion around her reflective lyrics that you can't help but be drawn in.

*Been living for the weekend*
*Maybe that's shallow but it's what I do*

*Who cares about the dead ends?*
*Does it even matter where I'm running to?*

I didn't expect her to be this good. The song could compete with any major artist's heartfelt stadium anthem and her performance of it is astounding. I want to crawl into my computer screen and be right there in the audience for a better view.

*The future's always gonna be there*
*Nothing lasts forever so I'm OK with now*
*Don't we all just figure it out somehow?*
*If we take it one day at a time*
*One day at a time ...*

By the chorus, I am in no doubt whatsoever – I am an Alana Howard fan. I'm swaying in my seat, humming along with the end chant because it's ridiculously catchy. It's like catching up with a long-lost friend I didn't realise I'd been missing.

This is the girl I work with. The girl who I honestly thought was more suited to holding a yoghurt pot than a guitar. I should have given her a chance so much sooner. Because she's amazing. She's more than amazing. She's a hit artist waiting to be discovered.

I don't know how long I sit there having a one-girl listening party to the video on repeat before I notice my brother standing in my doorway, watching me with a steely, scrunched-up expression.

'Hey, whose song is that?' he asks.

Of course. If there's music happening in this house then it has to pass through Baron Von Casshausen first. He must give written permission for every note that dares to reverberate on the premises. Which is another reason why he's never, ever going to hear a single bar of any of my songs.

'I thought you were off in a strop?' I say, refusing to flinch. I will not be embarrassed about waving my imaginary lighter above my head. It's my room and I'll imagine lighters if I damn well want to.

Caspar rolls his eyes. 'I'm not in a strop. I'm just sick of how much pressure Mum's putting on me about doing stupid interviews. It's annoying.'

'Yeah, so much pressure,' I reply, mirroring his eye-roll. 'You get the house to yourself, producers on tap, Mum and Dad doing literally everything for you ...'

'Suffocating me more like.'

Oh, boohoo. Suffocated with love and attention. Poor little Cass Cass. (I don't say that bit out loud, obviously. I just give him a sarcastic look and hope that it conveys the sentiment.)

'So whose song is that?' he repeats, flopping onto my bed. 'You been talent scouting or something?'

'No, nothing like that. This is a girl I've been working with at my new job.' Caspar looks blankly at me. 'At the yoghurt shop. You know, my summer job?'

He shrugs. 'I dunno what you're up to, do I?' If only all the Caspar fans could see us now. They think he's the perfect big brother and that our relationship is soooo cute. But the reality is we're barely more than passing ghosts in this house.

'Well, I'm working at Dodo Yoyo down in The Lanes and the girl training me is a singer-songwriter. She's really good, check it out ...'

As I replay the video, my bedroom fills with Alana's wonderful voice again. I grin with excitement as the song builds up. It feels more and more familiar to me with every listen, like a classic ballad I've known for years.

I watch Caspar watching the video – his head nodding slightly. I can tell he's enjoying it. Alana will be thrilled to know he took the time to listen to her.

At the middle eight, I turn the volume down slightly. 'What do you think? She's good, right?'

'Yeah, not bad,' Caspar nods. 'Huge potential with her songwriting.'

'That's what I thought,' I say, smiling. Wow. Caspar and I actually agreed on something. Something *musical* no less. This is nothing short of a bloody miracle. 'I reckon she could get signed if all her songs are this good.'

Caspar makes a loud, spluttery guffaw. It catches me off guard. And before I have time to process his reaction, he's already sauntering out of the room.

'Hey, what's so funny?' I call out after him. 'She's talented!'

'Yeah, I guess,' he answers, with a smirk. 'Just a shame she's so fat. Such a waste.'

By the time the words reach my ears, he's gone.

Maybe it's for the best. I'm so shocked that I wouldn't have known what to say back anyway.

# CHAPTER NINETEEN

'So, it's just you and Caspar, right? You don't have any other famous siblings hidden away do you?'

Alana is perched on a stool on the wrong side of the counter, after helping herself to a scoop of double chocolate swirl. For once I'm glad she's being nosy about my life, because it means we're not talking about her songs. There's no way I'll be telling her about Caspar's bullshit 'advice'. It would break her heart.

I can't believe he'd dismiss her incredible voice like that. But ... is he right about her image? Ugh. I feel like a traitorous bitch for even thinking it. Why is the world more obsessed with what people look like than their actual talent? It's not frickin' fair.

'Nope, it's just the two of us.'

Alana is now spinning around on the barstool like a human tornado. I feel dizzy watching her. 'So does musical genius run in the family?'

Great. Back to music. The one thing I categorically *don't* want to discuss.

'Well, yeah. I don't know if you ever saw Caspar's early videos, but it was Dad who recorded him and taught him everything he knows. Mum not so much. I mean, she *thinks* she can sing but ...'

'No, I mean you,' Alana cuts in with a booming laugh. 'Do you dabble in songwriting?'

I freeze. No one has ever asked me this. Everything is always me in relation to Caspar. Do I like his songs? Which one is my favourite? What's life like growing up with a famous brother anyway? But no one ever asks me if *I write music myself*. So I honestly have no idea what to say. This is completely unchartered territory.

Alana stops spinning, looking straight at me. 'Well?'

I blink out of my daze, laughing nervously. 'Erm, yeah. Sorry. Songwriting? Not really. That's Caspar's thing, not mine.'

'You are blatantly lying!' she exclaims. 'Tell me the truth.'

Red alert. Sirens screaming in my brain. How on Earth does she know? What the hell do I do now? I have not kept my songs a secret my whole life for this girl to figure me out after one week.

'Well, you know, I used to help my dad with lyrics when I was younger, for fun. But nothing serious.'

There. That sounds totally plausible. So why do I suddenly feel like a germ under a microscope? Must be because Alana is now scrutinising every cell of my being with a disbelieving stare.

'You're from this hugely musical family and you've never written a proper song yourself? How come? Haven't you ever wanted to try?'

Oh, for crying out loud! She is not going to let this drop. I've never had to deal with this kind of interrogation about my music before. Well, only from BandSnapper but he doesn't count.

'It's not really my thing,' I answer, vaguely. I'm hoping it's enough to kill the conversation dead, but Alana has other ideas.

'How can it not be your thing?!' she squawks. 'It's music! It's amazing! And it's a part of your whole family, so don't give me that.' Her words are a helicopter's massive searchlight glaring down on me. There's nowhere to hide and the intensity of it is making me sweat. 'Is this something to do with those girls from yesterday? Are you worried they'll bully you about it?'

'No!' I exclaim. 'Come on. I get tons of hate mail day-in, day-out from crazy Twitter followers. It's not like I'd let anyone's opinion stop me doing what I want.'

Yes I would. I let people's opinions stop me doing *everything* I want.

'Not everyone can be as musically gifted as Caspar. We might be related but that doesn't mean we can both write songs.'

'Well, you should try writing something. I bet you'd be good at it.'

I lean back against the counter, avoiding Alana's eyes. 'Yeah. Maybe one day.'

'I don't mind giving you some lessons. We should jam together! That would be awesome!'

Oh God. I think I liked it better when she was endlessly going on about Caspar instead of me. 'Did you listen to any of my songs yet by the way?'

I'm grateful to spot a group of girls lingering outside – their eyes flashing with excited recognition when they see me. 'Customers!' I cry. 'Better get back to work.'

'They're not customers, they're your fans. And they'll totally buy your record when we write it together.'

I smile at the girls entering the shop, hoping Alana will get the hint that I don't want to talk about this anymore. But annoyingly, hints don't appear to exist in her world.

♪

'You do listen to music, right? I mean, music that isn't just Caspar?'

'Of course I do!'

'What kind?'

'All kinds. Pop, obviously. Indie bands, EDM, singer-songwriter stuff ...'

'Ooh, singer-songwriters! Now you're talking. Name some you like. Come on, let's see if we match.'

The girls who entered the shop only provided a temporary distraction, and now it's back to the questioning. At least this time we're on to other musicians and not our own stuff so I decide to go with it.

'Dodie is one of my favourites. Then there's Billie Eilish, Taylor Swift ...'

'OH MY GOD, I LOVE TAY TAY! Which songs do you like?'

'All of them really. I love the whole *folklore* album, especially "invisible string".'

Alana's eyes light up with glee. 'That's the best album track! It should have been a single right?'

As usual, her enthusiasm cancels out her spatial awareness. I step backward. 'Yeah, totally!'

She steps forward. 'Do you know any of Ingrid Michaelson's stuff?'

I step backward. 'Yeah! *Be OK, Everybody ...*'

She steps forward as we both say, '*You and I.*'

'Are you kidding?' Alana laughs crazily. 'It's one of the songs that made me want to write in the first place!'

Excitement flutters in my stomach and before I know it, words are tumbling out of me, eager to catch Alana's wave. 'She writes in such a clever way; her lyrics are so quirky but heartfelt. Do you know any more American female writers? LP? Sara Bareilles? Grace VanderWaal?'

'Yes and yes and yes. I literally love them! Are you living in my brain right now or something?! They are so underrated.' I'm on a roll now. There's a whole encyclopaedia of singers in my mind and I want to compare them all against Alana's checklist. 'Do you know Oh Wonder? They're a London-based girl-guy duo – really chilled out and beautiful.'

'I saw them live last year!' Alana answers. 'I even met them after the show and Josephine signed the set list for me. I thought I was gonna die on the spot.'

'Amazing, I love her style! They're incredible!'

'How the heck can you listen to so many cool songwriters and not be inspired to write your own stuff?'

I realise I've let my enthusiasm get the better of me. Alana has managed to break down my guard without me even noticing. Damn it. 'I dunno,' I shrug, defensively. 'I watch a lot of movies too, but that doesn't mean I want to suddenly become a film director.'

Alana shakes her head. 'Nope. I'm not having that. Not with your musical genes. You've just gotta find inspiration. And I'm gonna help you.'

She's going to help me.

Yay. Well done me. Couldn't just stick to opening the till, could I? I had to go and open a massive can of musical worms. Somehow, holding back Caspar's nasty comments has resulted in a songwriting lesson from Alana being bestowed upon me.

Is it home time yet?

# CHAPTER TWENTY

I'm being lectured about the one thing I actually know something about. The thing I love more than anything. I'm so tempted to tell Alana the truth – scream it. *I'M A SONGWRITER, DAMN IT! I've written dozens upon dozens of songs and they're all on my laptop!* But my words stick in my throat. I can't do it. I have no idea why. I just can't.

'Inspiration is absolutely everywhere,' Alana is explaining, somewhat patronisingly. 'You just need to tap into it.' Her eyes flit to the window. 'Ah-ha! Look Meg! Your muse is calling you.'

I turn, expecting to see some hot, song-worthy dude, but I'm severely disappointed.

'Ewww. What the hell is that?' On the windowsill is the mankiest, sickest, dirtiest pigeon I've ever seen. I point at the bird-shaped mess. 'That mangy thing is certainly NOT my muse. It looks like it's about to die.'

Alana's powerful voice suddenly fills the room knocking me off-guard. *'There's a mangy pigeon on the windowsill ... He's looking at me all funny in the eye-eye-eye ...'*

Holy shit, is she wearing a hidden microphone? She has the loudest, clearest, most pitch-perfect voice I've ever heard and she doesn't care who hears it.

'*His wings are rotting and his beak is all diseased ...*'

I clap a hand to my mouth, erupting into uncontrollable giggles.

'*... I really think he's about to die-ie-ie ...*'

'Oh my God Alana. You're singing about a one-legged, red eyed, flying rat!'

Alana looks at me deadly serious for a beat before we both crack up laughing even harder.

'I'll sing about literally anything. You see, Meg, inspiration is everywhere if you just look for it!'

OK laughy time is over. I really don't need a lesson in finding inspiration, thank you very much.

'If I *was* going to write a song, it wouldn't be about bloody pigeons. It would be about my life or, like, a guy or something.'

'A GUY?!' Oh no. T.M.I. Alana's eyes light up like I've just handed her free tickets to Hamilton. 'What guy? Who is he?'

'No one! I just mean hypothetically!' Damn it, why did I open my mouth? She caught me when my defences were down with her stupid off-the-cuff mangy-pigeon singing.

'Don't fib, there's totally a guy. I could help you write your first love song for him! Does he live nearby? We could play it at open mic next week and invite him down ...'

Irritation prickles through every inch of my body. 'I told you, I don't write songs so can you please drop it?'

'If you come along to one of my music nights, you'll see what it's all about. You'd love it!'

'NO, ALANA. Why are you like this? I'm not going to change my mind and magically become a musician just because you keep going on and on at me. I don't sing, I don't write, so DROP IT.' My exasperated words are heavy bricks – each one rebuilding the wall around me.

But still Alana ignores my protests. 'Yeah, but have you even heard your own voice before? Why don't you whisper-sing and I'll record it on my phone? I bet you sound better than you realise!'

Her persistence is overwhelming. It's a real shame because we were sharing a moment there and having a laugh, but now she's pushed it too far.

'Can you chill out already?' I snap. 'I'm not singing in this shop. End of.'

There's no response.

'Alana, are you listening to me?'

She's staring at her phone. I'm ready to carry on with my stroppy outburst, but then I look at her face. I mean, properly look. The sparkle and fun is draining out of her and tears are brimming up in her big, blue eyes.

'Alana? What's wrong?'

'I ... I think I need to go,' she stutters running out to the back room, leaving me staring after her, dumbfounded. Laura appears a minute later, a tight smile on her face.

'Sorry about that,' she says. 'Alana's had a bit of ... personal news. I've said she can take the rest of the day off.'

I don't understand what's happening. Why did I have to go and shout at her like that? Why am I such a horrible bitch?

'Is she alright?' I ask in a small voice.

**145**

'Yes, she'll be fine,' Laura answers, brightly. A little too brightly for me to believe her. 'Anyway, how have you girls been getting on out here today? All going OK?'

I'm not sure how to answer. So I just nod and say nothing.

♫

**BandSnapper:** Hey, are you online? :)

**LostGirl:** Yeah, just got back from work! What are you up to?

**BandSnapper:** Not much. Wondering when you're going to tell me your Top 5 water related songs. I've been waiting ages now!

**LostGirl:** Sorry Snapper! Been crazy busy and haven't got to it yet.

**BandSnapper:** No worries! How's it going?

**LostGirl:** Not tooooo bad. You won't believe this: my co-worker is a singer-songwriter too.

**BandSnapper:** No way!! Really?

**LostGirl:** Yep. She even tried to get me to sing with her behind the counter today. I wanted to DIE!

**BandSnapper:** LOL, are you serious?! You should have joined her for a public duet!

**LostGirl:** No way! She doesn't even know I'm a musician ... I'm not gonna tell her.

**BandSnapper:** Wait, wait. What? Why not?

**LostGirl:** Because she's a blabbermouth. She'll try and get me to go to open mics with her.

**BandSnapper:** And that's a bad thing because ...?

**LostGirl:** I told you. You're the only one who gets to hear my music.

**BandSnapper:** But she's doing the same thing you are. You could support each other!

**LostGirl:** Yeah, or she could push me into stuff I don't want to do. Or steal my ideas.

**BandSnapper:** OK, now you're just being cynical

**LostGirl:** Life has made me cynical, BandSnapper Most people I've met haven't exactly been kind or supportive.

**BandSnapper:** Well, maybe you haven't given them the chance to be.

**LostGirl:** I am trying with 'Miss Music' (as she will now be known) but she seems like a very dominant personality, so I'm kind of wary. Anyway I think she got some bad news because she had to leave in the middle of our shift.

**BandSnapper:** Oh no! What happened?

**LostGirl:** I don't know. I was a bit off with her and now I feel bad. She's quite full on, but she's funny and a lot nicer than the girls at school

**BandSnapper:** Do you have her number? Why don't you message her?

**LostGirl:** And say what?

**BandSnapper:** Ask how she is?

**LostGirl:** I dunno. I barely know her ...

**BandSnapper:** So, why not get to know her?

**BandSnapper:** Sorry LG, but I've got some editing work to do.

**BandSnapper:** BTW, think about that open mic night offer ...!

**LostGirl:** Err, no, that's not gonna happen.

**BandSnapper:** Sure LG ...! You keep telling yourself that.

**LostGirl:** URGH! Later alligator x

**BandSnapper:** URGH! right back atcha. Talk soon! Xxx

# CHAPTER TWENTY-ONE

I sit holding my phone, unsure of whether to message or not. My natural instinct is to steer well clear of other people's problems. But then I remember how upset she was. I know that if I don't check in with her, I'll only spend the evening worrying about her.

> Hey Alana. You OK?
>
> M

Not my most poetic effort, I'll admit. Still, it gets the point across. Instantly, I see that she's typing.

> Hey Meg. So sorry for running out like that today. I had a bit of horrible news. I'm kind of shell-shocked, but I'm OK.
>
> A

I wait for her to elaborate, but she doesn't. What do I do? Does she want me to ask or is she specifically trying not to talk about it? It doesn't seem like her to withhold information. Then again, what do I know? It's only been a few days since I met the girl.

> What happened? Or would you rather not say?
>
> **M**

Alana starts typing. Then stops typing. Then starts again. I keep waiting until her answer pops up.

> **A**
>
> My ex-boyfriend overdosed.

I stare at the words, trying to process them. *Ex-boyfriend. Overdosed.* Neither are terms I can associate with Alana. Not bright, funny, eccentric Alana who is always smiling and sings out loud in the shop. How on Earth does this story fit together?

> I'm so sorry. Is he OK?
>
> **M**

Oh God. There I go with the feeble 'OK' again. Surely nothing about this situation is OK.

> **A**
>
> He's stable. Still in hospital but it was a close call.

> **A**
>
> His Mum found him just in time. She's the one who texted me.

**151**

> **A** Probably hoping I'll save him somehow.

> **A** Like I haven't already tried a thousand times.

My head is swimming. From everything I know about Alana, I'd guessed her bad news was more likely to be about a pet dying or a kindly Grandad breaking a hip. Not a dark, gritty past of drugs and heartbreak.

Looks like I'm not the only one who can keep secrets.

> Are you guys still close? Will you go and see him? **M**

> **A** We haven't spoken for months. The second I got that text, my first instinct was to rush to his side but then I told myself what a bad idea that would be.

> **A** It took forever to get Dylan out of my life – it's not a wound I need to reopen.

Dylan. He has a name. I don't know why that surprises me. It just makes everything real. How can any of this be real?

> **A** Sorry, I'm oversharing. This isn't your problem.

Oh no, I'm taking too long to reply. She thinks I don't care, but I do. I really, really do.

> **M** No, honestly, it's fine, you can tell me. I'm just so shocked to hear this.

> **A** He actually used to be a decent guy. No one understood what he ever saw in me.

I blink in confusion at the screen.

> **M** What do you mean?

> **A** He always had girls flocking around him. He could have dated anyone.

> **M** But he chose you!

> **A** Yeah, the dumb, chubby 16-year-old.

What? Is Alana really that insecure about herself? Am I even talking to the same Alana right now?

Hey, don't say stuff like that about yourself!

**M**

Just being honest. Anyway, he saw past all the superficial crap and loved me the way I was. Probably because he was a musician too. We used to write songs and gig together.

**A**

Wow, that must have been intense!

**M**

It was. He was three years older than me and people disapproved, but we were in love ...

**A**

You obviously had a special connection.

**M**

I dunno ... I feel like I should have tried harder. Like it was my fault.

**A**

I guess I got sick and tired of never feeling good enough next to him. I never really did fit into his world.

**A**

Woah, stop. Firstly, you're good enough for anybody! I know I haven't known you long, but I can

> clearly see that you're a catch
> Alana. And secondly, THIS IS NOT
> YOUR FAULT. If Dylan decided
> to do this it's on him. You aren't
> responsible for his actions.
>
> **M**

I'm about to bring up Caspar and how I can't blame myself for the stupid things he does either, but I check myself. This is hardly the same situation. God, why do I bring everything back to him all the damn time? Not everything is about Caspar, brain, despite what most people in my life would have you believe.

> I can't help thinking, what if I'd
> kept in contact? Or what if I'd tried
> harder to keep him on the straight
> and narrow? What if, what if, what if.
> I mean I did try. I did. Didn't I?
>
> **A**

How can I answer that question for her? I don't know what happened. I wasn't there and I can't visualise her in such an extreme situation. My instincts tell me Alana would've given all she had to this guy. She certainly doesn't seem like the type to hold back, so I try to reassure her.

> You loved him. You couldn't have
> done anything more.
>
> **M**

He used to drink and smoke all the time and at first I thought it was harmless. Worse, I actually thought it was cool. Not so cool when he'd get so drunk he'd pass out. And then he started getting into harder stuff …

Drugs. What a waste of time. I had A&R guys double my age offering me cocaine and MDMA at Caspar's gigs. They always seemed so sleazy, hanging out in manky club toilets shoving god-knows-what up their noses, then talking shit at everybody all night. It scares me to death to think of my brother getting tempted by that stuff. Maybe he already has. How would I ever know?

OMG, that sounds scary.

Yeah, it was. Dylan started hanging out with a crowd I hated. He was always partying. When I questioned it, he turned nasty on me. Really nasty. We lost all our friends because he drove everyone away. Venues didn't want to book us because he was so unprofessional.

It broke my heart but I couldn't keep trying anymore. He was dragging

156

> **A** me down with him and I didn't want to live that life.

> I'm so sorry Alana, that sounds awful! But you did the right thing. **M**

I want to help her, but I'm out of my depth. When my words matter the most, they seem to come out all wrong. Tears fill my eyes.

> **A** Did I? Maybe if I'd stayed, he wouldn't have got into this state. Maybe I could have stopped him self-destructing like this.

> It sounds like he was determined to go down that dark alley, with or without you. **M**

> **A** I'll never know for sure. I can't understand his choices. He has loads of talent but he's wasted it away, too busy blaming the world for his problems. I guess in the end I had to save myself.

A tear rolls down my face and I wipe it away, self-conscious despite the fact Alana can't even see me. For some reason I feel emotional. Maybe it's the realisation that everybody has a hidden story. Or maybe it's because somebody finally trusts me enough to confide in me.

> Anyway, I'm so sorry for dumping all this on you. You've probably got way more important things to worry about. I'm sure I'll be fine again next week and hey, at least I can channel all of this into my music xx

She's winding down to go, but I feel like we've barely scratched the surface. If only I knew how to help her.

> I'm glad you told me. Look, I know I can be a snarky cow at times, but it's all a front. You can always message me if you want to talk, coz tbh I don't have that many real friends.

As soon as I've sent the words, I realise that for once I haven't been second guessing myself. I've been genuinely caught up in what Alana has been telling me and it feels good to be there for her.

This is a first.

> Wow. Caspar McCarthy's sister as my own personal agony aunt? Got to say, I never saw that one coming

> What are the chances? You might even get me singing that Mangy Pigeon song ... 😛
>
> M

> A
>
> Now that I would LOVE to hear!!!!

She's getting back to normal and I'm smiling because of it.

Damn it. I'm going to have to tell her the truth now, aren't I? How is there even a choice anymore?

I type the words into my phone. *I've got a confession to make. About songwriting.* But she messages again before I can hit send.

> A
>
> Think I need to go process all of this. Thanks for everything, Meg. I'll see you on Monday xx

Too late. The moment has passed. It would feel weird to send my message now. But I do want to cheer Alana up. And I know exactly how to do it.

# CHAPTER TWENTY-TWO

**Top 5 Things I Should Be Doing This Weekend:**

1. Updating Twitter
2. Updating Instagram
3. Updating Facebook
4. Updating my knicker drawer
5. Avoiding Caspar

**Top 5 Things I Am Actually Doing This Weekend:**

1. Being
2. Anal
3. About
4. My
5. Cat-song (now one word)

I listen back to it seventeen times, trying to imagine Alana's reaction. She's going to love it. I bet she'll laugh so hard that she snorts. But suddenly, the thought of sharing it with her has sent me into a meticulous meltdown of Caspar-sized proportions. I've spent an hour tweaking the EQ on my vocal and re-recording the ukulele. I want it to sound exactly right.

A loud knock on my bedroom door jolts me out of my nerdy nitpicking and back to reality. I scramble to get my headphones off and tentatively open the door.

'You making music in here?'

It's TJ. Arms folded with a cheeky smile teasing his lips. Damn it. Usually no one hears me when I work on my songs. I got a bit carried away.

'It's nothing serious,' I say, trying to sound vague. 'Just a silly thing I'm recording for a friend.'

He eyes up my Røde microphone. 'You've got a nice little set-up in here. I didn't realise you did home recording.'

'Yeah, Dad set it up for me a few years ago, showed me the basics, you know ...'

Mum is bustling about next door doing the laundry. To my horror TJ calls out to her. 'Joanna! Did you know your daughter is writing music in here?'

Her blonde head pops around the door. 'Oh she's often up here noodling around, aren't you Megs?'

'Sure,' I mumble. 'Like I said, it's nothing.'

'Right, you're just noodling around ...' TJ edges closer to my mini studio, peering at my Logic session on the screen. I watch him taking it all in. 'Can I hear it?'

I rush to my seat, minimising my work with one click.

'No, no it's really stupid and it's not even finished yet.'

'Oh, go on. I've never heard you sing before, I'm curious.' From the way he's looming over me, I can tell he won't leave until I do as he asks. Should I press play? No one has ever heard my voice before apart from Matty. I feel sick even thinking about it.

Oh whatever. Fuck it.

I hit the space bar and my voice rings out over the carefully recorded chords. I suddenly find my oatmeal carpet incredibly interesting and stare down at it intensely. TJ is abnormally silent. This is excruciating. What the hell is he thinking?

'See, I told you it was stupid,' I mumble, cutting off the song by verse two.

'Are you kidding me?!' TJ exclaims, eyes widening. 'It's GREAT! You sound fantastic, Meggy. I had no idea you could sing like that! Did you record it by yourself?'

'Well, yeah,' I say, instantly turning the colour of Alana's lipstick. 'But, like I said, it's not a real song or anything.'

'Sure sounds like a real song to me.'

He turns to the door, looking for Mum. Only Mum isn't there. She's long gone. I can hear her fussing in Caspar's room across the hallway. Big surprise. Oh well. I didn't want her to hear it anyway.

'You'd better get back to kicking Sir Cassington up the bum,' I say, giving him an escape route. 'Otherwise you'll be living here forever, right?'

'Right. If only he was being as productive as you.' TJ claps me jovially on the shoulder. 'Let me know how you get on. I'd love to hear the finished result.'

'Sure,' I answer. Which we both know translates to *no way*.

I put my headphones on, trying to get back into the zone. I want to get this as good as I can for Alana and, although I can hardly even admit it to myself, I want her to be impressed. Just as I pick up my ukulele, TJ reappears in the doorway.

'Will you go away already?!' I shout. 'And close the door behind you!'

'I've got my eye on you, little lady,' he says with a wink. Then, just like that, he's gone, leaving me to finish my cat love song in peace.

♫

**LostGirl:** Hey Snapper! I finally have my list of water related songs for you.

1. Sea – Ina Wroldsen

2. Oceans – Seafret

3. Waves – Dean Lewis

4. Cry Me a River – Justin Timberlake

5. Stop The Rain – Ed Sheeran

**LostGirl:** I also have a VERY IMPORTANT UPDATE. Miss Music has had some tough news, so I've decided to cheer her up by sending her Maximoo. (Not my actual cat. The song.)

Yes, I'm showing her my music.

No, we're not making a big deal about this.

Your next category is top 5 songs with numbers in the title. Go! Xxx

I close Discord and switch to WhatsApp. Alana's not online but I take a deep breath and attach the song. I can't undo this once it's done. Alana won't be able to unhear my voice or my dodgy recording skills. This is it – there's no turning back. She's going to know my massive secret. Just like TJ now knows.

Oh, whatever. Fuck it – for the second time today.

After hitting send, it takes approximately six seconds for panic to clog up inside me like a blocked toilet.

For my own sanity, I decide to close my laptop and pretend this never happened.

♫

I pick up a half-read graphic novel from my desk and collapse on my bed. Three minutes later, my phone starts vibrating. I might be imagining it, but the buzzing sounds more urgent than usual. Before I even look at the screen, I know exactly who it is. I mean, who the hell else could it possibly be?

'Hel-'

'OH. MY. GOOOOOOD!'

As if on speaker, Alana's loud, booming voice fills up my bedroom like a hyperactive American talk show host. Here we go. 'Look, don't make a big deal out of th–' I start to say, but Alana cuts me off.

'Err, hello?! This is a MASSIVE deal! Because OH MY GOD, MEG. Literally. Oh. My. God. You're a SINGER?!'

What have I done? The regret is real. So, so real.

'It's just something silly I thought would cheer you up ...'

'No, no, no,' Alana interjects. I can practically see her wagging her finger at me. 'Don't give me any of that. You're a real, proper singer. And a songwriter! I knew you were. I totally knew it.'

'Ugh, don't say that. Please don't make this into a thing.'

'But it IS a thing. Your voice is incredible. And the recording sounds so professional. I could never make something as good as that. It's so cute and catchy, and the lyrics are hilarious!'

I can't stop myself smiling. And it's not the fake kind of smiling I do for my Insta-followers. This is the real deal. 'You liked it then?'

'I bloody LOVED it. Please tell me you have more stuff to send me.'

This is surreal. I'm used to reading compliments from BandSnapper on a computer screen but I've never heard such positive feedback out loud. My music is an abstract thing floating around in cyberspace somewhere. It's not something that actual human people comment on.

'I have stuff,' I mumble. Am I really admitting this? What's wrong with me? 'Loads of stuff actually.'

Alana gasps with excitement. 'Send everything to me. I want to hear all of it. Also, why don't you sing it live?! There's an open mic at Latest Music Bar every Sunday. I was planning to go down tomorrow anyway.' She's shaking my phone, my room, my whole world upside down. 'How awesome would that be?'

OK. This is why I don't show anyone my music. This is why sending that bloody song might be the biggest mistake in the history of my life. I should've remembered that if you give Alana an inch, she'll take a mile. Or rather, if you give her one little song she'll plan a whole performance!

'No, that would not be awesome. I've sent you this in absolute confidence. I don't want anyone knowing I make music. No open mics, no nothing. Alright?'

'What if we did some songwriting together? We could build up your confidence a bit then go and perform!'

'ALANA. What part of NO don't you understand? I don't want to!'

There is a beat of silence. Oops. Was I too harsh? Did that come out too snarky?

But then Alana carries on ignoring the fact that I just snapped her head off.

'I don't understand why you want to keep it a secret. You obviously sent this to me for a reason. Come on, show me the other stuff. The real stuff. I absolutely wanna hear it.'

I groan loudly. Wait ... I just made the exact same noise Caspar is always making. The spoiled brat groan. I seriously need to check myself. 'I don't know,' I say, digging deep and trying to be nice. 'Maybe.'

'What have you got to lose by showing people anyway?'

The one outlet that's purely for me and not the entire bloody world? The sanctity of the *McCarthyBrand*? My dignity?

'No offence, but you don't know what it's like growing up with a prodigy brother. It piles a lot of pressure on. I'm not ready to put it all out there yet.'

At this point, she laughs at me. She actually laughs, like this is meant to be funny. 'Oh, Meggy, Meggy. Don't worry. I know all about the precious male ego when it comes to making music.'

Oh wait. Is she laughing with me?

'I take it you mean Dylan?'

'Who else?'

I tread cautiously. This is still unknown territory. 'How is he? Have you heard anything?'

'Not a lot. Only that he's awake and alive. Apparently.' She sighs. 'I've decided I'm definitely not going to see him. That might sound mean, but it's not worth the heartache.'

'It's not mean. Honestly. You've got to look after yourself.'

I think I just heard her smile. 'Thanks. And you really did cheer me up with that song.'

'Good. That was the aim.'

'Come see me tomorrow,' she blurts out. 'I'll be playing at around 8pm. You don't have to sing or anything. Just come listen.'

I almost tell her that I've watched her videos on YouTube and that I think she's exceptionally brilliant, but I stop myself.

'I'm kind of busy tomorrow,' I lie. Lying seems like the safest option when being put on the spot like this. 'It depends on what's going on in the house, with Caspar's schedule and everything.'

'Quit making bullshit excuses and get your arse down there!' she commands.

'Fine. I'll think about it,' I answer.

Alana knows she's getting nowhere, so the conversation winds down. But when we eventually hang up, I'm true to my word. I do think about it. All of it.

I think about it a lot.

# CHAPTER TWENTY-THREE

> **BandSnapper:** LostGirl! I'm doing a shoot tonight for our local newspaper so I don't have much time to message, but ... WELL DONE on finally sharing a song with someone!!! Did Miss Music like it? Tell me! xxx

> **LostGirl:** Thanks, BandSnapper 😊 She loved it. And congrats on getting the photography work! No rush on the reply. I sort of have plans this weekend too.
> Laters xx

♫

I arrive at Latest Music Bar at 7.53pm. Cutting it a bit fine, I know, but it takes me the entire day to decide whether I'm actually going or not. I nearly flake out about five times before my curiosity finally gets the better of me. The venue isn't far so it would be pretty feeble of me not to check out at least a song or two. Besides, Alana asked me to come and I want to see her play, which is ultimately what leads me down the winding steps to the café basement.

The tiny, candle-lit room is heaving. There's a cute little stage at the back covered in the usual messy tangle of microphone leads and instrument stands. It's empty. I hope I haven't missed her. I squeeze my way to the back of the room hoping that my black button-down dress will act as an invisibility uniform. Not that anyone would recognise me in a place like this.

Suddenly, the room goes quiet and my attention snaps to the stage. Alana appears, looking glorious in a fitted black bolero top, a bold floral print skirt and to-die-for heeled aqua blue sandals. She can't see me, but I can certainly see her. Shining, sparkling, confident, and ready to perform.

'Good evening, everyone! How are you all doing tonight?'

The YouTube videos didn't do her justice. In real life, her whole brightly burning aura is visceral, tangible, drawing every person's attention to her.

'I'm gonna start off with an old favourite. Sing along if you know it.'

She slings her guitar strap over her shoulder and begins to strum. The action comes as naturally to her as blinking or breathing. The chords ring out and her pitch-perfect voice launches into song.

*Watch another door swing open*
*Calling like an invitation*
*And yet I don't walk through it*

*Waiting for too long, I find I'm*
*Scared to write the words down wrong*
*Why do I always do it to myself?*

This one must be popular with the local crowd because everyone in the room seems to know it. Alana's delivery is full of humour, acting out every word as her eyes dance and spark off her audience. As she hits the chorus, her voice soars across the room.

*These are the songs you've never heard*
*all these unspoken words are*
*From my heart*
*From my heart TO YOURS*

I can't help smiling. *These are the songs you've never heard*. Wow, how apt. I guess I'm not the only one to hide my lyrics, melodies, and emotions away from the people I've written them about.

*These are the songs I've never played*
*These are the sum of wasted days apart*
*From my heart TO YOURS*

Do you ever hear a song and feel like someone has reached right into your brain and pulled out everything you've never been able to express yourself? Because right now, she could be singing my own inner thoughts. Damn you Alana Howard and your amazing, fearless, relatable songwriting skills.

*But OH OH*
*I'm ready now*
*OH OH*

*So ready now*
*I think you deserve*
*Songs you've never heard*

I'm so transfixed that the final lines catch me by surprise. I only know the song is over by the roar of excited cheering that erupts from the crowd.

I'm clapping and whooping and I don't care who sees me. It was so good that I want to be a part of it. Even if all I can do is applaud in the aftermath.

Alana grins. 'Thanks so much guys, it's always fun playing that one.'

She takes the guitar from around her neck. Oh, is that it? My stomach drops in disappointment. I wanted to hear more. I guess everyone has to get a turn at an open mic, but three minutes was not enough. I want to shout for an encore.

But then, Alana crosses the stage and sits at the piano. Her mood seems to change and the atmosphere in the room shifts with it. 'So, err, this is something totally new,' she tells the audience. She sounds different. Cautious. Dare I say, nervous? 'I literally only wrote it yesterday, so please be kind to me.'

The crowd laughs. Someone lets out a cheer of encouragement and my heart pounds in anticipation. I think I know what, or rather who, this is going to be about.

I'm not sure I can take it. This feels too personal. Like I'm about to read Alana's secret diary without permission. Only she's giving her permission willingly to every single person here.

'This song is about someone I used to know,' she announces, her tone soft and genuine. 'Someone I tried to help, but I ...' her voice catches and I feel my own breath catching too, '... but I couldn't.'

As she plays a few gentle chords she introduces the song. 'This is called 'Didn't I?"

*You turn away*
*I'm talking to your back again*
*And my words have turned to dust, floating out the window*

*And each time you go*
*Cuts my heart a little more*
*Think I've died a thousand times*
*Trying to keep this love alive*

The accompanying chords are simple, but somehow – underneath Alana's strong, heartfelt voice – they invoke an entire orchestra.

*Now I got nothing*
*Nothing but a question*
*All I do is ask myself ...*

Her eyes are closed, barely glancing at the piano keys, let alone the audience. The fragile, delicate emotion of her performance is pouring straight from her heart into mine.

*Didn't I try my hardest?*
*Didn't I do my best?*
*Didn't I hold you when you hurt?*

*Didn't I say I love you more*
*Than anyone else that's gone before?*
*Didn't I mean every word?*

I feel her hurt. I feel her pain. I feel every frustrated thought that must have been running through her head all weekend. Her entire heartbreak, perfectly captured in one achingly beautiful chorus.

*But when the night comes down*
*And the light fades out*
*All that's left are the shadows and the doubt*

The song continues to grow and evolve, Alana's voice rises through the second verse and chorus. The melody has changed now, weaving through doubt and anger until she is singing from a place of pure passion with nothing holding her back.

*Didn't I give everything?*
*Didn't I keep on promising?*
*Didn't we walk side by side?*

*When did your hand stop holding mine?*
*Have you been slipping away all this time?*
*But at least inside my heart I know I tried*

She pauses, blinking back her tears. Taking a last vulnerable breath, she finishes the line in a soft whisper.

*... Didn't I?*

She's totally lost in her moment and the rest of us don't exist. Time is suspended. The room is silent. Stunned. Captivated.

Before I realise what I'm doing, I step out of the shadows, drawn to her light. I'm clapping and cheering and pushing my way to the front.

As Alana finally turns to the crowd she catches my eye. Blinking in surprise her tears turn to laughter.

The tiny club is filled with deafening applause, which must be spilling out across the whole of Brighton. I'm clapping loudest of all and I couldn't care less if anyone recognises me. Because there isn't a shred of doubt in my mind: Alana Howard is the greatest songwriter I've ever met.

And I have to write with her.

# CHAPTER TWENTY-FOUR

Somehow, the rest of the room has disappeared. The musicians, bar staff, and audience have all faded into the background, taking my self-consciousness with them. The only person I see right now is Alana. Before she's even gathered up her guitar, I rush to the side of the stage, cornering her with a stream of worryingly-out-of-character, excited babble.

'OhmyGod, ohmyGod, that was so, SO amazing! That was one of the best songs I've heard in my life. Your voice is incredible, Alana. I can't believe how talented you are!'

I throw my arms around her neck and give her a giant bear hug like she's one of my oldest, dearest friends. What is wrong with me?! I'm not a hugger! The beautiful music has turned me into a cringey *fangirl*.

Luckily, Alana doesn't make it weird. She laughs and hugs me back.

'I can't believe you actually came! I was looking out for you, but I couldn't see you.'

'I was hiding at the back, like a vampire.'

'Of course you were.' She keeps squeezing me. 'Did you honestly like the song?'

'I totally loved it.' Not going to lie, this hug is getting socially awkward now. But perhaps I'm just overthinking it. 'I loved both of them, but 'Didn't I?' was just so ... beautiful. It was perfect.'

It feels impossible to put into words how much her song meant to me, but I have to try. There's a whole dictionary of glowing adjectives in my head and I'm desperate to reel them all off, only a blinding light suddenly interrupts my thoughts. I blink in confusion and pull away from Alana as the room starts coming back into focus.

'Wait, can you keep hugging a second longer? I'm not sure I quite got the shot and it's so lovely.'

Woah. Hang on. I know that voice.

I know those earnest blue eyes, that mussed-up blonde hair and lopsided little grin. I even know that faded Johnny Flynn T-shirt.

'What the hell are you doing here?' I shout, barely concealing my panic.

Matty Chester lowers his camera and lets out a browbeaten sigh. 'Hi, Meg. Nice to see you too.'

It's him. My favourite person. Here. In my actual real life. All I want to do is run and hug him, like I did to Alana. But even the power of her magical song can't change me *that* much. I fall into the spiteful caricature version of myself all too easily.

'How many times do I have to tell you not to take my bloody photo? It's bad enough you stalk me at school with that stupid thing, now you're harassing me when I'm out for the night too?'

Alana is looking back and forth between us in complete confusion, unsure if this is a joke or not. 'Oh, you guys know each other?' She flashes Matty a clueless smile. 'It's fine, snap away dude! I love getting photos taken.' She throws an arm around my neck, posing shamelessly. 'Here, get one of us together!'

I am not even slightly prepared for dealing with this. My heart is pounding as I wriggle out of her grasp and try to pull her away from the stage. But she refuses to budge.

'Ooh, did you get any pictures of me playing?'

Matty holds up his viewfinder. 'Yep, check this one out. It'll look great in the paper.'

'Wow, that's stunning!'

'It was a stunning song. I was lucky to catch you right in the moment.'

NO! This is not happening. This is like two worlds colliding in an explosion of hellfire. Oh, God. If she breathes one word to him about my cat song then it's game over. I have to stop them talking by any means possible.

'Right, you've got your picture,' I interrupt, barging between them. 'Now can you please just give us a moment? I need to talk to Alana.'

Alana is gawking at me in total shock. She knows I can be a rude cow sometimes, but she's never witnessed me at my worst. I can't look at her or I'll break.

'Maybe I'd like to talk to Alana for a second too,' Matty counters, boldly. 'So whatever problem you've got with me can wait a minute.'

He's so assertive. I could seriously kiss him right now ...

'Well, excuse me if I've had enough of you shoving your wanky camera in my face. I didn't give you permission to take my picture so get rid of it!'

'Woooooahhhh,' Alana cuts in. 'Woah, woah, woah. What's happening here? Guys, chill!'

Matty turns his camera screen to me and exaggeratedly deletes all the shots of me with Alana. Us laughing, us talking, us hugging. My guts twist tighter with each erasure. They're such good photos.

'There,' he snaps at me. 'Happy? I guess it's not enough to humiliate me at school, you've got to carry on your vendetta in public too. What have I ever done to you, Meg?'

I've hurt him. I've really hurt him. The realisation absolutely kills me.

'Quit being so overdramatic, Matty. It's pathetic.'

'Meg,' Alana murmurs in horror, putting a hand on my shoulder. 'What on Earth is all this about?'

'Welcome to the wonderful world of Meg McCarthy,' Matty mutters, rolling his eyes. He touches Alana's arm. 'You were honestly fantastic tonight, Alana. Give me your email and I'll send you all the photos.'

He takes a business card out of his pocket and hands it to her. Business cards? When did he get those made? I feel hurt that I don't know every little detail of his life from our *Music Hunger* conversations. But then, why would I? I share nothing

**178**

with him so I can't complain if I only get back what I give.

He glares at me. Disgusted that someone as vile and mean as Meg McCarthy is hanging out with someone as talented and positive as Alana Howard.

What's wrong with me? Why am I even like this?

'MEG ...' Alana says my name again. Hard this time.

I turn to her, feeling the world move in slow motion. 'Yes?'

'Emergency girl meeting. Now.'

With that, she grabs my arm and drags me towards the ladies toilets before I have a chance to object.

♫

'OK, so that was a revelation. You never told me that Meg was actually short for Mega-Bitch.'

The ladies loos are cramped and unglamorous. Alana is blocking the door, arms folded, judging me silently. Her guitar is propped against the wall, taking up what little space is left in here.

'What?' I spit out defensively. 'I wasn't that bad.'

We both know, without a trace of doubt, that I was indeed 'that bad'. I was worse than 'that bad'. I was my worst self. I was horrific.

'That guy was only trying to be nice and take our photo. Why the hell were you such a psycho witch to him?'

I stare down at her feet. Those shoes really are splendid. Maybe if I stand here counting the sparkly straps this conversation will just go away by the time I finish.

'Has he done something to you? What happened?'

'Nothing,' I say, concentrating on my strap counting. 'He's just ...' Think of a valid reason, Meg. Any valid reason. 'He's just ... super annoying. He goes to my school and he ... he winds me up.'

Valid, Meg. Real valid.

'Is this about me? Are you trying to sabotage me or something? Don't you want my photo going in the paper?'

'What?!' I exclaim for a second time. 'No, that's not it. Don't be stupid.'

'You seemed pretty determined to get me away from the camera, and you made him delete those gorgeous pictures.'

I can't believe she's reading the situation like this. This is getting more and more messy.

'I've had this kind of thing happen before you know ... Girls trying to put me down because they feel threatened by my music. I really don't have time for silly mind games. If you don't want to be friends then just say so.'

'You're being totally paranoid,' I reply in exasperation. 'Alana, I bloody love your music. I didn't tell you this, but I listened to your stuff online, and hearing it live was even better. I'd never want to sabotage you. Are you crazy?'

'So what the hell was all that about then?' she demands. 'The way you were with that photographer guy. I don't get it, you were so, so ...'

'I'm in love with him,' I blurt out. Just as she says the word *mean*.

'What?!' she screeches.

My hands are shaking. 'Shit. Did I say that out loud?'

'Yeah, you kinda did.'

The walls of this tiny bathroom are closing in and crushing me.

'You're in love with him? Is this the guy you mentioned to me?'

I groan. All I want to do is take the words back, but it's too late. They're spewed all over the floor for everyone to see.

'Wow. He's not what I expected.'

'Why, what's wrong with him?' I ask, defensively.

Alana holds her hands up. 'Nothing! He's lovely. I just didn't think he was your type, what with all the fashion-conscious Instagram posts and everything. I thought you only liked cool, model guys.'

'Not everything is about looks, Alana.'

'I know,' she replies. 'Trust me, I know!'

'He's nice to me.' I say debating whether to elaborate. Do I? Don't I? Oh, who cares anymore? I've come this far. 'I send him all my songs and he actually listens to them.'

Alana's eyes widen like a bewildered bush baby, 'So he knows you write?!'

'No, well yes, I mean ... He doesn't know it's me.'

There is a flabbergasted pause. 'Huh?'

'I talk to him under the username LostGirl,' I mumble. 'But he has no idea it's me. I don't know why I'm so horrible to him in real life. We got off to a bad start and it just kind of snowballed from there. Now I'm so bloody deep in the lie that I can't find a way out ... I'm a terrible person.'

Alana's mouth opens. Then closes. Then opens. Then closes. Then she finally speaks. 'That's messed up.'

'Don't,' I say, warningly. 'Please don't lecture me. I already know. It's a disaster.'

'Why can't you just tell him the truth?! You're Meg flipping McCarthy. What have you got to be worried about?'

Everything. My mad family, my nasty Internet trolls, the fact everyone thinks they know everything about me, right down to what kind of guy I want to date. Where do I even start?

'It's complicated,' I say, pathetically. 'He knows things about me I could never share with anyone else.' I step towards Alana pleadingly, 'You can't tell him who I am. Please, please don't tell him!'

For once, I'm the one in her personal space. She edges backward. 'OK, OK. I won't breathe a word.'

I exhale in relief.

'But *you* need to tell him.'

'Look, can we stop talking about this now? I didn't come here to discuss my tragic love life. I came here for you. To finally hear you play.'

OK, so maybe I'm purposefully changing the subject here, but it is the truth. For the first time ever I see a hint of shyness in Alana. 'You really liked the set?'

'I *really* liked the set. I liked it so much that I want to try writing a proper song with you. Like, in the same room. If you're still up for it?'

'Really? Really?! REALLY?!!' By the third 'really' she's reached the whistle pitch that only dogs can hear. 'Whenwhenwhenwhenwhen?'

I shrug. 'Whenever you want to. We could go to mine. I have a mini studio in my bedroom.'

'Are you seriously being serious right now?'

'Yep,' I grin. 'I'm seriously being serious right now.'

Alana looks like she might self-combust with joy. 'Can you send me your songs? Tonight? I know I'm not as cute as camera-boy, but I'm dying to listen to them.'

'Only if you send me yours too,' I answer. 'I want to hear everything.'

A double dose of excitement has just been poured into the blender and switched onto high-speed mix. I hope what comes out of it is something more appealing than Dad's gross green smoothies.

'Are you free after work tomorrow?'

More questions. Endless streams of questions. But for once, I don't mind answering them.

'I'll check if the house will be empty.'

'OK. Let me know as soon as you get home.'

'Sure. I'll send you stuff, and you send me stuff.'

'I will! I've got loads.'

In this closed-in little bathroom I've become a different person – someone open. I want to share everything I've ever written. And more than anything I want to be friends with this marvellous, loud, space-taking, insanely talented girl. I'll probably regret all my blabbing and confessing the minute I'm home. But at the moment all I hear are a thousand melodies that are waiting to be written; all the notes we're going to make our own, one by one, together.

'Shall we go back out?' Alana says, nodding to the door. 'I feel bad that I'm missing the next act.'

I nod. 'Yeah, sure.'

She picks up her guitar to leave. 'By the way,' she adds, 'you're telling me this whole camera-boy story in thorough detail tomorrow. In-between the songwriting.'

I'm not able to give any kind of comeback. She's already out the door, singing along to the acoustic Dua Lipa cover currently being performed on stage.

# CHAPTER TWENTY-FIVE

Inspiration is a wonderful thing. It's been so long since I saw live music in such an intimate setting. Just local people playing songs with passion and humour and creativity, for no other reason than that they love them. It almost made me want to push through the blind terror and get up on stage myself.

Maybe that scenario isn't as impossible as I thought only a few hours ago. Not with Alana beside me. Holy shit. We're going to write a song together. Tomorrow! It's only just dawning on me how daunting that prospect really is, but for once I'm not running away screaming, I'm actually seizing the opportunity.

Mum's so desperate for me to make a new friend that she's agreed to get everyone out of the house for the afternoon. (Even His Royal Cassness.)

It's late, but I switch on my laptop and choose my favourite songs to send to Alana – a playlist that tells the story of my life so far. I don't even flinch as I hit send. She's obviously doing the same thing because her folder of songs arrives almost simultaneously.

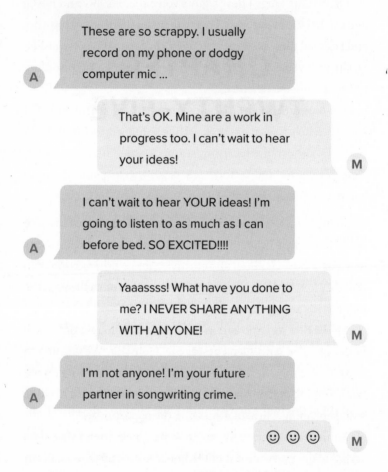

> **A** — These are so scrappy. I usually record on my phone or dodgy computer mic ...

> **M** — That's OK. Mine are a work in progress too. I can't wait to hear your ideas!

> **A** — I can't wait to hear YOUR ideas! I'm going to listen to as much as I can before bed. SO EXCITED!!!!

> **M** — Yaaassss! What have you done to me? I NEVER SHARE ANYTHING WITH ANYONE!

> **A** — I'm not anyone! I'm your future partner in songwriting crime.

> **M** — ☺ ☺ ☺

When the download is complete, I eagerly drag the entire folder into iTunes. The recordings are grainy and a little distorted, but they're enough to show me the inner workings of Alana's mind. I flick between chirpy acoustic guitar, melancholy piano chords, soulful humming, and a few unintelligible voice memos with traffic noise in the background.

On certain songs I hear a guy's voice too. It's low and husky and catches me by surprise. Their voices flow effortlessly together and I can tell there is serious chemistry between them. It must be Dylan. I scroll past these tracks quickly, feeling like I'm intruding on something too personal.

The songs are rough but there's an endless amount of potential in them. Lately Caspar has been getting so hung up on production that he's forgotten what is most important. The heart of the song. The lyrics and melody. It's all very well spending hours and hours getting the right kick drum sound or the perfect vocal compression, but that should all come afterwards. The hard thing to find is the magic, the idea, the seed.

Alana has an entire garden of seeds. I can hear so many ways to make them grow. Strings and drums and harmonies and synthesisers. A thousand different directions and possibilities.

I get to the last song 'Invisible Monsters'. I love the title and it's much better quality than the others. It must be what she recorded when she won that free studio time earlier in the year. All the emotional nuances of her voice shine through, and it proves how good she can sound when a professional producer gets involved.

*I know*
*Poisonous words, they can echo*
*They cling to your doubts and then they grow*
*Like oceans they never end*

*And I could believe it, but wait*
*I don't want to drown in their hate*
*And if they destroy I'll create*
*I won't let them stop me again*

I hit replay and let the words sink in. Underneath all of Alana's jokes, laughs, and confidence, she has the same insecurities as I do. The only difference is she doesn't let them stop her performing.

*Invisible monsters at my door*
*Don't wanna believe in them anymore*
*Invisible monsters in my mind*
*They've stolen too much of my precious time*
*I'm gonna leave them*
*Gonna leave them behind*
*My invisible monsters*

I've got plenty of invisible monsters of my own. Alana is telling me exactly what I need to hear and she doesn't even realise it. Songs are funny like that. Sometimes they come into your life at the perfect moment. Just when you need to hear them the most.

I start typing a ridiculously over the top, enthusiastic message to Alana, but then I notice a *Discord* notification. Matty's back home and online. I don't want to read it, but there's no way I can ignore it. So reluctantly, I open the tab.

**BandSnapper:** Hey LostGirl! Quick reply before I go to bed. Firstly ...

**BandSnapper:** My top 5 songs with numbers in the title:

1. Seven Nation Army – The White Stripes

2. 6/10 – dodie

3. One More Night – Michael Kiwanuka

4. good 4 u – Olivia Rodrigo

5. Three Little Birds – Bob Marley and the Wailers

**BandSnapper:** Your next category is top 5 songs about bullies/haters. I know it's a negative topic, but I'm feeling uncharacteristically miserable tonight. I've just had another run-in with the vile Meg McCarthy. She was at the open mic night I was shooting. I swear she's like a bad smell that won't go away. Since summer started she's been EVERYWHERE. I can't seem to avoid her.

**BandSnapper:** All I did was take a photo of her and her friend – a great photo, can I add – and she went crazy on me. It was so embarrassing. There were loads of cool musicians around and she humiliated me in front of all of them. Worst of all, her friend Alana was absolutely incredible. Probably one of the best live musicians I've ever seen and now she thinks I'm some creepy camera guy. I wasn't trying to be rude or anything. I only wanted to help her with promotion. Wish I'd never bothered now.

**BandSnapper:** I just don't get why Meg hates me so much. I've tried to be friendly to her. I've also tried doing the opposite and staying out of her way. Nothing works. She loathes me whatever I do and I'm getting bloody sick of it. I know her family are rich and famous with the perfect life, but that's no reason to treat everyone like dirt on her Jimmy Choos.

**BandSnapper:** Bet she's jealous that her new mate is getting the attention, not her. What is she famous for doing anyway? NOTHING. Pouting into a camera phone. Her brother is clearly the talented one. All she does is scowl and insult people. It's pathetic! Wish she'd leave town already and move to London with all the other shallow, bimbo Instagram models.
Shit LG – I'm sorry for the rant. She just really, really winds me up.

**BandSnapper:** On another note. Alana Howard. Wow. I mean, WOW. You need to look her up right now and get inspired. Seriously, you'll thank me.

**BandSnapper:** Let me know what's happening with you and your new friend. What did she say about your Maximoo song?!
Sorry again for the massive dump of negativity.
BandSnapper xxx

I read the message two, three, four times over. First I scan it as quickly as possible, hoping the faster I read it the less it will hurt. Then I take it one paragraph at a time, letting myself feel the pain fully.

*Vile. Shallow. Pathetic.*

Each word is a stab in my heart.

*No talent. Ugly. Pointless. Rude. Bitch.*

I don't reply.

I can't reply. What would I even say to him? It's my own stupid fault. I started all of this.

Feeling empty and deflated I climb into bed. My newfound happiness has been eclipsed by a dark shadow of my own creation.

I try to focus on Alana and how much I'm going to need her help if I'm ever going to fix this total mess known as my 'perfect' life.

I try not to replay Matty's words over and over in my mind.

# CHAPTER TWENTY-SIX

**Top 5 Things I Talk About at Work With Alana:**

1. Songs
2. Her songs
3. My songs
4. The songs we're going to write together
5. The Matty situation (and the tragic songs I've written about it)

At the end of our shift, Alana and I walk back to my house together. Her voice is an endless river, gushing on beside me.

'So you wrote "Second First Impression" about Matty? That was definitely the stand-out track for me. I can feel so much emotion from you, it's bloody beautiful. I can't believe no one in your family has heard it. How can you hide this kind of talent from the ... OH MY GOD. Is this where you live?!'

She cuts off mid-flow, stopping to stare up at our three-storey, red-brick, Victorian semi.

'Yeah, welcome to The House of McCarthy,' I say, rummaging for my keys. 'Or The House of McCrazy as I prefer to call it.'

'It's a mansion!' Alana cries. 'You've got a whole flower bed and a keep-out wall and ...' she cranes her neck upward, '... there's like thirty-seven bedrooms in there. Jeez Meg, how big is this place?!'

'There's only six,' I say, opening the door and shrugging.

'Oh right, *only six*. Because obviously the cat needs his own room and a walk-in wardrobe.'

'It's not that posh. It's where we've always lived,' I explain, uncomfortably. 'We're not, like, rich or anything. Well, not like some people.'

'Right ... And you're not poor like some people either ...'

Alana hovers in the hallway, taking in her new surroundings: the expensive artwork on the walls, the bookcase filled with limited edition hardback books, the polished, stripped wood floors, and the designer light fittings.

'Remind me never to invite you over to my house. Our hallway's got rising damp and fifteen-year-old IKEA furniture.'

'We've got IKEA furniture ... I think ... In the guest room.'

'Naturally,' Alana sighs.

Before I can stop her, she's nosing at every little thing on display. She hones in on some framed childhood photos. 'WOAH, pictures of you and Caspar! That is so WEIRD. Hey, has Caspar touched this? Am I touching things he's touched? Can I steal some of his DNA?!'

Oh dear Lord.

'Put it down,' I say, gently prising Caspar's Brit award photo from her hand. 'I'll go grab some supplies and then we can get started.'

I check every downstairs room then sweep the kitchen for snacks. Mum has been true to her word, there's no sign of anyone anywhere. Thank God. This is definitely not a family-listening-in scenario.

Alana is still giving a running commentary. Her eyes are huge and her head is swivelling like an owl's. When we get to my room, her mad owly-ness only intensifies.

'Is this your set-up?!' she shrieks, gawking at my mini studio. 'This is proper nice stuff!' Then she starts touching everything. Without permission.

'Argh, don't mess with the mic stand, it's in the perfect position.'

'Sorry,' she says, picking up my notebook and flicking through it. I'm beginning to think this was a bad idea. Breathe, Meg. Just breathe.

'Take a seat,' I say, attempting to channel the welcoming, patient Meg who I know is in here somewhere. Alana perches on my bed as I load up Logic. 'So ... We're gonna write a song.'

'Yes!' Alana cries exuberantly. 'We are!'

'Awesome. Where shall we start?'

There is an epically long pause. I look at Alana. Alana looks at me. I look at Alana some more. She looks blankly back at me.

'I have no frickin' idea.'

Fuckballs.

♬

Here's the thing, when I'm writing alone my ideas flow so naturally that I hardly have to think about what I'm doing. It's like a sudden rush of creativity takes over my body and I have no choice but to pour everything out via the piano or a guitar or my voice into a microphone. I don't have to explain why I'm writing what I'm writing. It just happens. I'm a lightning rod that conducts melodies and I have no control over how fast they strike. I don't think the songs into existence. They simply exist. Through me.

Writing with another person, however, and a person you've only known for a week at that, is like being expected to play thrash metal guitar when you've only learned classical cello. My lightning rod powers have completely corroded, and the longer Alana keeps staring at me, the wider the expanse of nothingness grows inside my brain.

'Right, OK,' I say, breaking the loaded silence. My voice sounds shrill and unnatural to my own ears, like every syllable is on display for scrutiny. 'How do you normally start then?'

Alana is kicking her legs against my bed frame so hard I think she might propel it across the room. 'Finding a melody, I guess. Or ... lyrics.'

'Lyrics, great!' I say, desperately clinging to any starting point we can find. 'Have you got those ideas we scribbled down at work?'

Alana retrieves a scrappy, ripped piece of stock-sheet paper from her bag. It's covered in song titles from our mid-shift brainstorming session earlier. I stare down at all the words. 'Dazzling'. 'Fierce'. 'Imperfect world'. '100%'. 'Time is now'. 'Waiting to speak'.

'These all sounded way more inspiring a few hours ago,' I admit, forlornly.

'Yeah,' Alana agrees, looking around the room. 'Can I borrow your guitar? When I used to write with Dylan, he always started with a chord sequence.'

'Sure thing.' I pass her my beaten-up old acoustic, suddenly embarrassingly aware of the fact that I've had it since my eleventh birthday and it's covered in stickers of the rainbow, fairy, Disney, unicorn variety. My perfectly-pieced-together image is suffering a tragic and rapid deflation as I realise evidence of my loser status is all over this room. My lucky hippo on the shelf above my laptop, a heart-shaped picture frame with a photo of me and Dad in it, my koala bear slippers, my dance competition trophies. I've even still got Big Panda on my bed for God's sake! It's like I didn't see any of it until someone else came into my girl-cave. But now they are all flashing into sharp, uncomfortable focus.

Alana takes the guitar without any comment and begins to pick an aimless melody. It's sweet, but to be honest, totally forgettable. She catches my unimpressed vibes and starts strumming random chords instead. 'This isn't a proper idea – I'm just ... warming up.'

'Right, no problem,' I say, trying to sound encouraging.

Time passes painfully slowly and we still have nothing but odd, jarring chords ...

'No pressure Alana, but an idea would be helpful any time now ...'

Her aimless strumming clunks to an abrupt halt. 'I can't think of anything,' she wails. 'This is like peeing with the door open. I can't go with you watching me.'

'What a beautiful analogy!'

'Well, it's true! I feel like all my creative juices have completely stopped flowing!'

Why is this so bloody awkward?!

'Enough with the peeing and the juices!' I groan. 'Maybe this was a bad idea.'

The very fact that Alana is in my room at all is bizarre. She looks weirdly out of place sitting on my bed, holding my guitar – taking over everything with her Alana-ness. Squashing my Meg-ness in the process. She doesn't fit in here. Our energies are not matching. This is like putting Kanye West on stage with Kae Tempest.

But then Alana starts strumming a persistent rhythm and suddenly, out of nowhere, I catch a strand of melody. Quietly, cautiously I start humming the tune that has appeared in my head. There's something here. Ideas are forming.

'What's that you just sang?' Alana encourages me 'Go on, do it again, it was good ...'

'I don't know where these words have come from but I've got this idea. *Line 'em all up in a row ... Line 'em all up in a row ...*'

'*Like dominoes, Like dominoes?*'

'YES. Dominoes ... it's the domino effect!'

'*What did you expect?*' She rhymes back.

It's a scrap of a melody, a fragment of lyrics. A single seed. But it all fits together perfectly.

And just like that, we're off.

♫

I'm not used to the process of co-writing. All my choices are being examined under a magnifying glass and so are Alana's. The song becomes a giant jigsaw puzzle with both of us scrabbling to fit the pieces. Sometimes one of us gets completely side-tracked, but we work together – carefully crafting side-by-side, analysing words and rhythms until we've created our musical picture.

'I think we should leave more space here, let it breathe a little.'

'Are you sure *trucking on* sounds OK? Maybe *pushing on* sounds better?'

'Should we go back to the pre-chorus again after the middle eight?'

We record onto my laptop as we go. Our voices harmonise in a way I hadn't expected. It's as though we've been singing together our whole lives. I've lost all my inhibitions and I don't care if the whole neighbourhood hears me.

*I've been moving forward*
*No point in looking back*
*I've been pushing on like a train on a track*
*It's getting everyone excited*
*But if you haven't bought a ticket*
*Then you're never gonna ride it*

*I've been growing gardens*
*Yeah I've been planting seeds*
*But nothing's gonna bloom*
*'Til I clip out all the weeds*
*And now you're telling me it's not fair*

*Well I guess you shoulda been there*
*You shoulda been there*

*Lining up my dominoes*
*I'm good to go, I'm good to go*
*Line 'em all up in a row ...*

It's totally different to how I usually work, but it feels so real to me – so natural, so inevitable. Alana listens to me. She takes my opinions on board. She brings ideas that I would never have thought of myself. Brilliant ideas.

*Look out for what's coming next*
*You'll be feeling the domino effect*
*Coz I've started it falling down*
*Falling down*
*One, two, three*
*Better keep your eye on me*
*What did you expect?*
*You'll be feeling the domino effect*
*Coz I've started it falling down, falling down*
*Falling down*

With our finished lyrics on the floor in front of us we sing the whole song through together. We're bouncing off each other's energy and excitement, addicted to our own creation. We made this! A few hours ago this specific combination of notes and words didn't exist and now they do. It's a mad kind of magic that

I'll never be able to get my head around.

I'm having so much fun, I've forgotten about time and space, and everything else around us. It's just me and Alana, singing as though we're headlining the O2.

Suddenly we hear a loud thump. I shush Alana, my heart pounding. 'Shh, I think I heard something.'

She mutes the guitar in alarm. 'What was it? Was it your cat?'

I shake my head and hold my breath. No. This was a very human kind of thump.

'Hello?' I call out. 'Mum? Dad?'

I tiptoe to the door silently, cursing myself for leaving it open. Then, I let out a huge, panicked scream as I come face-to-face with a total stranger.

# CHAPTER TWENTY-SEVEN

The random bearded dude is so freaked out by my freak out that he freaks out and drops the pile of stuff he's holding. A tangled mess of extension cables, plugs, and adaptors fall to the floor like spaghetti, topped off by his iPhone.

'Who are you?!' I squeak, my voice coming out like a Mariah whistle note.

'Sorry love, I'm with the crew,' the guy says, fumbling to pick everything up. 'I was looking for the bathroom.'

I stare at him, dumbfounded. 'What crew?'

There are more noises coming into focus now. Clanging, banging, and chatter.

TJ's voice is booming out orders. 'Mind the paintwork in the hallway! And we're going to need another camera in here so we can get a full-body shot. Those shoes were a freebie, the brand wants them to be seen.'

Oh no. This is not good.

I shove past the hipster intruder and race down the stairs. A crew of strangers are acting like they own the place, laying cables across the floor and setting up lights in our living room.

Mum emerges from the madness, smiling widely at me. 'Hi love! Are you having fun with your friend?'

'What's going on?' I ask, ducking as a guy with a stepladder swings past me. 'Mum, you promised there'd be no one in the house this afternoon.'

'I know, darling,' she replies with an apologetic pout. 'I tried my hardest, but TJ had this amazing interview opportunity come up for Cass. It's with BuzzPop TV! They thought it would be cool to show him in his natural environment. You know, a familiar, homely feel.'

Right. Because nothing says homely like an entire film crew in your front room.

This is so frickin' unfair.

Through the half-open living room door, I see Caspar perched on a stool, hair gelled, face powdered and jeans slung low. He's scowling as TJ shouts instructions. 'Remember, stick to music. Tease the album. You don't have to give anything away, but let people into your writing process.'

Dad is stuck to TJ's side like a loyal Jack Russell. Oh Lord. He's carrying a pint of fruit-infused water with a straw so he can personally quench my spoiled brat of a brother's thirst between takes. I don't think I can bear to watch another second of this so I turn around and stamp back upstairs, hoping it will disrupt the mic check.

'Meggy, where are you going?' Mum calls after me. I ignore her, bumping into the annoying cable-carrying camera guy again. I'm so angry that it's hard to resist pushing him down the stairs. He scurries away at my dirty look.

'Session's over,' I sigh to a bewildered-looking Alana. 'The Duke of Cassbridge has taken over the whole house. There's no way I can sing now I know they're all down there.'

I start shutting down our recording session. Alana is crestfallen. 'Oh no. I was really getting into it.'

'Me too,' I reply, letting a small smile break through my disappointment. 'I'll send you what we have so far and we can finish it another day, yeah?'

'Yes, send it to me! Maybe we can ...' She stops. *Please don't say what I think you're going to say.* 'Maybe we can show it to your family when it's done?'

I should have known this was coming. Alana isn't like me. She's not the kind of girl to write a song and hide it away. She's going to want to show the whole world.

'I think my family are somewhat preoccupied at the moment.'

'OK. But you have to promise me we're building up to something here. A gig or a video or *something*. It's too good not to share it.'

'Alright, I promise. But you could always sing it without me.'

'NO WAY,' Alana booms back. 'It needs both our voices or it doesn't count.'

I cross my arms defensively. 'Easy for you to say. You don't have a musical-genius sibling to contend with. Everyone's going to be judging me times a thousand and comparing me to him.'

'You're just as talented as Caspar. In fact, I think you're better than him.'

I shoot her a sceptical look, but she's smiling encouragingly at me. Wow, she really means it. And she has no idea how much it means to me that she means it.

Suddenly, her eyes widen. 'Wait. Caspar.' My brother's name has unlocked a separate part of her brain. 'Did you just say he's downstairs?'

'Err, yeah. Doing some stupid interview.'

Alana's eyes bulge like an astonished tree frog. Oh God. I know that look. Cue crazed fangirl meltdown in three … two … one …

'Caspar McCarthy … IS DOWNSTAIRS?' She lets out a high-pitched, dog-like yap. 'I know I'm being embarrassing and I get the feeling you kind of hate him and everything, but can I meet him? Pleasepleasepleeeeease?!'

I see this happen a lot where Caspar is concerned. Rational, normal girls – and sometimes boys – behaving like mad, hyperactive bubble-heads the minute they get the slightest inkling that he's in the vicinity. It's the biggest cliché in the book.

'Are you serious? Don't be that girl, Alana. You're cooler than that.'

'PLEEEEEASE!' she begs, crawling off the bed and literally grovelling at my feet. 'I'll leave as soon as I've said hello and I won't mention anything about us writing music. Just please, please let me meet him, pleeeeease! I've been a fan of his forever!'

I stifle the urge to kick her in the face. 'GOD! OK. But make it quick because he's about to start filming.'

Alana is out the door so fast I can see cartoon speed lines

behind her. Jeez. What happened to me being better than Caspar? Guess that was only true before she realised he was in the building.

'I don't hate him, by the way,' I admit, following her downstairs. 'He's my brother and I love him. It's just that he really is incredibly irritating.'

'Oh, it's normal to feel like that when you're close to people,' Alana answers, dismissively. 'I'm sure you'll say the same about me one day.'

'I'll say it to you right now. You're really, incredibly irritating Alana. And also, at this precise moment, completely mortifying.'

Alana ignores my insults. She only has one thing on her mind, and he's posing pretentiously in our living room. The sight of him causes her to turn the colour of Mum's carmine scatter-cushion collection.

'It's really him!' she yelps in a manic whisper. 'Oh, my, Gooooddddd.'

'Yeah, yeah, the wondrous chosen child,' I huff. 'Real-life, flesh and bone Caspar, sweepy hair and everything, blah, blah, blah. Let's get in there and get this over with.'

I push her towards the door. The cameramen, the lighting people, the make-up lady, the BuzzPop Barbie TV presenter, TJ and my parents all look up simultaneously. None of them seem particularly thrilled to see us, but I carry on regardless.

'Hey, sorry to interrupt,' I say, not sounding sorry at all. 'Just wanted to introduce you to my new friend, Alana.'

For the first time, possibly ever, Alana is speechless. I nudge her in the arm and she manages a pathetic, shaky wave. 'H ... hi.'

In the centre of his fussing entourage is a thoroughly pissed-off Caspar. He looks Alana up and down with barely contained contempt. It's so spiteful, it makes me physically wince. Luckily, Mum swoops in, serving as a well needed distraction to his less than desired reaction. 'Oh, hello, hello. It's wonderful to finally meet you.' To my embarrassment, she grabs Alana and gives her massive air kisses on either side. 'Meggy's told us all about you and your music.'

Funny. I seem to remember her eyes glazing over every time I mentioned part of my life that's not Cass-related. Selective memory there, Mum.

'Look, can you two get out of here?' Caspar barks at us with eyes of steel. 'We're kind of busy.'

Alana is caught off-guard and trips over her words. 'S-S-Sorry, I know we shouldn't have interrupted. It's just that I'm such a huge fan of your music and I wanted to say hi ...'

'Yeah, I can see you're a *huge* fan. But in case you didn't notice, there's a whole film crew in here waiting to do their jobs and you're holding everyone up.'

The presenter gives a nervous giggle beside him while the entire crew shuffles and looks at the carpet. They're all pretending not to notice Alana's crimson cheeks and trembling lip.

'Well ... hopefully we can chat another time ...' she squeaks.

How dare he? This has to be a joke, right? I'm half-expecting Caspar to break into his camera-ready grin – the one he reserves for fans and photoshoots – but the snide stare refuses to budge from his face. He's looking at Alana like she's rotting fish on legs.

I take back what I said about loving him. I bloody HATE HIM. Everything in me wants to violently push him off that stool, but TJ cuts in before I completely lose it. 'Wait a second, let me give you something.' He hurries over to Alana, simultaneously handing her a voucher card, escorting her out of the room and explaining away Caspar's appalling behaviour in hushed tones. 'Sorry, Cass is under a lot of pressure right now. Please take this. It's annual membership to The Caspar McCarthy VIP virtual fan lounge. Access to all-exclusive news and recordings, free album downloads, and you can even order half-price merch.'

This is what is known in the business as damage limitation. After years of working for my brother, TJ has become a polished expert at it. The fact that he's now using the same old spiel on my new friend has made a little bit of sick come up in my mouth.

I grab Alana's wrist and pull her out of the room. 'Save it TJ. We're out of here.' I glare over my shoulder at Caspar before walking out. 'Thanks for making our family look totally sane and welcoming, Cass. And by the way, you need more concealer on your eye bags.'

I see him snatching a mirror from the make-up lady as I slam the living room door on all of them.

Alana stands in mute shock, turning over the voucher card in her hands. 'I told you he could be awful,' I say apologetically. 'Not quite the charmer you were expecting, huh?'

'Yeah, talk about never meeting your heroes.' She pulls her shoulders backs and wipes her tears away. 'What a dick! Is this what you have to put up with on a daily basis?'

'Pretty much. He's the biggest diva I've ever met. And yet the whole world thinks he's bloody perfect.'

Alana waves the voucher at me. 'Got a bin?'

I hold a hand to my open mouth in faux shock. 'You mean you want to throw away your membership to Caspar McCarthy's fan club? *The* Caspar McCarthy?!'

She dramatically rips it in half with a grin. It's a grin that lets me in. A grin that I'm part of too.

'Meg, by the time we're done, Caspar will be the one begging to join *our* fan club.'

# CHAPTER
# TWENTY-EIGHT

**BandSnapper:** Hey LostGirl, you online? You've been very quiet. I hope I didn't offend you with the massive Meg rant the other night. She just really got under my skin. You OK?

**LostGirl:** Hey. No, it's fine. Sorry she was so horrible to you 😠 Didn't mean to ignore you, just been v. busy!!

**BandSnapper:** No worries, I'm over the drama now! What you been up to?

**LostGirl:** Stuff and things.

**BandSnapper:** Music related stuff and things?

**LostGirl:** Mayyybeeeee ... 😊

**BandSnapper:** I can't wait to hear! BTW, did you check out Alana Howard yet? She is AMAZING.

**LostGirl:** Not yet, I'll look her up. In the meantime ...
Top 5 Songs About Bullies/Haters:
1. Mean – Taylor Swift
2. Don't Kill My Vibe – Sigrid
3. The Bully – Sody
4. Praying – Kesha
5. Shake It Off – Taylor Swift (she needed two entries, come on!)

**LostGirl:** Your category is top 5 songs about friendship.

**BandSnapper:** Haha, nice answers! And intriguing theme ... are you and Miss Music becoming friends?

**LostGirl:** Mayyybeeeee ... 😊

**BandSnapper:** Wait, are you writing together???

**BandSnapper:** Don't leave me in suspense LG! Have you got a new song?

**LostGirl:** Not yet. Besides, I'm in suspense too. I need more details about your photography job.

**BandSnapper:** There's not much more to tell. I think they're using a shot in a review. But hey, one snap at a time until I'm backstage at the Brighton Centre.

**LostGirl:** I have no doubt that you will make it happen ☺

**BandSnapper:** Will you ever come to Brighton LG? You can't be that far away. When can I meet you?

**LostGirl:** Not this again ...

**BandSnapper:** We could go to a gig together! Next time Alana plays you should come with me.

**LostGirl:** I'm not sure ... I'll think about it. OK?

**BandSnapper:** OK, I understand. I think.

**LostGirl:** I'm sorry.

**BandSnapper:** No ... I'm sorry for being pushy. I'd just love to meet you.

**LostGirl:** Like I said ... I'll think about it.

**BandSnapper:** Well, that's a step in the right direction at least!

> **LostGirl:** One day I'll make it up to you. I promise.

> **BandSnapper:** I'll be right here waiting ... ☺

> **LostGirl:** I hope so. Anyway ... better go, work in the morning!

> **BandSnapper:** Yeah me too. Sweet dreams, LostGirl xxx

> **LostGirl:** Sweet dreams, best friend x

♫

The best thing about working with your brand-new collaborator is that boring shifts serving yoghurt suddenly become packed with inspiration. The day after our epic songwriting session, Alana and I are both suffering from the musical equivalent of a sugar rush, firing plans and thoughts back and forth in-between all the mundane shop tasks.

As we're talking about how to re-arrange the middle eight of 'Domino Effect', a group of excitable, foreign exchange students burst into the shop, giggling and snapping photos as they order. They can't speak much English, but they're clearly fluent in the language of selfies.

The leader turns her camera lens onto Alana as she pays. 'We love you, both of you. Beautiful singing video! Trop bien!'

Huh? I side-eye Alana who looks as confused as me. Have they somehow heard her music? Is she big in Brussels?! 'Sorry, what video?'

'Ouiiiiiii, la vidéo! Beautiful duo! Merci pour la photo, Meg and your friend. Vous êtes adorable!' She blows us a kiss and the girls all pile out of the shop in a flurry of excitement.

'Meg,' Alana says, the second the door closes, 'what the hell was that about?'

'I have literally no idea,' I answer. 'Have they got their wires crossed or something?'

Alana shrugs. 'What did they mean "beautiful duo"? And why the hell were they taking my photo too?'

Something seriously weird is going on here. I get the sudden urge to check my phone, only it's locked away in the staffroom. Before I can open the back door, Laura comes flying out of it. 'GIRLS!' she shouts, her voice a high-pitched shriek. 'The Dodo Yoyo Twitter account is going crazy! Look at this!'

She places her phone on the counter. There's a YouTube video playing. Of me and Alana. Sitting in my bedroom. Singing our song.

My mouth drops open. Alana's mouth drops even wider. We exchange a look of complete horror.

'Can you believe this?!' Laura exclaims. 'You're going VIRAL!'

Intense nausea is rising in my stomach, but I force myself to take a closer look at the screen ...

**MEG MCCARTHY & MYSTERY GIRL SINGING ORIGINAL SONG!!!**
EXCLUSIVE footage of Caspar McCarthy's sister Meg and unknown friend writing and performing together.
Caspar fans have been waiting endlessly for his second album. Is Meg hoping to follow in his footsteps and release her own music first?!
Watch out, Caspar! These girls sound great!

There are over two minutes of footage of Alana playing guitar and me singing next to her. We're a bit obscured as the angle is just outside my bedroom door. However, the audio comes across loud and clear.

The comments section has been disabled, but the view count is high. It's already at 9,437 and it's only been up for around an hour. Nearly 10,000 people have heard my voice, my melodies, my lyrics. Nearly 10,000 people know my secret. I think I'm going be sick.

'How has this happened?!' Alana cries, gaping at the clip as it loops back around. 'We didn't give permission for this to go out. Who even filmed it?'

The answer hits me immediately. 'That camera-guy,' I say with a groan. 'He was right outside the door with his phone, remember? I knew he looked dodgy; he must have been secretly filming us.' I peer at the account username. It's some kind of celebrity gossip channel. 'I bet they paid him for the clip. What a douche.'

I can see Alana's innocence dissolving before my eyes. 'But that's horrible! Why would anyone do that?'

'Welcome to the world of showbiz,' I reply, dryly.

Laura shakes her head at us in disbelief. 'Girls, what's with this negative reaction? This is amazing news! Your song is being heard by thousands of people. Look!' She refreshes the page. The view count has now jumped up to over 13,000. 'It's shooting up! People are sharing it. This could make you stars!'

My heart rate is climbing as rapidly as the views. All I feel is panic. Absolute blind panic. 'We haven't even finished writing the song yet. It's nowhere near ready for anyone to hear it.'

'It sounds great to me,' Laura replies. 'You two are so talented. I can't believe you've found each other like this, and in MY shop! It's destiny!' She beams at Alana. 'All those years of hard work, Lan, and now you finally get your moment. I know your name's not on the video, but people are figuring out who you are already.'

If Laura's words are supposed to be supportive, the intention is getting thoroughly lost in translation. Alana has turned pale. 'I'm not sure I'm ready for this,' she gulps. 'Oh God, Meg. What are people saying about it?'

'Let me check,' I reply, heading to the back door. I'm not sure I'm ready for this either.

When I grab my phone from my locker, it's flashing with a never-ending stream of notifications – tweets, Instagram comments, emails. It is blowing up. I take it back into the shop with shaky hands, too afraid to read them on my own.

'Go on then,' Laura urges. 'What's the feedback? Has anyone tweeted about it?'

Alana is wringing her hands together anxiously. I forget that she's not used to thousands of virtual eyes watching her. Judging her. Not that it's something you ever really get used to.

'OK,' I say, taking a deep breath. 'Here goes nothing.'

I dive into the sea of tweets. There are a good few hundred or more waiting to be read, so I go from the top of the page and work down.

 WOW! **@MegMcCarthy** has a voice! I had no idea! She's AWESOME and so is her friend!

OK, I NEED the full-length studio version of this song by **@MegMcCarthy** and mystery girl. When's the album out?

Relief starts spreading through me as I read them out loud. Alana and Laura are hanging on my every word, their eyes bright and brimming with delight.

 So shocked IN A GOOD WAY. **@MegMcCarthy** is a singer like Caspar! I totally knew it! Ur voice sounds so fresh, and the girl singing with u!

'They like us,' Alana laughs. 'Meg, THEY LIKE US. I can't believe this is happening.'

I feel the knot in my stomach loosen a little. 'Yeah, I guess they do.'

But then I make the oh-so-familiar mistake of scrolling a bit further down the screen.

This is the Internet. An anonymous soapbox where anyone can say whatever they want, with zero repercussions. A place for people to spew out every negative, judgmental, and critical thought that pops into their minds without seeing the hurt that it causes. A consequence-free arena for all the bullies and the haters. I don't know why I'm even surprised. The nervous, vomitous feeling returns.

 WTF?! Does **@MegMcCarthy** actually think she can sing now? LOL! Don't give up the day job, you'll never be a star like your brother!

216

OUCH **@MegMcCarthy** my ears hurt after that clip. And who the hell is that nobody on guitar? You are both crap and the song SUCKS.

EW **@MegMcCarthy** who is that WHALE in ur vid?! Song is ok, but think u need better guitarist.

Every one of them stings, but somehow the last one is the worst of all. It's going to take all of my restraint not to reply. Alana's done nothing wrong. Why are people so cruel?

'What else are they saying?' Alana asks, enthusiastically peering over my shoulder. I can feel her radiating oblivious excitement, and there's no way I can pop her bubble. What good would it do anyway? Time to lock all those nasty comments in a box and bury them in the very back of my mind. I'll deal with them later when I'm more prepared.

'There are so many tweets, I can't keep up with them all,' I say. 'Maybe we should look later, on the computer.'

I slip my phone into my back pocket and force a smile. Judging by Laura's huff of exasperation I don't think it's very convincing. 'Come on Meg, get a little excited about this. Hundreds of people are loving what you two made. It's incredible!'

'Yeah, it's great. I just ...' I catch Alana's eye, hoping she understands my trepidation. 'I just wanted people to hear our music when it was actually finished. We don't even know what we're doing yet, so how can we explain it to the whole world?'

This is what always happens in these kinds of situations. People get totally carried away. Everyone is waiting for the magic

TV moment when someone suddenly rises from obscurity to stardom. In real life those moments take time and planning and a lot of hard work. We're not ready. Not even close.

Alana touches my arm encouragingly. 'Hey, it's OK. I know this wasn't how you wanted to announce your big secret. We don't have to say anything public about it if you don't want to. We're just giving everyone a clue.'

'A clue?' I repeat, making the effort to smile. 'I kind of like that.'

It's weird. If this was happening to me by myself, some leaked video of me singing solo in my room, then I think I'd be having heart palpations and collapsing on the floor right about now. But with Alana beside me, I don't feel as wobbly as I thought I would. I feel like maybe we can actually handle this.

'I think more fans are coming,' Laura cries, peering out of the window. Sure enough, there is a gaggle lingering outside of the shop, working up the courage to come in. 'The word must be spreading. Let's get them in here. I'll cover the till and you two make sure you chat to them all.'

It must be Laura's lucky day: two local celebrities for the price of one. That's double the advertisement, and double the froyo sales.

'Uh-oh, Alana. Here we go ... Are you ready for this?'

She glances nervously at the crowd and then fixes a determined grin on her face. 'Only one way to find out. Let's see what it's like being Meg McCarthy for the day.'

Somehow, Alana and I fall into a rhythm with each other, taking turns to answer questions and joke with the crowd. When our shift ends it's an anti-climax to simply say goodbye and go our separate ways. It feels like we should be planning our next song or our album or our world tour.

See what I mean? It's easy to get carried away.

# CHAPTER TWENTY-NINE

When I get home Caspar is blocking the landing, pacing up and down, ranting obnoxiously into his phone. I feel sorry for whoever is stuck on the other end of the line.

'No, you listen to me ... I want the name of every crew member from that shoot or I'm getting my lawyers involved. That video was leaked and you had absolutely no right!'

I guess he's heard the news then. Along with the rest of the entire world. I nervously sneak a glance upwards at him as he leans against the banister. He's too busy barking orders to notice me. I haven't seen him quite this mad for years – not even during his teen-angst rows with Mum and Dad. Even his hair seems angry, sticking up all over his head in messy outrage.

'No, nobody gave permission for it to go on YouTube ...'

Wait. Is he protecting me? I stay frozen in the hallway, eavesdropping with a swelling heart.

'That crew were supposed to be there for *me*. Not my little sister and her amateur friend.'

Oh. Consider my swelling heart well and truly deflated.

'My manager sets things up through his hard-earned connections and they are nothing to do with Meg whatsoever. Do you know how badly such unprofessional footage reflects on my brand?'

Yep. Burst, dried up, and disintegrated like ash.

Internet trolls are one thing, but hate from your own sibling is quite another and I'm not in the mood for it. I dump my bag in the hall and try to find some space for myself in the living room instead.

Mum, Dad, and TJ are huddled on the sofa, deep in conversation about something. No prizes for guessing what that something is.

Mum is the first to speak, literally leaping up and running at me with open arms. 'Oh, Meggy. We had no idea ... No idea at all!' I'm hit with a wall of Chanel N°5 as she pounces on me. 'Your voice, your songwriting! It's so wonderful! How have you been hiding this talent from us?!'

Dad attacks from the other side, pulling me and Mum into a bear hug. 'We're so proud of you, babygirl. Have you seen? You just hit the 40,000 mark! I can't believe you've been writing songs like this. I thought you were just playing around in your room. Why didn't you tell us?'

'I knew it all along,' TJ says, joining in on the group hug. 'From the first moment we met, when you were a kid, I knew there was something special about you.'

I wriggle out of the triple-adult rugby scrum so that I can breathe. 'Woah, woah, time out. I'm glad you're all excited, but can you not smother me to death, please?'

'We can't help it!' Mum cries. 'This is such a shock. I mean, a brilliant, amazing shock, but still a bloody shock nonetheless. When I saw you singing away in that video I just couldn't believe it!'

Oh no. I think she might be crying. Wait, what am I talking about? Mum blubs her eyes out at emotional dog food commercials. Of course she's crying.

'Why didn't you tell us, darling? You could have confided in us. Is it because of Cass?'

Err, yes.

'No, of course not, Mum. Not exactly ...'

'So this is a new thing then?' Dad asks. He's bouncing on his heels, visibly brimming with pride. 'Is your new friend showing you how to write songs?'

'Well ...' I answer, trailing off into nothingness. I should probably lie. But I can't. The box is open now and there's no point in slamming it shut again. 'She's been encouraging me for sure, but I've been writing for ages. I just didn't show anyone.'

TJ stares me down – his demeanour all business. 'OK, how long? How many songs?'

I blush. This day has taken a sharp turn down what-the-fuck-is-going-on street.

'Erm, ages,' I stammer. 'Years. And I don't know how many songs. Like, thirty?'

'Thirty?!' Mum exclaims. 'I'm a terrible mother! My daughter has been writing for thirty years and I didn't even know!!'

222

'MUM. How old do you think I am??'

'I had to find out from a tweet like I'm *just anyone* ...'

Here we go, over the top as usual. I shake my head at her. 'This is why I didn't want to show you guys in the first place. You have to go and make such a big deal out of everything. I didn't want *anyone* to know. It's that stupid camera guy's fault.'

The viral video flashes into my mind again. Caspar's not wrong with his criticism of it. Our performance wasn't exactly professional. I mean, we didn't even know we were being filmed. I dread to think of how many hateful new tweets have popped up since the last time I looked. But then again, we had plenty of positive comments too. Maybe they'll balance each other out?

TJ grabs my hands, leads me to the sofa and forces me to sit so we're eye-to-eye.

'Meg,' he says, his voice even and reassuring. 'Forget about the video for a second. Forget about your parents and everyone else, and just answer me one question ...'

I feel like this moment was inevitable. 'Shoot,' I say.

'Is music something you love doing?'

I don't know why I hesitate before replying. There's only one answer I could ever possibly give. 'Yeah, of course. It's the only thing I'm really passionate about.'

'OK,' TJ nods, squeezing my hands. 'And is it something you want to pursue as a proper career? Like Caspar?'

I pull my hands away feeling a mixture of irritation and dread. Caspar, Caspar, Caspar. It's always to do with bloody Caspar, even when it's supposed to be about me for once. The trouble is that as soon as his name gets mentioned, any confidence I was starting to feel shrinks like a woolly jumper in a hot wash.

'I don't know! I can't answer that kind of question. I'm not Cass. I don't know what I want to do with any of this yet. I didn't ask for that stupid video to be put online!'

'Meg!' Mum snaps. She and Dad are looming over us, desperate to be involved in the conversation. 'TJ's only trying to help you. We all are!'

'Sorry,' I mumble, guiltily. 'It's been a bit of a weird day, OK?'

TJ continues, unbothered. 'OK, OK, OK. So you may or may not want to go further with this. That's totally fine, Meg. If you want that video to go away then say the word and I'll do my best to make it disappear. Or, if you want to do the opposite, well, I can help with that too.'

I stare at him, bewildered. 'I don't get what you mean?'

'I've been an extended part of your family for years, Meg. I may be Cass's manager, but that doesn't mean I can't help you out too.'

I take a deep breath and try to focus on what TJ is actually saying. He really knows his stuff and if anyone's going to give me some solid advice right now, it's him. After all, TJ is a master of PR and marketing.

'Thanks,' I say, meaning it. 'I won't lie, it would be pretty helpful to get your words of wisdom right about now.'

TJ leans back on the sofa, crossing one long leg over the other, assessing me like he's the big-shot boss at a job interview. 'Well, little lady, if you want my advice, I suggest you start showing me the whole story. What can I hear, how can I hear it, and most importantly when? And the answer had better be *now*.'

'Erm, well, I've got everything recorded on my laptop ...' I'm trying not to look directly at anyone in the room.

'Excellent,' TJ cries, bounding up from the sofa like a massive spring uncoiling at full force. 'Let's go fire it up. I want to hear everything.'

'I want to hear it too!' Mum squeals.

'And me,' Dad joins in. 'I want a front row seat!'

Oh God. Why are parents always so cringey? No. Stop it Meg. They're being supportive. This is what you've always wanted. It's difficult, but I force myself not to give them my usual sarky eye-roll. Instead, I smile and give a tiny, awkward nod. 'OK. Come up and listen.'

Alright, if I'm being honest, maybe I'm secretly thrilled. They're proud of me. All they've heard is one tiny, badly-recorded snippet of a song, but they're so proud they're ready to fly out of the window and let the whole city know that I'm their marvellous daughter. For the first time in as long as I can remember I'm not invisible to them. I've got to admit, it feels pretty good.

As we follow TJ up the stairs Caspar is squatting on the landing like a furious frog. He catches TJ's eye. 'They've left me on hold,' he seethes. 'I'm not hanging up until someone their end has been fired. If they can't figure out who the rat is then they should sack the bloody lot of them.'

'Cass, just leave it,' TJ replies, taking on the smooth tone he reserves solely for my brother's temper tantrums. 'You won't get anywhere with them; you'll only make things worse. I'll handle the snitch my end and we'll get compensation for it. Don't you worry.'

'I need more than compensation,' Caspar spits back. 'I need justice. This whole thing has been utterly humiliating.'

Mum bites her lip, clearly wanting to console Caspar, but thinking better of it. Dad is blocking it out completely by humming excitedly to himself on the staircase.

'You do what you gotta do, mate,' TJ says, clapping Caspar on the shoulder. 'We'll be in Meg's room if you need us.'

Caspar glares at each of us in turn. 'Erm, OK? Why?'

Mum can't contain herself and beams at him. 'We're going to listen to Meggy's songs! She's got loads of them! Why don't you come in and listen too?'

When I think of all the people I've tried to keep my songwriting life secret from, my brilliant brother is top of the list.

Caspar. The musical genius.

He's a giant shadow that has hung over me since the day I was born, terrifying me into silence for the majority of my seventeen years on this Earth.

He's also my biggest inspiration – the one who taught me guitar. My musical hero. I want him to be proud of me like Mum and Dad are right now. I want him to put our stupid sibling rivalry aside and tell me what he thinks of the songs I'm finally brave enough to play.

'I'm on the phone, Mum,' he snaps with a patronising tutting sound. Then he turns away from us, tapping his free hand manically on his knee.

Mum gives me a 'ho-hum, typical Cass' smile and follows TJ and Dad into my room. I pause to pick up Maxi, and as I do so Caspar spins around to face me. He burns me with his darkest, meanest look, killing my confidence on the spot. Without saying a single word, I get the message loud and clear. *There's only room for one musical genius in this household. And it is NOT YOU!*

For a few moments, I crumple. I almost believe it. I can feel that shadow sucking me in and suffocating me.

But then I think of Alana, her loud laugh, her beautiful guitar chords, and the way she threw her Caspar McCarthy fan-club card in the bin without even flinching.

I'm not on my own with this anymore. Not if I don't want to be.

Stroking Maximillian for reassurance, I give Caspar my most confident smile.

'Have fun on the phone,' my voice is sweet but taunting all at once. 'And say thanks to Buzzpop for helping us out so much.'

His dark expression erupts into pure, unadulterated rage. I close my bedroom door before he can reply.

# CHAPTER THIRTY

Playing my songs out loud to my parents and TJ is possibly more excruciating than the time I walked into Chemistry in Year 10 with my school skirt tucked in my knickers.

As I load up my top five songs and hit play, I don't know where to look. Do I watch them while they listen? Do I nod my head and hum along? Both options make me feel thoroughly ridiculous so instead I fix my gaze on my laptop, following the time bar on iTunes as it moves slowly along the screen. These songs are so familiar to me that it's impossible to imagine hearing them for the first time.

Finally, the last notes of the last track fade out and I dare to take my eyes off the screen and look up at my audience of three.

'Wow,' TJ exhales. 'I'm speechless. You did all of this by yourself? In here? On your laptop?'

'Uh-huh ...'

'You're a dark horse Meg – this is bloody brilliant! I'm so impressed. I can't understand why on Earth you haven't played me these songs before. No wonder people are going crazy for that video. With the right production that "Domino" song could be a hit.'

Woah there. For someone who is speechless TJ has a lot to say.

'Your songs are wonderful, darling,' Mum interjects. 'You should release them! We could help you get proper studio time, set up interviews, get the promo sorted ...'

'Mum, calm down,' I sigh, slumping back in my seat. 'Not everything has to be part of the flipping McCarthyBrand. *I don't even know if I want to release these songs ...*'

She blinks at me, wounded. 'Oh. Well. What are you aiming for with all of this then?'

I know she only wants to help, but why does there have to be an *aim* at all? Why can't I write a song just because I want to – for no other reason than the pure, creative satisfaction it gives me?

'I just want to write songs Mum; maybe do a performance. See where it leads.'

TJ smiles at me. 'Correct answer young lady. I think that's exactly what you should do. Start building from the ground up'

'Yes, you girls sound fantastic together,' Dad chimes in enthusiastically. 'You don't need to go booking expensive studios. Everything sounds great already. Must be those mixing lessons I gave you, huh Meggy-moo? Did you hear how good those vocals sound, TJ? She got the compression just right. That's my girl!'

My parents and TJ get swept up in a detailed discussion of my songs. Mum's voice catches in her throat as she mentions 'Firework Display'. 'I hope *we* didn't make you feel like that,' she asks teary-eyed for the second time this afternoon. 'Darling, I can't bear it if we did. I know Caspar's whole career must have been terribly disruptive for you over the years ... It's not that we didn't see your firework display ... we just ...' She pauses, her lip wobbling. 'We just didn't even know you'd brought so much as a sparkler to the bonfire party ...'

As frustrating as she is, I can't stay cross with her. 'It's OK, Mum. And thank you. For coming up and listening I mean.'

Her perfume fills my nose as she squeezes me. 'We'll always listen sweetheart. And if we don't, please just shake us until we do.'

'Got it,' I whisper into her shoulder.

TJ stands up – his signature move whenever a meeting with a client has come to an end. 'I think we should give Meg her space now.' He turns to me. 'And I suggest you ring Alana and sort out another writing session. You need to explore this partnership and then, when you're ready to take it further, you know where I am.'

The realisation that TJ is serious slowly sinks in. If he gets behind us, it could be the start of something very, very exciting. For the first time in my life, I'm starting to wonder what a future beyond being Caspar McCarthy's little sister could look like.

At the mere thought of my wonderful brother, he materialises in my doorway. I appear to have summoned him, like a demon.

'Oh, hello son,' Dad says. 'You off the phone now? We've been listening to Meg's songs and they're absolutely cracking!'

Caspar's eyes narrow, seething with barely concealed fury. 'Oh, great,' he says flatly, tossing his hair back like some kind of battle taunt. 'Well, sorry to interrupt and everything, but I'm getting nowhere fast with BuzzPop. TJ, it would be nice if you acted like my manager for once and helped me sort this out.'

My manager. *As in belonging to Caspar, not to Meg.*

'Duty calls,' TJ says, holding his hands up in surrender.

'By the way Dad,' Caspar adds, hanging off the door frame like he owns the whole house, 'I was thinking about our song. Maybe we could take another look at it?'

Seriously? He's going to sink this low? I'm positive my parents won't bite after pledging their allegiance to me no more than two minutes ago, but both their faces light up as they fall hook, line, and sinker for his massive attention diversion.

'Really?' Dad exclaims. 'I'd love to rework it with you. I think it's got so much potential.'

'Ooh, is that the one you showed me the other week?' Mum asks. 'I liked that one. It could be a contender for the album.'

'Yeah, let's see if we can get it right,' Caspar says, feigning interest. 'Are you free this afternoon?'

'Of course! I've got a few emails to send, then I'm all yours.'

Mum and Dad don't mean to be cruel. They do at least pat my shoulder and give me a thumbs up as they immediately snap straight back into orbit around Planet Caspar.

Poor Dad. Caspar is never going to use that song for anything. He just can't stand a shred of attention being on anyone other than him. Still, as much as it should sting, I'm surprisingly desensitised to the pain. I'm way too excited. No, I'm beyond excited. I feel free. That's the word I'm looking for. *Free.*

Before I do anything else, I text Alana, trying to condense my immense rollercoaster of emotion from the last hour into one quick message.

> Guess what Alana? I played our song to my parents and my bro's manager ... EEK! Can't believe they finally know everything! They were all v. impressed & think TJ will help us if we want him to. We've GOT to write again ASAP. This week?? Xx **M**

She replies almost immediately but it is the total opposite of anything I expected from positive, sunny Alana. I am completely unprepared for the message smouldering in my hands.

>  Hi Meg. I can't. I don't think I want to write a song ever again.

What. The. Hell?

🎵

'Oh ... Hey, Meg.'

Alana's voice sounds flat and far away. Most un-Alana-like. I wasn't sure if she'd pick up the phone, and now I have no idea what to say to her. I decide to cut the chit-chat and dive straight in. 'What was that message all about? I don't get it. I thought you'd be excited?'

For a moment, all I hear is Alana's shaky breathing down the line. Then finally, there's a tearful gulp. 'It means what it means. I don't want to do this anymore. I wish no one had ever seen that stupid video. I'm not cut out for this. I've just been deluding myself.'

'Woah!' I cry. 'What's happening here? Where is this coming from?'

'I bet everyone's been laughing at me this whole time. Why did no one at open mic ever take me to one side and tell me to give it up?'

'Don't be crazy! No one's been laughing at you; people love you. What the actual hell are you going on about?'

'There's no point trying to persuade me, I've made up my mind.'

'Why? What do you mean?' I wish I could reach through the phone and shake her out of this.

'I've seen the comments, Meg,' she answers, her voice breaking into a proper sob now.

'Alana, don't …'

'They're tearing me to bits. It's awful.'

Oh God. Twitter. I scramble for my laptop and scan the reviews, which are still flooding in. Certain words stand out in the river of text, as if they've been underlined in red. *Terrible. Ugly. Fat.*

They're not the only words. There are kind comments too – beautiful compliments and messages of hope and support. Unfortunately, the positive sentiments are totally drowned out by the toxic sludge of the negative.

'You can't pay any attention to that crap,' I sigh down the line. 'There's always someone who isn't going to like what we're doing. That doesn't mean their opinion is worth listening to.'

'But there are loads of bad comments,' Alana whimpers. 'Loads and loads. And they're *right*. I am fat and ugly next to proper artists. What have I been thinking? Going out performing and acting like I can actually get anywhere ...' Her words are fast and frantic, running and crashing into each other. 'Maybe I can't even write music. Maybe our song is complete rubbish ...'

I cut her off sharply. 'No. Enough. You have reached a Level 5 Doom Spiral and you need to be diffused immediately.'

She actually laughs a little at this, despite the tears. 'Level 5 Doom Spiral?'

'Text me your address,' I say. 'I think we'd better go through this in person.'

♬

**Top 5 Stages Of A Doom Spiral:**

Level 1: Shock

You've been working hard on a project, whatever that project may be, and you're super proud of it, but you read a nasty comment. The idea that someone doesn't love it as much as you is like a 1,000-watt shock to the system. And let's face it, a jolt that strong can bloody hurt.

Level 2: Anger

Piercing anger is almost always the next emotion. How dare this stranger, who doesn't even know you, criticise something you love so much? They don't have any context. They don't know how hard you've worked, how many gruelling hours you've put in or how much passion flowed out of you to create this wonderful, amazing thing. In short, said stranger is a total idiot who has no idea what they're talking about.

Level 3: Doubt

But ... what if they have a point? What if your thing isn't nearly as good as you think it is? Maybe there are parts of it that do need some serious improvement ...

Level 4: Crippling Doubt

Actually, come to think of it, your thing is absolute rubbish, isn't it? Look at other people's things. How could you ever think your thing was anywhere near the level of their thing? Your thing is TERRIBLE.

Level 5: World-Crumbling, Inescapable Doom

Your whole life is a lie. Everything you do is useless. You will never find any success or happiness and you must go live in a cave where you'll never bother anyone with your terrible thing ever again. There is no meaning to anything.

Yep. That is pretty much the gist of your average Doom Spiral. I should know. I've lived through enough of them.

# CHAPTER THIRTY-ONE

I am greeted at Alana's house by a large, welcoming lady with flowing brown hair, and I see the family resemblance immediately.

'Oh, you must be Meg,' she says, ushering me in. 'I've heard such a lot about you.'

Alana's whole house could probably fit into our kitchen extension and it's totally teeming with clutter. An overfilled shoe rack is spilling its contents onto the floor. A wonky sideboard is bursting with piles of magazines and ornaments, and the magnolia-coloured, wood-chip paper walls are covered with an array of family photographs in mismatched frames. If ever there was an antithesis to my Mum's ideal home aesthetic, it's this. She would break out in hives if she walked in here.

'Alana's in her room if you want to go up.' Mrs Howard is wringing her hands without realising it. 'I really do appreciate you coming over. She's been a bit overwhelmed by all this YouTube business.'

'I'm kind of feeling the same way,' I answer, truthfully. 'But it'll be fine, honestly. I'll go and talk to her.'

She gives an easy smile, like the one I'm used to seeing on Alana. 'Thank you, Meg. She's been so thrilled to meet another girl who's into music. She's never had anyone to share it with properly. Well, not anyone who's ever been good for her anyway.'

It's obvious she's referring to Dylan. I like that guy less and less the more I hear about him.

'She's *such* a talent, you know. Everyone in the family is so proud of her and she deserves a break. I want her to enjoy this moment, not get all upset about it.'

'Don't worry,' I say with a tight smile. 'We'll figure it out. I promise.'

I've almost convinced myself I have all the answers when the truth is, I don't have a clue. I get torn down by Internet bullies all the time and I've hidden the thing I'm most passionate about for years because I'm terrified of what people will think. But weirdly, seeing this happen to someone else has given me a mighty feeling of determination.

When I knock on Alana's door, I'm ready to start fighting back.

♪

'Knock, knock ...'

Alana is sitting on her bed, clutching her phone. She glances up dejectedly as I open the door. 'Hey ...'

Unlike my dorky bedroom, Alana's room is an epic expression of her personality and love of music. Forest green walls are covered with gig posters, tickets, and a massive photo collage. Her guitar leans up against a fluffy sofa and fairy lights circle the top of the room casting a warm glow on her brightly coloured bed sheets. I'm drawn towards a framed, signed set list hanging above her desk. 'Whose is that?'

*Please don't say Caspar*, I think automatically.

'Aurora,' Alana answers. *Phew!* 'She played at Concorde 2 a few years ago. Me and Mum were right at the front.'

'Cool!' I'm genuinely impressed. 'Your Mum seems lovely by the way. I just met her.'

Alana sighs, still grasping her phone, eyes glued to the screen. 'Yeah, she is, but she doesn't get what's going on right now. She hasn't seen all *this*.'

I watch as Alana scrolls up and down her Twitter feed. Hundreds of hateful words flying past in a blur.

'Stop looking,' I order. 'Or you'll give them power over you.'

'Don't you care?!' she wails. 'They're saying stuff about you too, Meg. They're ripping our song to pieces.' She pauses her scrolling, honing in on one particular cluster of tweets. '*Total mess of a song. Unrehearsed drivel.* Oh, and this is the worst one. *Didn't think I could hate acoustic music more, then I heard this shit.*'

OK, hearing such harsh criticism out loud hurts. Of course it hurts. But I've reached my limit now. I refuse to keep allowing these total strangers to wrap me in chains. I'm not going to hide my voice just because some people out there don't like it.

'Give me that,' I say, snatching Alana's phone from her. 'Why should we care what these idiots think? What are they doing that's so brilliant?'

I click the username of the first hater and scan through his Twitter profile. It's filled up with cartoon screenshots, gaming memes, and endless whining about all the music that offends him.

'This person is like ten years old,' I say with a snort. 'They can hardly spell. Look, he complains about every single song in the charts. He's probably just some bored kid with no mates.'

Alana peers over my shoulder, assessing the evidence. 'Hmm. Yeah, he does seem kinda young.'

'Do you actually care what some bratty little kid thinks about us? What makes him qualified to judge how good our song is?'

Alana's defence is dropping. She edges closer to me. I decide to keep sleuthing and bring up the user profile of another hate comment. It's a middle-aged woman from Michigan who runs an entire blog dedicated to slating new releases.

'Are these all her posts?' Alana gasps. 'Wow, she's vicious! Why would anyone spend so much time writing all this hateful stuff?'

As I keep snooping around her blog, I find a bio page which includes a photo of her with a guitar. '*Sharp-talking Michigan Mom who tells it like it is. Also an aspiring songwriter, hoping to finally put out that album one day ...*'

'OK, now it makes sense,' I say, shaking my head. 'Hoping to *finally* put out that album *one day*... She's just a sad, frustrated musician. Clearly she's got resentment issues.'

'Let me see,' Alana snatches her phone back. 'I don't get it. Why doesn't she record her own music then? Surely that would be more constructive than cyber-bullying people she's never met?'

I can't help but laugh, both with exasperation and a strange sense of relief. Because even though I'm doing this for Alana's benefit, I'm facing my own fears in the process. I can hardly believe I've been afraid of these negative, bitter people for so long.

'It's much easier to destroy than it is to create,' I say. 'That's why everyone's a critic.'

'We should keep a watch on this woman,' Alana blurts out. 'Wait for her to release her own song and then tweet about how terrible it is. Give her a taste of her own medicine.'

'That's the thing,' I say. 'This woman will never release her own material. People like her never do. They're way too scared of failing. They know they're going to meet trolls like themselves on the Internet, so they'd rather not even try.' I point at the never-ending stream of poison on Alana's phone. '*This* is the only thing Michigan Mom is going to be known for. *This* is her legacy.'

'Wow.' Alana replies, under her breath. 'How sad.'

'Exactly. So why should we let these losers stop us making something we're proud of?'

For a while Alana continues silently scrolling, lost in contemplation. I wait for her signature giant grin to light her face up again. But something still isn't right.

'It's not just about the music,' she finally says. 'People are saying really mean things about *me*, as a person. About my weight.'

Oh no. I was hoping she hadn't seen those types of comments but of course she has. They weren't exactly hard to miss.

'*Walrus. Miss Piggy. Fatass.* Oh, and loads of mock concern about my health and how someone should bring my mammoth size to my attention.' A humourless laugh escapes her lips. 'As if it never occurred to me that I'm fat. I only have to live with it every day of my bloody life.'

'Don't read that stuff. Don't you dare let it knock your confidence, OK?'

She throws her phone onto the bed and lets out a moan. 'Meg, you don't get it. You're practically a supermodel. You don't have to worry about bad angles giving you a double chin or clothes looking like crap on you.'

'OK maybe it's not exactly the same ... but do you know how many filters and outfit changes I go through to get one nice picture? The answer is a lot. And someone usually ends up slagging me off anyway.'

We're side by side on the bed, trying to read each other – trying to see ourselves from the opposite perspective.

'But you're not *fat*,' Alana sighs. 'You don't know what it's like living with that label. I can't deal with tons of strangers analysing my every move on video, laughing at me.' She shifts on the bed, wilting before my eyes. 'Everyone tells me I should lose weight, but I've tried so many different diets and nothing ever sticks. I love food too much. And my metabolism *sucks*.'

'So don't change then,' I say. 'Not if you don't want to.'

'I don't think I do want to. To be honest, it never really bothered me until everyone else had a problem with it.'

'Here, I want you to see something.' I pass my phone to Alana.

Somewhat suspiciously, she takes it and looks at the screenshots I saved earlier. Enthusiastic, appreciative tweets and comments, all of them raving about us and our song.

'These are the people we need to do this for. They're connecting with our vibe and they're on our side.' I nudge her playfully. 'They want to hear more from us. Look ...'

Alana reads aloud. '*OMG, who's that singing with Meg McCarthy? Amazing voice! So inspiring to see someone representing us plus-size girls. Makes me want to get out there too!*'

As the words sink in, her anxiety slowly melts into a warm glow. I fold my arms with a triumphant smile. 'See? You can't give up when people like her are watching you. Imagine if she actually saw you playing live. Seriously girl, no one is thinking about what size you are when you get up on that stage. You own it!'

'Yeah? I am pretty good, aren't I?'

And just like that, the original Alana is back in the building. Confident Alana who joyfully takes up her space in the world, whether it's the shop or on a stage, in front of one person or 100.

'You know you are,' I laugh. 'You throw yourself into your songs like you're invincible.'

'Yeah, well. I can't help it. I get lost in the moment.'

'So that's what we've both got to do now. Forget all the white noise around us and get lost in our moment.'

Then it hits me. My username. It's absolutely perfect. I know I won't be able to take it back if I say this. I know it could start a chain reaction that gets me found out. I know it's risky and dangerous and stupid but I also know I don't care anymore.

'This might be a crazy idea,' I say, 'but *Lost Girls*? What do you think about that as our duo name?'

The two words spark then settle, like they've been waiting for us to find them.

'I love it,' Alana beams. 'Meg and Alana, aka. Lost Girls.' She lets the phrase linger in the air, testing it out. 'It feels like us, doesn't it?'

Two girls, lost in the music, lost together. Lost but not losing.

I leap off the bed and grab Alana's blue guitar. She watches in bemusement. 'Um, what are you doing?'

'I'm kicking off our second writing session. Have you got pens and paper?'

'Yeah, of course I have,' she replies, looking a little confused. 'But I don't have any proper recording stuff like you do.'

'It doesn't matter, we can record on our phones for now.'

'But what are we gonna write about?'

'This conversation!' I exclaim. 'We're going to take all the things we've ever wanted to say to the haters and the fat-shamers and people who knock us down, and we're gonna put them into a song. Turn this whole thing into something positive.'

I'm already getting ideas as I tune the guitar. She smiles and starts humming – her own creative energy escaping into the magic alchemy of the space between us. Our eyes lock, and in this moment I know I can face this. I know we both can. Because we're not fighting our invisible monsters alone anymore. We're fighting them together.

So we go ahead and write a bloody brilliant song.

# CHAPTER THIRTY-TWO

**BandSnapper:** Hey LostGirl. Was hoping you'd be online tonight, but you're not ... Are you hanging out with Miss Music? :) I've been thinking about my category. Top 5 songs about friendship. Here we go.

1. Me and My Friends – James Vincent McMorrow
2. Real Friends – Camila Cabello
3. All My Friends – Dermot Kennedy
4. All My Friends Are Falling In Love – The Vaccines
5. None of My Friends – Liz Lawrence

**BandSnapper:** Your theme is top 5 duets.

**BandSnapper:** There's a reason duets are on my mind. Have you seen the video going around online today?! I'm in total shock, to be honest.

**BandSnapper:** Meg McCarthy, as in my horrible, spoiled, cyber-celebrity classmate who constantly yells at me for no reason, is a SINGER. Not only that, she's been making music with ALANA HOWARD, the amazing girl I told you about from the gig. There's a video of them harmonising on a song they've apparently written together.

**BandSnapper:** I say 'apparently' because it's so hooky, I'm almost certain Alana is the mastermind behind it. Although, I have to admit, their voices blend together really well. I had no idea Meg was musical. It makes me even sadder that she's never given me the time of day. I bet we have more in common than she realises.

**BandSnapper:** You should definitely check it out – it might inspire you and Miss Music. Seriously, it sounds like something you could have written, LG.

**BandSnapper:** Hmm ... Speak soon xxx

♬

**Top 5 Problems That I Didn't Have This Time Last Week:**

1. The viral video has now gone past 200,000 views. (Positive.) At least 150,000 of those viewers didn't say anything nasty about it. (Positive.) As for the remaining 50,000 ... Let's not go there.

2. Caspar is back in a door-slamming phase. Me taking up the tiniest bit of space seems to mean his enormous ego no longer fits in our house. He's in a stadium-sized bad mood and he wants us all to know it.

3. There are now hundreds of photos online of me and Alana wearing those revolting cerise polo shirts and the accompanying Satan-endorsed beak hat. Beak-chic is definitely not the aesthetic I was hoping to launch our duo with.

4. Having to think about my new, somewhat overwhelmed, friend. Alana is constantly firing unanswerable questions at me: *What's going to happen next? How many views will we get? When will we record the song? Does Caspar hate me? How long will we have to work at the yoghurt shop? Why isn't Adele answering my tweet?*

5. Why the hell did Matty sign off his last email with a *Hmm*? What the hell does *Hmm* mean?! I don't like it. I don't like it at all.

Breathe Meg. Just breathe. I'm not thinking about this. I'm not thinking about any of it. I'm living in the present moment.

Namaste.

♫

Alana has come home from work with me so that we can get stuck into recording our new song. My headphones are up so loud that

I don't hear TJ knock on the door. When I turn around, he's just standing there like a creepy Madame Tussauds exhibit.

'Jesus, TJ! You could warn me before sneaking up on me!'

Alana is falling off the bed laughing. 'He did knock, Meg! I thought you heard him come in.'

'No, I was listening to the bass line,' I say, ripping the headphones off. 'Trying to find the right sound.'

TJ smiles and leans over me to look at my Logic project. 'Is this a new song?'

'Yeah, we wrote it last night,' Alana answers. It's impossible to miss the tone of pride in her voice. 'It came out really easily, too. We seem to be on a creative roll.'

'Well, you'd better play it to me then,' TJ demands, shunting me out of my chair. 'Right, I'm in peak listening position. Lay it on me.'

I switch on my speakers and take a steadying breath. 'OK. It's called "And What?"'

'"And What?" I love it already.'

It would have been easy to write a woe-is-me ballad about the haters and the trolls, but we decided to take all the hurt and channel it into something feisty and fiery instead. Into something *funny* – because everyone knows, the second you laugh at a bully they lose all their power.

TJ's face gives nothing away, however, I spot his foot tapping after the first few bars. This is a good sign.

*Well you've been scoring me out of ten*
*And you've given me a big fat zero*
*You're playing judge and jury again*

*From the comfort of your keyboard*
*When you're bored*
*But I got to say*

*At least I did something*
*At least I tried*
*At least I opened up the door and stepped outside*
*At least I'm not bitter*
*At least I'm not stuck*
*I'm out there*
*Doing my thing*
*Coz I don't give a ...*

Our voices exude fun and confidence, going round in a call and response pattern. Then, as the chorus hits, we come together in harmony, chanting our incredibly-hooky-if-I-do-say-so-myself battle cry.

*OK, so you don't like my face*
*No you don't like my style*
*Oh you don't like my song*
*And what? And what?*
*I'm not making this for you*
*I don't care if you approve*
*You hate every little thing that I do ...*

*And what? And what?*
*What you gonna do about it?*

*And what? And what?*
*What you gonna say about it?*
*And what? And what? What you gonna think about it?*
*And what?*
*If you think you're getting through*
*You're not*


When the track ends, it loops back to the beginning. I reach out to stop it, but TJ grabs my arm in mid-air. 'Wait, can I listen again?'

The second time round I start to relax. We made this, all by ourselves. We took a horrible, upsetting situation and turned it into something amazing. I have to admit, it feels pretty good.

TJ spins around to face us. 'That … ' He says jabbing his finger at my computer. 'That has confirmed it for me! I am *seriously* impressed with the standard of your songwriting, girls. Sure, you need a bit of help on the production side and I've got a few suggestions for the arrangement, but ultimately I think these could be hits.'

Alana stares at me with wide eyes, asking me telepathically whether she heard him right. *I'm* not sure that I heard him right. This is a big deal coming from someone like TJ.

'Meg. Alana. You two have talent. The views on YouTube say it all, and this new song proves it's not a fluke. You've got something here. I know it's still very new and raw, but that's what makes it so exciting to me.'

Goofy TJ has suddenly left the building and Business TJ has taken over proceedings. My heart starts fluttering with anticipation and I can sense Alana's nervous energy beside me.

It's ridiculous that this is happening here in my dorky bedroom.

'So here's the bottom line,' TJ says, his voice level and controlled. 'I want to manage you.'

Alana takes a sharp breath … or is it my breath? I'm not sure anymore. I'm not convinced any of this is even real. Did I fall asleep mid-writing session? Am I having a lucid dream? TJ wants to manage us?! It can't be possible. TJ is the reason that Caspar is a massive pop star and … and TJ's the reason a whole load of singers are now massive pop stars and he's talking to us like we could be his next massive pop star project … and … and … WHAT?!

# CHAPTER THIRTY-THREE

Offering management deals might be all in a day's work for Todd Elliot Jackson (aka. TJ), but to Alana and I it is a world-altering bombshell. Before we've even remotely recovered from the impact, he casually drops a second one.

'How would you feel about playing some songs at my showcase night in London?'

Kaboom. Nuclear explosion. Right in our faces.

'London?' I stammer.

'Yep.' He checks the calendar on his phone. 'Next Friday.'

'Next Friday?!' Alana squeals

'Yeah, why not?' TJ casually replies. 'It's my monthly networking night at the studio. Lots of mates are coming down and some of them are worth impressing, if you know what I mean. Especially when you've just gone viral!'

A business card materialises out of nowhere as he assesses our shell-shocked reaction. 'Here, take my card, Alana. Meg's known me forever, but it's important you're happy with what I do, too. You can check out my credentials on my website and if anything needs explaining feel free to call me.'

Alana stares at the card in disbelief, as if she's been handed a golden ticket by Willy Wonka himself.

'I manage quite a few other acts as well as Caspar and I also do one-off promotional deals for artists wanting to break the UK market. I ran a big campaign for Jessa-May Jones earlier in the year.'

'Jessa-May Jones?' Alana gasps. 'The one who does the "Love On Fire" song? That was never off the radio.'

'600,000 copies sold,' TJ holds his hands up in a mock-humble gesture. 'Her best-selling single to date and her gateway to US audiences.'

It's easy to forget that TJ has a huge, successful business that operates beyond the realm of my brother. He's achieved big things in all sorts of McCarthy-free areas and he knows loads of interesting people. The kind of *interesting* that could launch a whole career in music.

'So what exactly are you proposing here?' I ask. 'Are you looking to get us signed or something?'

'Well, that would be the ultimate goal. But first I would want to create some hype with the right PR companies, look for sponsorship deals, support slots, a booking agent. You know, start getting your name out there.'

OK, this is more serious than I thought.

'But TJ, we've only written two songs together!' I exclaim,

feeling that familiar twist of panic in my gut at the thought of singing in front of people. 'And we don't even know what our sound is yet. I've never even done a bloody gig before!'

As the excuses tumble out of my mouth, I catch Alana's eye. This has been her dream since she was a kid so who am I to turn it down for her? I can tell she senses my inner turmoil as she turns to TJ. 'This all sounds amazing, but we can't get a set together by next week. It's impossible.'

'OK girls, I know it feels quick. It *is* quick. But your video is on fire right now. It's being shared all over on social media and the mystery of what you're working on is keeping everyone interested. We can capitalise on that. It could be the biggest chance of your career!'

'But what if these companies are only interested because we've gone viral, not because they like our music?' I ask.

'Can't they be interested for both reasons?' TJ answers, pacing the room. 'Record companies want people who can create a buzz.' His hands gesticulate wildly. 'You've proved you can do that and it's caught their interest. It's got you the job interview, so to speak. Now showcasing your talent to them could take everything to the next level. But if we don't strike now, we might be too late.'

His words buzz around my head like flies. It would be so easy to swat them away, but part of me knows he's right. The music industry is fickle. It moves fast. If we wait for too long the perfect timing might not be so perfect anymore. I've seen it happen countless times to the artists TJ manages. Wrong timings can break promotion deals, lose headlines, and be the difference between charting or flopping, which is why TJ is so frantic about

Caspar finishing his second album before time finally ticks out.

'Can't we make another YouTube video?' Alana asks. 'You know, go viral again? Once we've had some time to figure out our sound.'

'You can't ever predict how these videos are going to take off,' TJ replies, shaking his head. 'The moment you start actively trying to go viral is the moment you lose authenticity.'

'But we could make it authentic,' Alana tries again. 'Me and Meg, introducing ourselves on camera, playing our song when it's been, you know ... rehearsed.'

'I hear what you're saying, I do. But this is why it would be smart to get a label involved at an early stage. They can help you launch yourselves properly with a decent budget. And it doesn't have to be straight away, you can spend a year or more developing your sound. Under the right guidance.'

The thing about TJ is that it's pointless arguing with him. He always gets his own way. Even though I have a hundred logical reasons why it would be completely ludicrous to play his showcase night next Friday, I already know that we'll be playing his showcase night next Friday.

Oh God.

I turn to Alana, 'What do you think?'

'I ... I don't know. Is this really what we want to do?'

'Look, look, look,' TJ sputters, 'it's just playing some songs and meeting a few people. You don't have to decide right now. Both of you sleep on it. Have a talk about it. Have a think.'

*Then sign your lives over to the music industry. In perpetuity. Throughout the universe. In legally binding contracts.* Obviously that all goes unspoken.

'OK,' I say. 'We'll think about it.'

'Yes, thank you, TJ,' Alana adds. 'It means a lot that you believe in us.'

'I do believe in you,' TJ echoes back. 'I think you're both capable of big things.' He grins his totally disarming cheeky, boyish grin. 'By the way, I've got one more request before I leave you lovely ladies to get back to work.'

'And what might that be?' I ask, raising an eyebrow.

'I've had a track from a big producer. Fancy working on it?'

Wait. Is he asking us to write a topline? Like real, actual songwriters?

'It's pretty basic, not much more than a few piano chords, but I'm sure you girls could do something creative with it.'

'How would that work then?' I ask cautiously. 'I mean, we've only ever written from scratch.'

'Well, whatever you come up with, it'll be a three-way split,' TJ replies. 'But that's a small price to pay for getting your stuff out there and tied to a big name.' I can't get a word in edgeways because he keeps on talking while heading for the door. 'I'll email it over, Meg. Take a listen when you can. I'll let you get on with finishing this song first.'

'Wait, is this one of Caspar's cast-offs?' The thought suddenly hits me like a slap round the shins with a wet hockey stick.

TJ pauses in the doorway momentarily. 'No, no, not a cast-off per se. Just something he chose not to use.'

Funny, that sounds an awful lot like a cast-off to me.

'He'll go mad if he hears we're working on this,' I say. 'Actually, he'll go mad that you're talking to us full stop.'

'And?' TJ answers mischievously. 'Maybe that boy needs a bit of fire under his arse. Nothing like a healthy dose of sibling rivalry, is there?'

Alana is looking increasingly uncomfortable. After her hideous encounter with my darling brother, she must be realising she's stepped straight into a McCarthy minefield.

TJ winks conspiratorially. 'Leave him to me. You two stay focused on what matters, OK? Now have a great session and we'll talk more tomorrow.'

With that, the musical genie drifts away like smoke, leaving us both with a head full of questions and a stomach full of nerves.

# CHAPTER THIRTY-FOUR

Alana and I worked on 'Domino Effect' all evening, perfecting the vocals and getting the harmonies as tight as possible. It was challenging, absorbing and, I admit, a welcome distraction from the intensity of TJ's offer.

Now that I'm alone, however, my head is spinning, trying to make sense of everything that has happened in the past week. The Meg of seven days ago would rather have taken all her clothes off and streaked through Tesco than sing a single word in front of anyone. The Meg of seven days ago was a friendless loser. The Meg of seven days ago most definitely did not have managers, viral videos, and showcase possibilities on her mental radar. I'm exhausted just trying to process it.

My messy mind-swirl is interrupted by the ping of a new email. TJ's sent the backing track. I forward it to Alana then take a sneaky listen.

A pulsing electronic beat ebbs out of the speakers – deep, dark bass and light, airy strings. This was obviously made by a pro. I instantly hear melodies and wish Alana was still here so that we could get straight on with writing to it.

The track has only played for a minute, barely long enough for me to start humming my ideas, when the hurricane hits. I shouldn't be surprised. Not when I forecast this myself.

'What the hell are you doing?' Caspar flings my door open and his foul mood wafts into my room like a rancid dog fart. 'I said, what the hell are you doing?'

I stare him down fearlessly. 'I'm listening to a track. Got a problem with that?'

'That's MY song!' he bellows. 'Where did you get it from?'

Thanks, TJ. You've done a swell job of communicating with your client here.

'TJ sent it.' It seems pointless lying. And besides, I'm not doing anything wrong. From Caspar's reaction you'd think I'd started a bonfire with his guitar collection.

'Why is TJ sending you stuff? I've got ideas recorded for this; he had no right!' Before I can stop him he's snatching my laptop from me. 'What else has he sent? I can't believe this. You've been having little meetings behind my back, haven't you?'

I lunge forward furiously, trying to grab my laptop back. 'No! He's just interested in what I'm doing with Alana.'

'Oh, your dumb little video,' Caspar scoffs refusing to let go of his grip. 'Newsflash, Meg: people only give a crap about that because of me. Because you're MY sister. No one will care by the end of next week.'

'Yeah? Well, TJ thinks a lot of people will care actually.'

Uh-oh. That was the wrong thing to say.

'So you *have* been talking behind my back! You fucking traitors.'

This is ridiculous. We're now wrestling back and forth like we're in a school sports day tug of war. This is suddenly about so much more than a stupid laptop.

'How are we traitors? We're not hiding anything from you. It literally only happened a few hours ago!'

Caspar finally releases the laptop, sending me flying backward. I come dangerously close to dropping it.

'You can't stand things not being about you, can you?' he hisses at me. 'You've always got to take everything I've got. Well enough is enough, Meg. The free ride is over. I draw the line at you taking my manager.'

A shocked, humourless laugh falls out of me. 'You're kidding me, right? I've supported you my whole entire life. I've moved schools, I've been to hundreds of events, I've posed in family photos for magazines, I've stayed invisible to everyone in this house, and somehow that's making it all about me? Cass, you are totally fucking delusional.'

For a second, his jaw gapes in stunned silence trying to force out a retaliation that isn't coming. Then his eyes narrow into that steely, immovable stare I know all too well.

'My career has given everyone in this house an incredible life,' he says, his voice low and menacing. 'You included, so don't give me some pathetic sob story. You've got tons of attention from being my sister. Oh, but now you've magically become this poor, overlooked songwriter? Give me a break.'

'Newsflash, Caspar,' I say, blasting his own sarcastic words back at him. 'You're not the only member of this family who can write songs. I've been working on my music for years. Besides, I didn't ask for any of this. It was your stupid camera guy who leaked the footage.'

We're standing face-to-face, animosity raging between us. Years of hidden resentment sparking from the embers.

'So why is TJ sending you my backing tracks? You think you're some kind of professional writer now after one little song? You're out of your depth, Meg. Do you seriously think you can handle being famous? Having your life picked apart by millions of people?'

His hostility winds me and causes me to hesitate. But, unlike the Meg of seven days ago, it doesn't take me long to recover. 'I don't know, Cass. But I *do* know that I'm sick of being paralysed into silence. I'd rather put myself out there and fail than keep doing nothing at all.'

As always Caspar twists my words so that they're all about him. 'Don't you dare start attacking me and my album. You don't know anything about this business. One bullshit chat with TJ doesn't make you an industry expert all of a sudden. Everything is riding on my next move, Meg. Our lifestyle, our finances, our reputation. *Everything.*'

'So just write something then,' I shout back, frustration seething through my veins. 'Get in the studio and write instead of freaking out about what I'm doing.'

With that, Caspar throws himself back onto me, scrabbling for the laptop again. 'You're a total bitch, you know that? You're trying to ruin my life.'

I throw my whole weight back against him. 'Jesus, Cass! Get off, you're going to break it.'

'Good! That's what you get for stealing my song off me.'

'It's not YOUR song though, is it? You need to have, oh I don't know, an actual *idea* for it to be considered a song.'

Caspar shoves me and it bloody hurts. We've travelled back in time to when we were kids fighting over the TV remote. I cry out in pain, gripping my shoulder.

'I have ideas, OK?' Caspar yells in my face. 'I have tons of ideas. Brilliant ones. They're just not ready yet.'

'Oh, yeah, sure you do. Nothing says inspiration like a permanent hangover.'

'I've been working fucking hard on this album and you know it.' His face is getting redder and redder. 'So what if I want to blow off some steam? It's called having a life, Meg, something you know nothing about.'

Placing the laptop back in its rightful position on my desk, I point to it with a wild flourish. 'This is what's known as hard work, Caspar. Something *you* know nothing about. Which is why TJ wants me and Alana to work on the tracks you've been ignoring all year long.'

Caspar lets out an almighty roar and wrestles me into a headlock. I scream and bite his arm.

We've fully regressed. I'm ten years old and he is thirteen. Always that little bit stronger and bigger than me. Always that little bit unbeatable.

Suddenly, Dad's voice cuts through the room. 'What the hell is going on in here? Get off each other, right now! For God's sake!

How old are you two?!'

I wince as he grabs my collar and wrenches us both apart. 'What is this nonsense all about?'

'Caspar's trying to break my laptop,' I whine.

I don't get the dignity of a first name referral. 'She's trying to poach TJ!'

Dad does that rapid blinking thing he always does when he's trying to catch up. 'Sorry, what?'

Caspar melodramatically examines the bite mark I've left on his arm. 'TJ's been sending Meg my tracks and they've been having little meetings together behind my back.'

'No we haven't!' I protest. 'It's been *one* conversation, Dad, and Caspar's totally overreacting.'

'Really?' Dad says. But not in a *I'm-very-disappointed-in-you-Meggy* kind of way. Quite the opposite. 'Wow, that's brilliant! What fantastic news.'

I'm not going to lie. I laugh. Just a tiny bit. On the inside. And maybe a bit on the outside too.

Caspar double takes. 'What the ... No! It's not fantastic news. She's thieving my manager, Dad.' He swings a death glare straight at me. 'MY. MANAGER!'

Dad claps a hand on Caspar's shoulder, clearly not picking up the vibes of apocalyptic doom emanating from his son's entire being. 'Come on, Cass. Aren't you happy for Meg? This could be a wonderful thing – brother and sister sharing a manager, supporting each other through the highs and lows of the music industry.' He turns to me, eyes shining with McCarthy family pride. 'What has TJ said, babygirl? Does he want to sign you and your friend?'

'This is BULLSHIT!' Caspar screeches, barging past us to the door. 'Why do you always have to take her side with everything?'

Poor Dad. He looks thoroughly bemused by this whole situation. 'Hey, what's the problem here? TJ manages lots of people, Cass. It's not going to affect his work with you.'

'Of course it will,' Caspar replies through gritted teeth. 'Which is why it's not bloody well happening.' He rampages into the hallway, shouting the whole house down. 'TJ! TJ! Where the hell has he gone? TJ, I need to talk to you RIGHT NOW.'

Dad flounders around behind Caspar, trying to soothe him back to normality. 'Calm down, Cass! Look, let's all sit down and talk about this like adults.'

'TJ, I AM GOING TO KILL YOU WHEN I FIND YOU!'

I slam my bedroom door shut on both of them. There is nothing more to say tonight, whatever Dad thinks. Instead, I load up the backing track – the harmless three-minute pop track which has caused fury, violence, and actual death threats.

The melody ideas flow as naturally as my own breath.

I record them all with a defiant smile on my face and I don't feel the slightest bit guilty about it.

# CHAPTER THIRTY-FIVE

'Oh my goodness, girls, you're going to be famous! And just think, I can tell everyone that you met at *my* shop. Maybe I'll get to sell my story to the magazines ...'

We've been going around in circles trying to decide what to do, and Laura's self-obsessed wittering about our showcase offer is definitely not helping to alleviate our doubts. On top of Caspar's meltdown last night, it's all beginning to feel a bit ... much.

'OK, L-Dog, don't get too carried away,' Alana sighs. 'We don't even know if we're gonna do it yet.'

'What?! Of course you're doing it! Honestly girls, opportunities like this don't fall out of the sky. Look how much TJ has done for Caspar over the years. That could be you two!'

Something weird is happening here. I'm agreeing with Laura. I'm actually seriously considering doing this. Singing. In front of people. It's like Caspar's epic tantrum has spun me

180 degrees in the opposite direction.

'Maybe we should, Lan,' I say, surprising myself as much as her. 'I mean we've got two great songs already. Plus we could work on that backing track together …'

Alana slumps on the counter. 'I dunno. Maybe.'

It's not exactly the reaction I was hoping for. Or expecting. 'Hang on a minute, I'm the one with a history of crippling stage fright, not you. Shouldn't it be me freaking out and you convincing me to do it?'

She fiddles with her ponytail, not meeting my eye. 'But … what if I'm not good enough for a showcase performance?'

'What?! You perform all the time! I'll be the one bricking it. I've never played a gig in my life. You're the pro here.'

'In Brighton maybe – at open mic nights where everyone's nice to you – not out there in the big wide scary world.' She points to the door for dramatic effect, just as it opens and our first customer of the day walks in.

I look up and see horizontal white lines against black fabric with the 'no music on a dead planet' slogan. I know that shirt. My heart stops – genuinely freezes stone still in my chest.

'You're right! It is a big wide scary world out there. I just heard a busker murdering my favourite Hozier song and my breakfast bagel got stolen by a seagull.'

Matty Chester is standing in the middle of the shop. As in the shop where I personally work. As in the shop where I have to wear a dodo hat. It's too late. He's seen me. Shit.

He makes a beeline for Alana, ignoring me completely. 'I'm joking about the bagel by the way. Not about the busker, though.

I stand by my sneering derision when it comes to appalling cover songs. Anyway, do you stare and point at all your customers or am I special?'

Alana laughs nervously, shooting me a thousand and one urgent rapid eye movements in the brief milliseconds she thinks Matty isn't looking. 'Oh, uh ... Ha ha! Sorry about that. Err ...' Telepathic glaring in my direction. 'It's Matty, right? Meg's friend?'

Oh for crying out loud, Alana, don't use those kind of loaded words.

'I guess you could say that.' Matty nods his head to me giving me the coolest of smiles. And I mean temperature wise. 'Hi, Meg.'

I'm grateful that I'm mostly obscured by the counter because I'm shaking like a whippet in the snow. 'Hi, Matty.' I sound clipped, cold. Basically the complete opposite of how I'm saying the words in my head. *Hiiiiii Matttttyyyyy, absolute love of my freaking life.*

Laura is bobbing behind us, intrigued by the interaction playing out. Alana coughs, clearly unnerved by the sudden awkward atmosphere that has more layers to it than a Christmas trifle. 'So, err, what can we get for you?'

Matty pushes his glasses up his nose. He always does that when he's self-conscious. I could watch him pushing his glasses up his nose all day and never get bored of it.

'Sorry, I'm actually on my way to work so better not risk dropping yoghurt all down myself.' He laughs awkwardly. 'I just wanted to drop by to congratulate you on your video. I saw it doing the rounds online and it totally blew me away.'

For a disjointed second, I forget the fact I work at Dodo Yoyo is all over Twitter, and the fact that Matty knows Alana from open mic night. It feels like he knows me, as in Meg McCarthy me, as intimately as he knows LostGirl and he's casually come in to see me because it's something he does all the time.

Only it's obviously not me he's come in to see.

'Why thank you,' Alana smiles. 'It's still weird knowing so many people are watching it. We haven't even finished the song properly yet, have we, Meg?'

She's throwing me a lifeline into the conversation. I take it so loosely she may as well not have bothered. 'Yeah, we're still working on it.'

Matty assesses me warily, unsure how close he can get to the savage beast. 'Well, it's a brilliant song. You definitely need to get it out there properly.' Another push of his glasses. Yep, still enthralled. 'I was so surprised you sing too, Meg. All these years at school and you've never mentioned music once.'

There is an accusing undertone to his comment. I can't help but fill in the blanks. All these years at school *where you've treated me like shit* and you never mentioned *we actually had something in common. You horrible cow.*

I shrug, defensively. That's all I've got. Urgh. What is wrong with me?! The worst part is I probably would have said or done something way meaner if my boss wasn't currently breathing down my neck.

'Meg writes too,' Alana says, gesturing to me, smiling in my direction, all but holding up a neon sign pointing straight at me. 'She is *super* talented. I would never be getting this kind of opportunity without her.'

Matty risks a small smile at me, but I stare down at the floor.

He clears his throat. 'Yes, I'm sure Meg's contacts must be a huge boost for you both.' Ouch, backhanded insult. 'Anyway, I hope you're going to take all this further. It sounded awesome.'

Alana's cheeks are glowing now. I can't tell if she's embarrassed by all this attention from my crush or genuinely enjoying the compliments. 'Thanks. We're working on more songs at the moment so we'll see what happens.'

'If you ever want photography,' Matty adds, 'I'm more than happy to help. Promo shots, live gigs, anything you need. Just say the word.' He looks pointedly at me. 'Only if I have *permission*, of course.'

Before I can form a snarky comeback, Laura jumps in. 'Funny you should mention gigs. The girls are playing a showcase night in London. How exciting is that?'

My stomach clenches in a tight knot. This is classified information. *Very* classified.

Laura fails to notice the tense silence and keeps chirping on to Matty. 'Caspar's manager is setting it up. He obviously sees real potential in them. And can you believe they met here in my shop? I brought them together! Maybe I should get a finder's fee.'

As she cackles away to herself, Matty gazes awestruck at Alana. 'Wow, that's a big deal. A *huge* deal.'

'We might not do it,' Alana answers, waving a dismissive hand. 'It's only a little showcase for a few select people. I doubt it will lead to anything much.'

'Totally *not* the impression you gave earlier,' Laura bulldozes on. 'You said there would be labels and A&R people there!'

Shut up, L-Dog, shut up!

'We said there *might* be,' Alana lies. 'Let's not get too carried away. It's just one gig.'

Thankyouthankyouthankyou, Alana! She knows I want Matty thrown off the scent by any means possible. If he starts digging too deeply into the *Lost Girls* he's going to uncover the secret of his own LostGirl. I feel sick. This secret is slipping out of my control and there's nothing I can do about it.

'You should definitely do the gig,' Matty says. 'You've got nothing to lose and you obviously bring out the best in each other.'

He tries one more smile at me and this time I actually smile back. A teeny, tiny, blink-and-you'd-miss-it smile.

Maybe losing control isn't the end of the world. After all, this week has shown me that letting go can lead to good things. There's just one last secret I need to stop holding on to ...

'Better go,' Matty says, taking a small step backward. 'Hope you don't mind all the fan gushing.'

He's talking to Alana. I've been well and truly tuned out.

'Not at all. We appreciate it,' she answers. *We.* Bless her. She's really trying here.

As Matty reaches the door, he pauses. 'One more thing before I go. Top Five Beatles Songs. Go.'

It's our game. Mine and Matty's. *BandSnapper* and *LostGirl*'s. To hear him mention it in the real world makes my entire universe tilt so that I totally lose my bearings. I expect Alana to laugh in confusion, but instead she reels off her list like she's been waiting all her life for someone to ask her.

'That's easy ... "Blackbird", "Come Together", "Eleanor Rigby", "I've Just Seen A Face", and "Get Back".'

Matty grins as if he's been handed five signed albums by the ghost of John Lennon. 'Good choices. Very good choices.'

As he leaves the shop I feel my heart collapse. A piece of our sacred, private, hidden world just turned from diamonds to dust.

'Gosh, he was lovely,' Laura beams. 'Alana, he seemed to like you *a lot!*'

'Oh, God no,' Alana splutters back instantly. 'He's not my type. Not at all.'

'Well, the last fella worked out so well didn't he? You should give a sweet boy like him a chance.'

I know it's pathetic, but I suddenly feel tears sting the back of my eyes. It should have been me listing my favourite Beatles songs. It should have been me chatting and smiling and receiving compliments. I should be the one Laura is urging to give a sweet boy a chance.

'Meg ...' Alana says softly.

I don't blame her for any of this. She was trying to be a good friend. I can only blame myself for being such a coward.

*No talent. Ugly. Pointless. Rude. Bitch.* The tidal wave of negativity I've been convincing Alana we need to ignore crashes into my mind. Murky, suffocating waters taking over my entire brain.

'I spy more customers,' Laura trills, leaning over the counter to get a view of the crowd of tweens gathering by the window. 'Come on, best smiles for the fans now ladies.'

Saved by the selfie. Blinking back my tears and taking a deep breath I put on my bravest showwoman mask.

The popularity of our video isn't slowing down. We have so

many people streaming into the shop from this moment onwards that there isn't a chance to mention our showcase gig or Matty Chester again for the rest of the shift.

# CHAPTER
# THIRTY-SIX

**Top 5 Ways to Say 'I Don't Want to Talk About It':**

1. 'Mmm' or 'uh-huh' or some other non-committal noise.
2. 'I guess we'll see what happens.'
3. 'Oh God, did I tell you I had a massive fight with my brother last night?'
4. 'Shall we get on with the song now?'
5. 'I DON'T WANT TO TALK ABOUT IT!'

None of these tactics work when it comes to Alana's wheedling. Not even the unapologetically blunt option.

'But why can't you tell him?' she asks for the thousandth time as we enter my bedroom. 'What's the worst that could happen? You've fessed up to everyone else in your life, so why not Matty too?'

'Let's just try and write this song,' I sigh. 'At this moment in time it's more important than my disastrous love life.'

Alana folds her arms. 'What are you so scared of?'

I throw my head back and wail. 'He hates me, alright?! Matty Chester absolutely frickin' hates me. And he has every right to after the way I've treated him.'

'He doesn't hate you. He talks to you every single day.'

'He talks to LostGirl,' I correct. 'And half of the time he's bitching about Meg to her. What the hell is he going to think when he finds out we're the same person? It'll be game over.'

'You don't know that. Give him a chance. I'm sure he'll understand. He's going to figure it out sooner or later anyway, especially when he hears our band name.'

'Yeah, well. Let's make it later rather than sooner.'

There's a lingering silence. Stalemate.

'Your song about him is beautiful,' Alana eventually continues. 'There's no way he won't forgive you when he hears it.'

I shift uncomfortably in my seat. 'Second First Impression' is the one song I haven't dared to send to BandSnapper. The thought of him actually hearing it makes me instantly break out into a cold sweat.

'I think we should play it at the showcase.'

I swivel round in my chair. 'What?'

'It's gorgeous. I could put some harmonies on it.'

'So … we're doing the showcase then?'

Alana meets my eyes with a shy smile. 'I feel like Matty's right, we've got to go for it. We could play "And What?", "Domino Effect", and "Second First Impression". What do you think?'

'I dunno, you've got loads of amazing songs too. What about "Didn't I?"'

'Too raw. Come on, we've got to do your song. It's perfect and it shows off your skills.'

Oh great. So Alana doesn't want to sing her emotional love song and risk her mascara running, but she's quite happy for me to. The thought of baring the most fragile pieces of my soul in a room full of music biz royalty is utterly terrifying. But at the same time some small, strange, sadistic part of me might actually want to do it.

'OK,' I say. 'So ... we're actually doing this.'

Alana's whole aura lights up with excitement. 'We're actually doing this.'

Saying the words out loud doesn't make it feel any less surreal. But this is happening.

The Lost Girls are here and we're ready to be heard.

♫

For the rest of the afternoon, we work on our first ever topline. It's a whole new process, trying to follow the chords and structure of the pre-produced track, but once we get into the song, our melodies take new directions that we wouldn't have found with only guitar or piano. We seem to be getting the hang of this co-writing thing.

TJ knocks on my bedroom door halfway through our session. 'How's it going ladies? Got anything I can listen to yet?'

'We've written up to the second verse,' I say. He peers over my shoulder at my Logic project. 'It's a work in progress.'

'Great! Let's hear it then.'

I shoot him a sceptical glance. 'So ... we're not going to mention Hurricane Caspar first?'

TJ waves his hand dismissively. 'It's fine, it's all under control.'

'Yeah, that screaming fit he had with you last night sounded completely under control.'

'Screaming fit?!' Alana echoes. 'Oh God. He's really mad about this, isn't he?'

'It's honestly fine, don't worry about Cass. I'm dealing with him.' The fixed grin doesn't leave TJ's face. I can't tell if he's covering up some kind of internal breakdown or whether all these years with Caspar have simply left him unflappable when it comes to tantrums. I guess when they're a weekly occurrence, you start tuning them out.

'OK, here goes then,' I say, grabbing the mouse. 'This is what we have so far. The song is called "Scripts".'

'Great title. What's the concept?'

It's a question I'm strangely struggling to answer. When I first heard the track, it sent a whole flurry of lyric ideas into my mind – lyrics that were also shaped by Alana's own experiences.

It's the kind of song that is intensely personal to us yet, at the same time, held out at arm's length. It's about knowing you're never going to be perfect, no matter how much you want to be. It's about saying the wrong thing over and over, because reality is never as glossy as the movies. It's about pressure. It's about Matty. It's about Dylan. It's about how stupidly I acted *yet again* in the shop this morning. It's about this whole crazy musical learning experience. It's about nothing in particular and everything that is important to us, all at once.

'Basically,' Alana says, deciding to try and explain the unexplainable, 'the idea of the whole song is wishing you had, like ... a script.'

Or, yeah. You could just say that. If you wanted to be *literal* about it.

TJ claps his hands and rubs them together furiously. 'I love it! Go on, hit play.'

I turn up the speakers and start the track. The song springs into life, followed by our voices, hushed and breathy.

> *Expectations burning in your chest*
> *You're waiting for those perfect lines*
> *But you get what you get*
> *Leading ladies*
> *Breathing down my neck*
> *So well rehearsed and in control*
> *But I'm a nervous wreck*
>
> *Coz I've been breaking glasses*
> *Like I've been breaking hearts*
> *Trying to tell you how I'm feeling*
> *Is like reading in the dark*
> *And I know ...*

TJ is listening intently with his eyes closed. His face remains infuriatingly neutral as the song keeps playing.

*Scripts make every word*
*Sound beautiful*
*But I've got nothing to follow*
*Nothing to follow*
*And I will say the wrong thing*
*Every time*
*But now I know*
*The cliché you wanna hear*
*Is nothing but hollow*

Alana raises an eyebrow at me as if to ask *What the hell is he thinking?!*

I shrug. *I don't have a freaking clue, but I hope it's not bad.*

See. We are literally telepathic now.

After an over the top *who's-the-winner-of-Strictly* dramatic pause, TJ's eyes snap back open and he leaps up from the bed.

'Please tell me you've been thinking about the showcase.' He presses his hands into a prayer. 'Because I am dying for you to show this to everyone. This song is fantastic.'

'Actually, we have been thinking about it,' I reply, looking to Alana for approval. She nods eagerly, urging me to go on. I take a deep breath and blurt out our news. 'We want to do it.'

'YES!' TJ cries, punching the air. 'Fantastic news, girls. Brilliant. Now I can get the wheels in motion.'

'But, I'm not sure about this song,' Alana cuts in, her face a little anxious underneath the excitement. 'We haven't finished it yet and we don't have enough time to work out an acoustic version.'

'Never mind, you can sing to the backing track. We've got to present the strongest songs and it would be silly not to play this one.'

Backing track? I can't think of anything worse and Alana looks like she's inhaled a wasp, so I'm guessing neither can she. TJ pushes on, ignoring our hesitation.

'Ladies, don't worry. We can talk about this over the next few days, make sure you're both happy. In the meantime I'll arrange a photoshoot, then we can put a few teasers online to keep everyone interested.'

It's impossible to stay immune to the exciting future that he's laying out in front of us like a red carpet. Something about TJ's complete and utter confidence in us is like a permission slip to be excited. He's making things happen. In the real world. *Photoshoot. Teasers.* This is the vocabulary of a manager launching a brand-new act. A brand-new act that just so happens to be us!

I temporarily forget my personal body space rules and throw my arms around Alana, who lets out a squeal.

'This is what I like to see,' TJ beams. 'A bit of excitement! Now don't let me down. Get practising and finish writing that hit.'

'With *my* track you mean?'

I have no idea how long Caspar has been standing in my doorway listening in. TJ jumps at the sight of him. 'Oh, Cass! You alright mate? Did you hear what the girls wrote? Absolutely amazing, isn't it?'

Wrong thing to say. Absolutely, amazingly wrong, wrong, wrong.

'How dare you give away my tracks?' Caspar shouts in TJ's face.

'You have no right to go behind my back like that. And you two.' Oh God. Here we go. It's our turn in the spotlight of doom. 'YOU TWO. Who the hell do you think you are? Come on, Meg. You're better than this.'

With that, Caspar slams my bedroom door, causing my Taylor Swift calendar to fall off the wall and my mic to start feeding back in an ear-piercing whine. Awesome.

Alana gasps. 'Oh no! Oh no, oh no. Do you think we should stop writing this song?'

'No way,' TJ commands. 'You let me handle him. He always calms down eventually.'

'Does he?' Alana bites her lip guiltily. 'Coz I'm not gonna lie, it's a bit upsetting to know my former idol hates my guts right now.'

She said *former*. Good. That means she's learning.

'Don't worry.' TJ smiles, as though the last two minutes didn't happen. 'It's not personal. Cass hates everyone right now … equally.'

Way to put her mind at rest, TJ …

'He's given me a headache. I'm off downstairs for an Ibuprofen and a Berocca. Don't waste your time worrying about him. You girls crack on.'

Easier said than done. I mean, I know what an arsehole my brother can be because I've had to share precious breathing space with him for the last seventeen years. Alana, on the other hand, is totally new to all of this. Until a few days ago he was a voice on the radio, a face on the TV, a personality in the press. He was the 2D version of Caspar McCarthy, with the evil third dimension well hidden.

Reality can be so disappointing compared to the story around it.

'He doesn't really want it, Lan,' I say, trying to reassure her. 'He just doesn't want us to have it.'

I play the song again. I know nothing is ever perfect and there's always room for improvement, but as we listen to our melodies and harmonies, I realise there is a distinct magic in what we've created.

'I'm not being arrogant when I say this, but Caspar wouldn't have written anything half as catchy as this.'

She smiles at me. I suddenly realise that it doesn't matter how many tantrums Caspar has or how many names he calls us or how many different ways he tries to undermine us, we're loving what we're doing and we're not going to stop.

'You're not being arrogant,' Alana says. 'You're being right.'

# CHAPTER
# THIRTY-SEVEN

**BandSnapper:** LostGirl ... Are you there? I haven't seen you online much lately.

**LostGirl:** I'm here! Sorry, I'm so busy at the moment. The last week has been crazy.

**BandSnapper:** I think I might know why ...

**LostGirl:** Huh?

**BandSnapper:** LG ... I know. I've figured it out.

**BandSnapper:** ... LG? You still there?

**LostGirl:** Here's my top 5 duets:

1. exile – Taylor Swift and Bon Iver

2. Somebody That I Used To Know – Gotye and Kimbra

3. Shallow – Lady Gaga and Bradley Cooper

4. Let's Go Home Together – Ella Henderson and Tom Grennan

5. Under Pressure – Queen and David Bowie

**BandSnapper:** I don't want to play games anymore. Please be honest with me. I know you in real life, don't I?

**LostGirl:** I can't have this conversation, BandSnapper.

**BandSnapper:** I can't not have this conversation. You're Alana, aren't you?

**LostGirl:** I don't know what you mean.

**BandSnapper:** Come on LG! I knew it as soon as I saw that video. It had LostGirl's style written all over it. Then today you confirmed my suspicions when I came into the shop. It's you. It has to be you.

**LostGirl:** I have no idea what you're talking about.

**BandSnapper:** You don't work miles away at a library. You work here in Brighton, and Miss Music is Meg. That's why you get so cagey when I mention her, because she's your friend. She's been so horrible to me because she doesn't want me figuring all this out …

**LostGirl:** OK, now you're inventing a story that makes no sense. You've heard all my songs. Surely you can tell from my recordings we aren't the same person?

**BandSnapper:** But the video?! It sounded just like you. You're Alana, you have to be …

**LostGirl:** You're only hearing what you want to hear.

**BandSnapper:** I know it's weird to speak to each other in real life after so many years of messaging. But we had a connection today. This isn't going to change anything between us. I promise.

**LostGirl:** We didn't have a connection because we didn't even speak to each other!!!!

**BandSnapper:** You're finally getting the chances you've always deserved. I'm so incredibly proud of you and I want to be at every gig, cheering you on. Please give me a chance, Alana. You don't have to keep hiding anymore.

**LostGirl:** I'm not Alana! And I'm certainly not doing a load of gigs. Don't you know me after all these years? Because if you did then you would realise how completely wrong you are.

**BandSnapper:** I know your lyrics. I know your melodies and your passion for songwriting. It's one of a kind. That video is YOU, LostGirl. It has to be.

**BandSnapper:** LostGirl? Are you still there?

**LostGirl is offline.**

♪

It's easy to block things out if you really try.

I've got the perfect excuse because the showcase is now only two days away. Forty-eight hours to be precise, which is not a lot of hours when you've got songs to rehearse, shifts to work, fans to take selfies with, social media to update, a tornado of a brother raging against you at every turn, and an online not-quite-boyfriend demanding to know your true identity.

I'm not going to lie, it's been a stressful week so far.

Despite the looming pressure, Alana and I have been practising every afternoon and our set is sounding faultless. It took us a while to pick the set list. At first we were planning on performing 'Second First Impression', but once we'd finished writing 'Scripts', we knew there was no way we could leave it out. Besides, TJ had very definitely made up his mind on that one and I wasn't about to waste time arguing with him.

However, I did stand my ground on the issue of singing to a backing track. If I'm finally going to get up on a stage and face my fears, I am not doing it karaoke style. I'm doing it on my terms, with real instruments.

While we've been practising, TJ has been in full-on business mode. He's sorted out a logo, written our bios, and created Lost Girls social media accounts. He also arranged a professional photoshoot for us. A refreshing change from my usual lonely selfies.

Everything is hectic and exhilarating. It feels like some sort of out-of-body experience. If I were to stop and think too hard about it all I'd have a paralysis attack like one of those stupid freezing goats. Just like if I were to stop and think about Matty. Or the fact that he thinks I'm Alana. Or the fact he seems to be falling for the wrong Lost Girl.

I choose not to think about any of it though. I simply abandon my chats with BandSnapper and I don't mention a word about him to Alana. I hit pause on the whole situation and instead I only focus on what's right in front of my face. I sing so loudly during rehearsals that it drowns out every single trace of him.

See? I told you it's easy to block things out if you really try.

♫

At 4.27pm, with a little over twenty-seven hours to go until we hit the stage, I realise that I've stopped caring about who hears me sing. I don't care if Dad stands in the doorway and watches for a bit. I don't care if Mum does her overly-enthusiastic singing-along-wrong thing. I don't even care if Caspar hears me.

In fact, I hope he does. Because we sound good. Really good. And like anything in life, the more we practice, the better we're getting.

Our fiftieth run-through of 'Domino Effect' is interrupted by an email alert on my phone. My heart lurches, terrified it might be from Matty. But thankfully it's only TJ sending over the pictures from our photoshoot. I wave my phone at Alana, who has been bugging me every five minutes about them. 'They're here! Shall we check them out?'

'*Yes please,*' she sings doing a twirl and flinging her guitar on my bed. 'But let's look at them on your laptop. I want to see them on the big screen!'

TJ has sent a whole folder of images and I open them in a slideshow. The first one is the two of us back-to-back in the Brighton Pavilion gardens. The colours are vivid and beautiful. My black jacket pops against the greenery and I'm staring moodily into the camera with heavily-lined eyes. I've been transformed into a proper pop star and I couldn't be happier with the result.

'What has he done?!' Alana cries, her voice strangled. 'I'm *enormous!*'

Oops. I just remembered. I'm not the only one in this picture. And while the camera has been kind to me, the same cannot be said of Alana. She's standing at an awkward angle, her huge boobs protruding and her large bare arm taking up most of the space between us. Without wanting to sound cruel, it definitely isn't the most flattering of shots.

'Oh ...'

I don't know what to say. I don't know what to do. I'm stuck between the rock of not lying and the hard place of not wanting to hurt her feelings. 'Don't worry, it's probably a weird angle. There are loads more shots to pick from.'

I scroll to the next photo. Then the next. And the next. They're not getting any better. Alana's flowing red, sleeveless dress looked fabulous in real life, but somehow in these pictures it's morphed into a billowing nightmare.

Her eyes well up with tears. 'I'm a huge, fat tomato.'

'No you're not! It's just ...' I'm floundering for words. 'Let's keep looking through.'

I continue flicking, hoping that the next pictures will be better but they only get worse. As does the atmosphere. And my ability to find the right thing to say.

Eventually our pose changes. We're lying down on the grass, acoustic guitars resting beside us. My face is tilted upward, serenely staring into the sky, but Alana is looking downwards. Everybody knows YOU NEVER LOOK DOWNWARDS! What the hell was the photographer thinking?! Why didn't he say something?!

'This is even worse,' she wails through stuttering breaths. 'I've got a double-double chin and my belly is hanging out. I'm disgusting.'

'You're not disgusting! We just got put in the wrong positions.'

My feeble words of encouragement aren't doing anything to calm her down. 'Is this what I look like on stage? Why has no one ever told me? The tweeters were right. I'm a gross whale!'

'ALANA. Come on, you *know* you don't really look like that. You've got tons of lovely photos from gigs. This is just bad luck.'

'But this is the one photoshoot that actually counts!' Alana falls to her knees melodramatically. 'And I've ruined it. All the pretty filters in the world won't be able to fix this. I'm a mess!'

I pause the slideshow before it repeats and we are forced to relive the excruciating experience again. This is awful. I don't like it when Alana shrinks. She's only herself when she takes up all the space in the room. She's meant to be big. It's who she is and it's a brilliant thing.

'We can fix this,' I say, taking charge. 'It's honestly not as bad as you think ...'

'Easy for you to say!' she snaps back. There's a snarl in her tone, a jagged edge I've never heard before. 'You look like a frickin' supermodel in every single one!'

I open my mouth to retaliate, but nothing comes out. I feel like whatever I say will be the wrong thing. We meet each other's eyes and her hard edge softens. 'Sorry,' she says quietly. 'I'm just so mortified.'

'As you should be,' a voice cuts in directly behind us.

We spin around and there he is. Of course he is. His in-built trouble detecting radar was bound to seek us out the second something went wrong.

Caspar barges between us, inspecting the disappointing results of our photoshoot with a snide smirk on his face. We don't stop him. I've reverted back to pathetic little sister mode and Alana has become the awestruck, intimidated fan once again. I hate that he has this kind of power over us.

'I think perhaps it's time for a little real, true talk,' he says condescendingly, folding his arms. 'Not the fake, bullshit advice

TJ is gonna give you. My room. Let's go.'

I know from his whole toxic aura that following him is a bad idea. Whatever he has to say, I'm certain I'm not going to like it. And yet we both follow him to his room, drawn to his destructive light like two entranced moths. Why are we doing this?

Maybe it's because I know he will give us the cold, hard truth. Maybe it's because he's been so successful. Maybe it's because I've always looked up to him and despite everything, I do care what he thinks.

I guess there are some relationships that can't be blocked out or switched off.

# CHAPTER THIRTY-EIGHT

Caspar's bedroom is huge compared to mine. Being the oldest (and richest) he's always managed to get the best of everything. At the beginning of the summer he moved his whole studio set-up back down here. He must have at least ten different guitars, a brand-new Kawai upright piano, brand-new Yamaha HS8 monitors and a Neumann microphone that I know for a fact cost more than Dad's Vauxhall Insignia. It puts my sad little set-up to shame.

'Sit down,' Caspar orders, sweeping scrunched-up balls of paper off the bed. What I assume are unwanted song lyrics are scattered everywhere. Remnants of his latest artistic efforts no doubt. He's got all this amazing gear, but no ideas worth actually recording. It's infuriating.

'What exactly do you want, Cass?' I ask, reluctantly sitting down. 'Because if you're looking for an excuse to be horrible then we don't want to hear it.'

He gives one of his trademark dismissive, scoffing snorts and pulls up his plush, leather desk chair. 'I'm not trying to be horrible. I'm trying to help you. I've been in this industry for a long time. I know what I'm talking about, OK?'

I eye him cautiously. Every cell in my body is screaming at me not to trust him, but there's also a tiny voice in my head whispering *he's right ... you know he's right*. Caspar has ridden the almighty wave of pop stardom to dizzying heights of success. He's also been properly slammed by crushing lows, scandals, bad choices and mistakes. He's experienced all of it and he's a fully qualified expert on whatever might lie ahead.

'You've got a real problem on your hands here,' Caspar continues, a smile flickering across his lips. I swear he's enjoying this. 'No one else is going to be honest with you, but you need to know.'

I glance at Alana who is hunched forward, chewing ferociously on her thumbnail.

'Come on, Lan,' I say, wishing I'd trusted my instincts in the first place. 'Let's go. We don't need to listen to this.'

'No, let him say it,' she answers. There is a loaded pause. 'OK. I'll say it then. The photos are awful, aren't they?'

Caspar nods gravely like this is hard for him to tell us. 'I can't lie to you. They're bad. I'm sorry Alana, but your whole look is pretty problematic.'

OK, that's it. I can't believe I even contemplated taking advice from my snake of a brother. I leap up, ready to storm out of the room. 'You're an arsehole, Cass, you know that? Don't you dare say ...'

Before I can finish, Alana pulls me back down onto the sofa. 'Meg, it's OK. I can take it. Let's hear him out.'

'But he's being vile! It was one bad angle. We can fix it.'

'It's not just one photoshoot,' Caspar interrupts. 'It's the whole image.' He stares straight at me and only at me, as if Alana isn't there. 'Come on Meg, you're better than this ...'

If he uses that condescending man-phrase one more time, I swear I'm going to piss on his toothbrush.

'... You're a model with a legit fanbase. People expect a certain look from you, and it kills me to say it but Alana just doesn't fit.'

It kills him to say it? Funny, because he doesn't look very dead right now. He looks more alive than I've seen him in months.

And I'm more furious than I've been in months.

'So we're different? So what? That's what's unique about us. The most important thing should be the music, not all this other superficial, shallow crap.'

'It should be,' Alana mumbles beside me, still biting her nails. 'But that's not how the world works, is it?'

'No, that's not how the world works,' Caspar echoes. 'Because it doesn't matter how much people blab on about *personality* and *inner-beauty*. Ultimately, they only want to see young, slim, attractive people on TV. The public want celebrities they can *aspire* to and unfortunately overweight singers don't cut it.'

Every word is crushing Alana. I see her sinking into the sofa cushion like she wants to disappear. I have to do something, say something, anything to make this better.

'There are plenty of plus-size singers in the industry,' I state. It's a solid fact that can't be disputed. 'What about Lizzo? ... And then you've got Mary Lambert, Meghan Trainor, Heather Mae ... They're all proud of their curves and people love them.'

'They're exceptions to the rule,' Caspar shoots back, waving his hand as if to shoo my examples away. 'And my number one tip for starting out in the industry is *never* assume you're the exception. Most people aren't.'

Tears are streaming softly down Alana's face. I reach out and put my hand on her arm. I should never have brought her here. I can't seem to stop my hateful brother from injecting his confidence-destroying poison into our world.

'I know it's hard to accept, but it's better you think about this now before you get in too deep. People are cruel. And blunt. One bad photo can get you streams of hate. Can you honestly handle that? Can you handle your music getting trashed because your image is all wrong? I've been through it and trust me, it sucks.'

'Oh God,' Alana sobs, covering her face and refusing to make eye contact. 'I can't do this. Meg, you should play the showcase on your own. Caspar's right, I'm only holding you back.'

'Don't be so ridiculous,' I retaliate, my panic levels rising. This is getting out of control. My talented, funny, pretty, no ... not pretty, *beautiful*, new friend is being torn apart in front of me. I can't let this happen. Not now, not ever.

'It was one. Bad. Photo. OK? You can't let this be the end of us and our music! I mean, look at all the gigs and YouTube videos you've done. You get up on stage all the time and you're the most confident person I know. You're the whole reason I'm doing this and not hiding in my bedroom.'

Through her tears she tries to give me a smile, but it's shaky and unconvincing. 'I'm out of my depth,' she admits, 'I make out like I want to be a real artist and take my music further, but I've never even played outside of Brighton. I've always been too scared to even try.'

Her sincerity knocks the breath out of me.

It suddenly hits me how different our lives actually are. For years I've travelled around the world and been exposed to Caspar's celebrity lifestyle. Gigs, festivals, parties, label meetings, radio and TV appearances, magazine interviews, stylists, photographers, you name it. None of it really feels like a big deal to me. But for Alana, it's the total opposite.

All of this is a big deal. A huge deal. The viral video, the photoshoot, TJ's business talks, not to mention the fact that Caspar McCarthy is casually hanging around the house and being completely hideous to her.

I thought she was the reason I was doing this. I thought Alana was the confident one. But I'm slowly realising that in many ways it's actually the other way round.

'I'm such a fraud,' she whispers, her voice cracking. 'All I've ever done is crappy homemade recordings. Nothing professional. I thought being a duo would make me brave enough to take the leap. But I'm not. That photo just proves what I already know deep down. I'm not good enough to do this for real.'

Caspar is looking on as Alana pours her heart out, barely containing his smug satisfaction at how this is turning out. He lit the fuse knowing full well it would lead to an explosion. In this moment I hate him so much that I want to smash up his guitars, destroy his studio, and bury him under the wreckage.

Somehow, I manage to control the anger rising inside me and focus on Alana. I crouch in front of her so that we're eye-to-eye, blocking out Caspar in the process. 'Not only are you more than good enough, Alana Howard, but you've given me the strength to see I'm good enough too. I'm not going to play this showcase without you.'

I mean it. More than any song lyric could ever express. Alana looks at me sadly, shaking her head.

'You've only just met me,' she says, wiping her smudged mascara. 'I'm so happy I've inspired you to sing. Honestly. *So* happy. But you should take this forward without me. You're the real star. I'm just the fat girl with no direction who plays a few little open mic nights.'

'No, you're *not*,' I cry. Fury is surging through me. Fury at Alana for giving up so easily. Fury at Caspar for putting all these doubts in her mind. Fury at the whole horrible, shallow music industry and the judgmental trolls that lurk around every corner. Most of all, I'm furious at myself for letting my guard down. How could I have been so stupid?

'We've gone through more together in one week than some friends do in a lifetime!' My tone is bordering on hysteria now, but I don't care. 'And I know this is all a total whirlwind, but I honestly believe we were meant to meet each other and find this chance together. I can't imagine performing with anybody else.'

Alana bites her lip, tears still brimming.

'If you really don't want to do this then I understand. You've played solo your whole life and now I've come along and re-routed the train tracks. So if you'd rather go back to performing alone then I promise I won't be mad about it. But, please Alana, only do it if it's your decision. Don't give up your dreams because of my *idiot brother*.'

I throw the last two words sharply in Caspar's direction, wishing they were darts and his supercilious face was a dartboard.

'Fine, be angry with me,' he says, standing up. 'I get it. It's easy to make me the bad guy here. The truth is hard to take. Still, it's better to hear it from me than publicly embarrass yourselves. I'm doing you a favour.'

If this were an arm wrestle, my arm would be almost touching the table right about now. He's winning and he knows it. It's the story of my life. He's bigger than me, taller than me, and so overpowering that I can't protect Alana from him.

'I know it's really hard to hear it, but you're overweight,' he says, python-eyes honing in on Alana. His voice is sickly sweet, as though he's explaining a difficult concept to a small child. Like it's somehow hurting him to twist the knife right into her heart. 'You can pretend it's not a problem. But I think deep down, if you're honest with yourself, you know how much it matters. Those nasty Internet comments you've been getting are the tip of the iceberg. I'm not being funny, but Meg and I get people telling us we're fat all the time, and we're not even *fat*.'

Alana flinches. I can't believe he's saying this.

'They're going to eat you alive. No one will take your music seriously until you sort out the problem. It's difficult, but you've got to face up to it. Take a year or so out, lose some weight, I mean really *try*. I don't think the record companies will touch you otherwise. That's my honest, professional opinion.'

If I was furious before, I'm literally apoplectic now. This is exactly what Caspar wants – for us to conveniently disappear for a few years, to give up on our music before we've even begun.

Because we're a threat. Because we're *good*. Because we're better than he is and everybody's going to know it.

'But I find it so hard to lose weight,' Alana sobs, her breath catching in despairing hiccups. 'I only have to smell a pizza and I gain a stone. It's my metabolism.'

'Sounds like a bad excuse to me,' Caspar snipes. 'Clearly you don't want to make it as much as you think you do.'

With that, I finally lose control as pure, blinding sibling-rage takes over. I slam my full weight into Caspar, shoving him so hard that he stumbles backward into his guitar rack. He teeters and flails, trying to grab his desk for balance but it's too late. He falls, in slow motion, onto his favourite mahogany, Martin acoustic guitar and we all hear the heart-stopping sound of wood splintering.

'Jesus, Meg! What the fuck is the matter with you? What the hell have you done?' he yells. 'I was only trying to help you, you ungrateful little cow!'

'How were you EVER helping?' I scream back at him. 'My best friend is crying her eyes out because of you. I've seen her on stage and she's beautiful. You have no idea.'

'No idea? Well, how come I'm the one with number one singles and awards and you're the one working in an ice cream shop?'

'It's not an ice cream shop. IT'S A YOGHURT SHOP!'

'Look what you've done to my guitar, Meg! I'm gonna kill you. You've ruined it. Just like you've ruined everything ...'

'I've ruined everything? My whole life has been ruined by you and now you're jealous because finally I'm getting some frickin' attention!'

'Oh boo-bloody-hoo, Meg. Is that the sob story you told TJ when you went behind my back?'

Caspar picks himself up from the floor. Suddenly I'm not feeling so brave anymore. He's six foot and menacing and right up in my face. 'You think he actually cares about you two? He's just seen a chance to make a quick buck. When you crash and burn, do you honestly think he's going to stick around?'

'TJ's not like that,' I answer. But I wobble. Only very slightly and only for a moment, but I wobble. Caspar sees my hesitation and rants on vengefully.

'You know this is just his way of punishing me, right? Because I'm taking too long with the album. But guess what? I'm not naïve enough to believe that everyone's going to magically love whatever I write. So I'm taking my time, which is costing him too much money. TJ is a *money* man, Meg. Once he's proven his little point about how super-fast you can get a song released, he'll dump you two like a bag of hot sick and come straight back to me. After all, he's *my* manager.'

I've been stunned into silence. All the tears that I'm usually so expert at holding back are rising to the surface. My heart is palpitating from adrenaline and I'm shaking uncontrollably.

'Trust me,' he spits. 'I know TJ.'

'Oh, you know TJ, do you?' comes a stern, authoritative voice. 'I beg to differ judging by what I've just overheard.'

It's as if a bucket of cold water has been thrown on the fire. I blink and the room comes back into focus. We've been so busy fighting that none of us realised he was in the doorway watching this whole chaotic scene play out.

He strides into the room and assesses each of us in turn. Todd Elliott Jackson. Self-made music mogul. The man who launched my brother's entire career. The man who could quite possibly launch mine. Suited, booted, suavely handsome and angrier than I've ever seen him in my whole, entire life.

# CHAPTER THIRTY-NINE

I feel my cheeks burning red with shame and embarrassment. How long has TJ been standing there? And how much of this out-of-control argument did he hear?

Caspar steps away from me, thrusting his hands in his pockets. 'W-where did you come from? I thought you were doing admin.'

'Yeah, I was,' TJ answers, levelling his gaze on Caspar. 'But it's impossible to concentrate with World War Three going on in here.'

He calmly sits down next to Alana and speaks to her in a soft, comforting voice. 'Hey, hey, hey ... Don't go getting all upset. Come on, deep breaths. It's all gonna be OK. It's gonna be fine.'

'It's not fine,' Alana sobs. 'I ... I can't do this. Caspar's right, I'm not a star. I'm going to let everyone down. I'm going to lose you money. I ... I ...'

Woah. Doom Spiral Level 93. We have both seriously lost

control, but despite TJ witnessing our histrionics I already feel better in his presence.

'Caspar's been saying all this horrible stuff,' I blurt out. I sound like I did when I was ten, telling on him to my parents. *Mum, Caspar's kicking me under the table. Dad, Caspar broke your Beastie Boys album because he was throwing it like a Frisbee. TJ, Caspar's crushing my best friend's self-esteem so that he can totally dismantle our future career in music.*

Yeah, I think some things are worth snitching on.

TJ stands up and straightens his suit. I can see why he's such a successful man. When TJ walks into a meeting, everybody listens. They have no choice.

'I heard exactly what Caspar was saying, and I've got to admit, Cass, I'm feeling pretty disappointed in your behaviour.'

Ouch, the 'I'm disappointed in you' speech. Everyone knows it's worse than being yelled at. Worse still is that he's not getting it from Dad, he's getting it from his manager. Brutal.

'Whatever,' Caspar mutters studying the floor intently. He shrugs as if he doesn't care, his defensive energy trying to push us all away. 'I'm only telling them the truth. Someone around here needs to prepare them for reality.'

'Oh, you want reality?' TJ counters. 'Well, I've got a story for you. Meg, Caspar. Sit down.'

It's not a question, it's a command. I sit beside Alana and, after a stubborn pause, Caspar begrudgingly concedes and slumps back into his chair.

TJ towers over us in the centre of the room, waiting for our full attention. Then he begins.

'So ... where I grew up in south London there wasn't exactly a whole lot of opportunity for kids who were into music. Mum worked all hours as an A&E nurse and Dad did late shifts for London Underground. They didn't exactly have the time to drive us round to piano lessons and theatre school. Me and my brothers just had to get on with it and take care of ourselves.'

Woah. I thought we were all going to be told off. I wasn't expecting this.

'It certainly wasn't easy to stay on track,' TJ continues, pacing the room, lost in his memories. 'If our youth gave us anything, it was the endless opportunity to make really bad decisions. And that's just what my oldest brother did. He dropped out of school and went completely off the rails. Got done for theft in the end. So needless to say, people didn't have particularly high expectations for me.'

He clears his throat. 'But you know what? I made a choice.'

As he talks, I realise that I actually know nothing about TJ's life. His dark eyes pause on each of us in turn.

'When I started secondary school I decided that I was in charge of my own story. I wasn't going to be like my brother, who gave up before he'd even tried. I was going to make my parents proud. I was going to have a career. I was going to make something of my life.

'I buckled down at school, I got good grades, enough to study business for my A Levels. And all the while, I listened to music to keep me focused: pop, rock, jazz, hip-hop, R&B, country. I was listening to artists no other kids on my estate had heard of. It became my escape, my ticket out of there. Those singers were expressing things I couldn't put into words myself and I knew I had to be part of it. I *had* to work in the music business.'

'So how did you do it?' I ask, taken aback. 'How did you start your company?'

'As soon I was old enough I applied for internships in every music company in London. Publishing, management, record labels, sound engineer work – I didn't care where I ended up. That's how I found myself at Connect Music Management.'

I vaguely knew of TJ's roots at Connect. They have a lot of big names on their books, and the fact he used to work with them was a real selling point when he first approached Caspar and my parents. Connect isn't a company that messes around. They make stars.

'I started when I was eighteen. It was me and two other guys from local colleges. Two guys who, if you'll forgive my arrogance, didn't have half as much spark or passion for the job as I did. I mean, sure they wanted to meet celebs and go to parties ... but they didn't want any of the work that went with it. Yet they ended up in all the sessions and meetings while I got stuck with filing and doing coffee runs.'

'But that's not fair!' Alana says, indignantly.

TJ raises an eyebrow. 'Nope, it wasn't. Life rarely is, unfortunately. But you know what? I accepted it. I kept my head down and did my work well, biding my time until I could bring someone into the company. And that someone was Charlotte Madison.'

I hear Alana gasp. Charlotte Madison is a huge name. She's been around for a while, but even people our age know her songs.

'She played a lot around my area, in all the local pubs and clubs.

What a voice! And such magnetic stage presence. I saw something special in her – that magic X factor that I've seen in all the artists I've taken on over the years. And when I brought her into Connect, they saw it too.'

'You never told me you managed her,' Caspar interrupts. 'How come she's not on your CV?'

TJ shakes his head. 'Because I never did end up managing her. Connect stole my contact and put one of the other guys in charge of her. Johnny or Jimmy or whoever the hell he was.'

'What?!' I exclaim before I can stop myself. 'Why?'

'Because apparently they were a "better fit",' TJ replies, putting air quotes around the last two words. 'Connect told me this guy represented what Charlotte was all about ... and that I would be much more suited to a rapper or an R&B artist.'

The undercurrent of TJ's story doesn't hit me at first, but Alana gets it straight away.

'Oh My God, that's totally racist!'

TJ holds his hands up. 'Yep. Connect put me in a box. They took one look at me and my background and they decided how my time with them was going to play out. Because guys like me only worked on certain styles of music. Guys like me *never* got past certain rungs of the ladder, however much we deserved it. That was just the way it was. That was *reality*.'

Reality. The word Caspar used against us is echoed straight back at him. My brother is sitting motionless, giving nothing away.

'You know what I thought back then?' TJ asks, singling out Alana specifically. 'I thought to myself – why should other people dictate my life to me? Why do *they* get to decide?' He moves closer, squatting down in front of her. 'So when the company pushed against me, I pushed right back. I used Connect for experience and contacts. Then I started building up my own artist roster on the side – not just the token black guy assignments they wanted from me, but artists from all styles and backgrounds. Until, one day, I could go out on my own.

'It was hard, Alana. I had to work twice as hard for half as much, every step of the way. I'm not naïve. I know this stuff happens. This shallow, stupid stuff that puts everyone into little boxes and tries to keep them there. It's what cost me signings and sponsorships and God knows what else the second I walked into a meeting and didn't match up with the client's expectation.

'But I was talented. Like you two are.' He points his finger at Alana, then me, strong and determined – urging us to understand. 'And I refused to stop fighting for what I wanted, because you know something? They don't get to decide.' The words hang in the air before he repeats them a second time. '*They don't get to decide.*'

With that, TJ takes his phone out of his jacket pocket and brings up an image. It's one of the shots from our unflattering photoshoot, but it's been cropped and edited so you can only see our faces. A filter has been added, brightening our skin and eyes. Our elegant new *Lost Girls* logo is now the central focus.

'I fixed it up in Photoshop,' TJ explains. 'We can do a better shoot later, but I think this will work for the press pack.'

Alana grabs his phone, staring at the picture in bewilderment. 'Wow, this ... this is actually OK.'

'More than OK,' I add. 'You look beautiful.'

'But ... but it's fake. I don't really look this good.'

TJ shrugs. 'It's not fake. It's just good presentation. It's using the right tools to get noticed, then you can let your talent handle the rest.'

Behind him, Caspar is silent. There is a shroud of humility surrounding him – something I never thought I'd live to see. My brother is proud and spoiled, and too smug for his own good. He disobeys my parents. He rarely takes responsibility for his mistakes and he never says sorry. But something about TJ's story has humbled him. Because despite all the recent drama, he loves his manager. TJ is the one person in his chaotic world that he actually respects.

'You're right, Cass,' TJ says. 'I am a money man. Because when you grow up with nothing, money equals security. But it's not what drives me. If it was, hell, I'd be an accountant or a banker instead. No, the thing that motivates me is *passion for music*.'

Caspar winces but TJ hasn't finished. 'When I see artists who love what they write, it reminds me of all those amazing songs that put me on this path in the first place. They inspire me to be on the journey. That's the reason I want to manage *Lost Girls*. Not because of YouTube views, but because I see all that raw, unbridled passion burning inside them. The exact same passion that I *used* to see in you.'

The words cut deep.

'This storm cloud that you're carrying around over your head is affecting everyone. People who count on you. It's time you stopped worrying about what your sister is doing and started focusing on your own career, before you derail it completely.'

Caspar opens his mouth to protest. But for once, he can't pin his shortcomings on anyone but himself. As the words stick in his throat, something happens that I wasn't expecting in a million years.

My brother starts crying.

'I'm under so much pressure from everyone to get this album right,' he chokes out. 'For it to be a smash. But I can't do it. I have nothing meaningful to say anymore. I'm completely lost. Every time I pick up my guitar I go round and round in circles until I'm straight back to nothing again. I can't stop overthinking it, because I know what they're all going to say about me. The critics. The fans. I've left it so long that they're expecting some kind of masterpiece from me and now I'm just going to be one massive fucking disappointment.'

I'm stunned. Shell-shocked. His confidence has crumbled away like a sandcastle hit by the tide. I've never seen him like this before.

'I know you're getting impatient,' he confesses to TJ, trying to pull himself together. 'I know you're looking elsewhere for the next *me* because I'm getting too old and irrelevant. I know I've become the one-album-wonder. And since Meg apparently has infinite ideas literally pouring out of her, you're onto the brand-new McCarthy star and pushing me out. It hurts, OK? It really hurts.'

'No one's pushing you out,' I say. 'Cass, can you hear yourself? All I've ever done is bloody look up to you. I'm not trying to hurt you.'

'You need to hear those things,' he says quietly. 'You need to be prepared. No one told me any of it when I was sixteen and thrown in at the deep end. No one told me how much it would hurt to have so many strangers attacking me, harassing me, sending me death threats, just for making my music. No one told me I'd be hated for doing the one thing that I love.' He looks sadly at TJ. 'You never warned me it would be so hard.'

It feels like there is no oxygen in the room and I can't take a proper breath. Even after all the unforgivable things he's said and done, I just want to hug him right now.

'Mate, I know it's hard but I've always done everything in my power to protect you,' TJ answers. 'I never sugar-coated this industry and I never pushed you into anything you didn't want to do.'

'But I was just a kid! I didn't have a clue what I was getting into. Once it started, it was impossible to make it stop and ... I don't know, maybe I'm burned out ... Maybe I've just had enough.'

'Alright Cass. I hear you. I'm sorry you're feeling this way, I had no idea. We'll sort it out, OK? But right now this is about Meg and Alana, and it's not fair to take your stress out on them.'

Caspar doesn't answer. He looks at TJ, his bottom lip trembling, before turning his gaze to me. I've never seen so much hurt in his eyes before. So much doubt. So many glimpses of myself staring straight back at me.

'Just forget what I said,' he mumbles, grabbing his jacket from the back of the door.' Do what you need to do, Meg. I'm not going to stop you. And Alana, I'm sorry, OK? I was only trying to warn you. I just ... I need to get out of here.'

I want to go after him but I know this wound will need time to heal. If only he could have been honest with everyone instead of letting his worry turn to anger. I realise that I've been turning him into a villain in my head instead of seeing the lost boy underneath.

We hear the front door slam downstairs as Caspar leaves the house.

TJ sighs. 'Girls this business is tough, I'm not pretending otherwise. But you've got to know that I believe in you. And you've got to believe in yourselves just as much. Whatever you do, there will be people out there who want to criticise you. Caspar has obviously bottled things up for way too long, but you know what? You've got each other for support and you've got to make your own decisions and choices. So Alana, Meg, are you ready to grab this opportunity?'

It's funny. I've watched so many movies about people reaching for their dreams. They always beat the obstacle, win the crowd over, get the guy or girl, and then everything gets tied up in a beautiful, velvety bow ... Ta-dah! The perfect Hollywood ending.

In real life there's always more than one single obstacle, one knock-back or one bad review. Real life is about fighting, constantly, even after the credits start rolling. It's about knowing that sometimes you're not going to get validation from other people, even when you deserve it. And that's OK. You don't need anyone's approval to keep doing what you love. There are no right or wrong paths. No happy ever afters. Only moments. That is true reality.

And this is our moment.

I look at Alana and the fire is back in her eyes. I know then and there that she finally gets. I mean *really* gets it. We both do. It isn't going to be easy and we're not going to be perfect. Even taking this first step is a huge challenge. We've both got reasons to be scared, but it's still a step worth taking. And we're taking it together.

'Shall we get back to practising then?' she asks with a smile.

'Sure, let's do it,' I reply.

TJ gives a nod of approval. The fire from Alana's eyes has caught hold of my heart. It's spreading wildly and burning any traces of doubt. This is exactly where we need to be.

# CHAPTER FORTY

♫

**Top 5 Moments In Which I Realise We Are DOING THIS:**
**(And by 'Doing This' I mean actually playing the showcase!)**

1. Shopping for stage outfits

The disastrous photoshoot was clear proof that we are incapable of dressing ourselves. So the day before the showcase, TJ sends us shopping in the Lanes with his favourite London stylist. She buys Alana a gorgeous black wrap dress that looks great with her wide-brimmed hat, and I find a slinky, lace-sleeved pant-suit that matches her perfectly. We look like the real deal.

I guess TJ was right. It's all in the presentation.

## 2. Travelling to London

Normally I would pay £17.15 to stand on a crowded, dirty, hideously delayed Southern Rail train to London – usually while some loud moron gets in my personal space or, even worse, blasts their shitty music in my ear out of a tinny phone speaker. Because everyone knows artists spend weeks in the studio just to have their creations reduced to low quality MP3s, right? Anyway, I digress.

This journey couldn't be more different because TJ has hired a limo for us all to travel up in. An actual fresh-smelling, soft-seated, window-tinted limo!

Laura has closed the shop and spent the afternoon with Mum, getting pampered and primped. Dad has even managed to change out of his aubergine-purple Thai fisherman pants and put on an actual pair of jeans, so I suppose that's his way of making this a special occasion.

None of us mention the missing McCarthy. Mum asked Caspar this morning if he was going to come, but he refused to join us. He hasn't spoken to me since his massive meltdown so I'm hardly surprised.

Oh well. I don't miss him. There's a brilliant atmosphere in the car with everyone laughing and joking as we cross the Thames. Eventually, we pull up outside a warehouse building with 'Lonestar Music Management' on a plaque outside.

Here we go ...

3. Entering TJ's Studio

I've been to TJ's studio complex countless times over the years, but suddenly the place seems bigger, bolder, brighter, and brimming with possibility.

He gives us a quick tour for Alana's benefit, showing us the huge open plan, bare-brick meeting space with its jukebox, ping-pong tables, chrome countered bar, and platinum discs on display. There are glass-walled offices down one side of the warehouse with connecting doors leading to the in-house recording studio, and the spacious live rehearsal room where we'll be performing tonight.

TJ's assistant has made it gorgeous in here. A beautiful grand piano is the centrepiece of the room and in front of the stage are candlelit tables, making the atmosphere warm and inviting. Spotlights shine down on two mic stands where we will be performing. Yikes. I count the number of chairs. Sixty in total. Double yikes.

Sixty people are going to be sitting here, looking at us.

I feel sick.

I feel excited.

I feel sickcited.

4. Sound check

'Err, one-two?' I say hesitantly into the microphone. Why does it always have to be one-two? It's so predictable. 'Check, check.' Oh God. This is embarrassing.

The mic feels huge and ominous in front of my face while the walls of the studio seem to close in on me like I'm in some sort of trippy Alice in Wonderland nightmare music video. My echoing, reverby voice sounds unfamiliar to my own ears. My throat twists and constricts until I'm not sure that I even remember how to physically sing anymore.

From the piano, Alana booms a confident 'One-two' into her own mic. She's done this many times before and despite the high-stakes situation, I can see her nerves melting away and Dr Showbiz taking over. She belongs up here.

So that means I belong up here too … right?

## 5. People turn up

Lots and lots of people. People I don't know. People who aren't part of my family and have important music industry jobs. Well-dressed London type people. Enough people to fill the room. People with faces and ears and opinions and, and, and ... My newly discovered fear of microphones has been surpassed by people-terror!

I'm sure they're very nice, innocent, well-intentioned audience members who are perfectly normal, nice, innocent, well-intentioned people.

But what if they're not?!

What if they hate us?

What if they hate music?

Of course they don't hate music, Meg, you complete idiot. They work in the music industry.

But what if they're all living a lie?!!

I take deep, slowing breaths to keep my panic under control. This is really happening. We're going to be singing in front of all these people.

If I pause long enough for reality to seep in, I'm not sure I'll be able to go through with it so I keep moving, manoeuvring with Alana through the crowd. We're inundated with handshakes and industry-talk at every turn. *Current. Fresh. Development. Viral. 360 Deal. Plugging. McCarthyBrand.* I'm beginning to feel like a naïve goldfish swimming through a pool of very upmarket piranhas.

♫

We head back to Studio 2, which is our dressing room for tonight. Alana is flushed, wired, spun-out by the massive attention overload we've both been subjected to.

'You OK?' I ask.

After a beat, she nods. 'Yeah. Yeah, it's just ... This is a lot to take in.'

Understatement of the year. In the past two weeks, we've gone from being complete strangers to proper friends and from writing our first song together to potentially signing a record deal. Maybe this is some weird stress-induced dream and any second now I'm going to wake up behind the counter of Dodo Yoyo in my hideous beak-cap.

Oh wait. That *is* exactly what I am going to be doing tomorrow. Talk about double life.

'It sort of feels too good to be true,' Alana continues. 'Like we're a couple of anxious snowballs that have been rolling down some huge mountain all week getting bigger and faster and totally out of control.' She laughs, rolling her eyes at her own analogy. 'I know I'm being kind of dramatic, but you know what I mean, right? Like, what if we're rushing in the wrong direction?'

'We don't have to make any decisions tonight,' I reply. 'All we have to do is play our music.'

'Right. And we're gonna smash it!' Alana holds her hand up for a high-five.

I slap my hand against hers like a thunderclap. Ouch. 'Hell yeah, we are. And whatever happens tonight, I love making music with you. I just want you to know that.'

'I love making music with you too. So let's keep doing that, whatever happens tonight. OK?'

'OK,' I promise.

We take a moment to peer through the double soundproof window that connects our studio 'dressing room' to the meeting space. The crowd are buzzing as they queue for the bar, laughing and chatting like they're all besties. In a little while they will be nothing but shadows behind the stage spotlights.

That's when I see him. Slightly obscured, right at the back of the room, but I'd recognise that face anywhere.

His blonde hair has been getting longer over the summer. It's mussed up, falling slightly in his eyes. He's wearing his Bowie shirt and holding his Canon 5D. The camera he used to take that beautiful picture of me and Alana hugging at the open mic night. The only decent picture anyone's taken of us together. The picture I made him delete.

Alana spots him too. 'Oh my God ... Is that who I think it is?'

I'm already halfway to the door.

Because Matty Chester is here at our showcase. And I need to know why.

# CHAPTER
# FORTY-ONE

'TJ, what is Matty doing here?' My voice comes out an urgent, strangled whisper.

'Hmm?' he answers in confusion. He's surveying the room from the back like the regal head of a medieval dinner table. 'You're on in twenty minutes. Shouldn't you be getting ready?'

OK, he's distracted. I get it. This is a distracting situation. All his schmoozy contacts are here in one room and he has to keep up his reputation for introducing them to the best new talent. But the love of my life is in the crowd so I need answers and I need them now.

'Why is Matty here?' I repeat, hoping he'll listen this time.

TJ finally tunes in. 'Oh, the photographer kid? He emailed me those shots from Alana's open mic night – asked if he could take some more tonight. They were great! Better than that supposed professional I hired. Plus, I loved his initiative in coming straight

318

out and asking me. It's the kind of thing I would have done at his age.'

Matty emailed TJ?! But how did he ... Oh, right. Laura was gabbing her mouth off about the showcase when he came into Dodo Yoyo.

'I wouldn't be where I am now without people throwing me a few chances along the way, so I like to return the favour when I can.' He cocks an eyebrow at me. 'It's not a problem, is it?'

What am I supposed to do, scream and shout and make a huge scene? Get security to drag Matty out and ruin the whole night? Is it possible to want to kill someone and kiss them at the same time? Because right now that's kind of how I'm feeling about the sneaky, anxiety-provoking, beautiful BandSnapper.

'No,' I mumble. 'It just would have been nice for you to mention it to me.'

'I think you've got more important things to worry about than some boy.' TJ is suppressing a knowing grin. Damn it. As if this couldn't get any more humiliating. 'Go on – get backstage and warm your voice up. I'll introduce you at seven-thirty, so be ready to go.'

I'm in turmoil. There's no way I can get up and sing for the first time ever with Matty watching me. But there's no way I can miss this chance either or let Alana down. I don't want to do it. But I have to do it. But I can't. But I *have* to.

And now I have eighteen minutes and twenty-nine seconds before my whole world detonates, which isn't a lot of time at all when you think about it.

'Don't worry, you'll knock 'em dead,' TJ adds with a wink.

'See you on the other side.'

He turns away from me and I have no choice but to scurry back to Studio 2 hoping Matty doesn't see me. I wonder if he came to London by himself? I bet he did. He's confident like that. And there's nothing he wouldn't do to try and support LostGirl.

Then I remember. He thinks LostGirl is Alana.

What a mess. What an absolute bloody mess.

Seventeen minutes and thirty seconds.

'Lan?' I call out as I open the door. 'Where'd you go? This is a code red. I repeat, CODE RED!'

Ok. Weird. She's not here.

'Where are you?' I shout. 'I need you! TJ's letting Matty take photos tonight. What the hell am I going to do? I don't know if I can go through with th–'

I stop mid-sentence. Alana is on the floor leaning against a subwoofer, knees drawn in, head in hands, curled up like a giant woodlouse in stage makeup.

'What's wrong?' I kneel down beside her. I thought I had issues, but she's obviously got way bigger ones. 'Lan, what's the matter?'

'H-he's here,' she answers in a pathetic stutter.

I'm totally confused. 'Who? Matty?'

Shouldn't I be the one freaking out and hiding under the mixing desk? Anyway, Alana told me she didn't like Matty in *that* way. I sure hope she doesn't, because at the moment my brain can't process being one corner of a socially awkward, dysfunctional, potentially friendship-destroying love triangle.

Alana shakes her head. 'Matty? What? No! ... Dylan.'

Dylan. For a moment I can't place the name. But as Alana

crushes my hand in a panicked death-grip, something clicks. 'Ohhhh! Your ex-boyfriend Dylan? Wait. What? Where?'

'He's at a table by the right of the stage.'

'Are you sure? Maybe you're hallucinating from nerves or something ...'

'It's definitely him.' Alana holds her phone up to my face. 'See. He messaged me.'

I squint at the screen and read the text out loud. *'Hi Lana. I saw on your work's Facebook that you had a London showcase tonight.'* I let out a huge sigh, then make gun fingers and shoot myself in the head. 'For God's sake, Laura! That woman is a bloody liability.'

I have no doubt that TJ will have stern words with her about all this oversharing online, but we don't have time to dwell on it. Instead, I keep reading out Dylan's message.

*'I'm doing loads better. Been out of hospital a few days and I managed to get my name on the door, so thought I'd make the effort to come along. I've got to admit, I'm pretty hurt that you've been so distant. I kind of expected to hear from you ... But guess you've been busy with all your music. Reminds me of all the amazing times we had gigging together. I think there's still life in those songs we wrote and people would love to hear them. Anyway, good luck. I'll be watching.'*

Somehow, those last three words sound more like a threat than an encouragement. I glance at Alana, trying to gauge her reaction.

'He doesn't want me to have this without him,' she blurts out. 'He's trying to worm his way back into my life, Meg. I don't want him anywhere near our music. He destroys everything he gets close to and I can't go through that nightmare all over again!'

Her voice is getting higher and faster like one of those old cassette tapes on fast-forward. 'Woah, Alana. Calm down.'

'I don't know if I can play our set with him out there. He'll try and come between us. I can't do it Meg. I can't. I can't!'

She is practically hyperventilating now. Her Doom Spiral level is off the charts. And we are down to thirteen minutes and fifteen seconds before we're due on stage.

'Get up,' I say, trying to pull her off the floor. 'Come on, don't let him freak you out like this. So what if he's in the crowd? Let him see you. Let him see how far you've come without him.'

I'm more than aware of the irony of this situation. I was just about to indulge in my own boy-related hysteria. But that's totally different. Kind of.

'He's not going to come between us,' I add firmly. 'No one could ever do that.'

'How do you know?' Alana responds. She's rubbing her temples, blinking a hundred times a minute to stop herself from crying. 'What if he tries to sabotage us? I wouldn't put it past him.'

I shake my head defiantly. 'He's not going to sabotage anything. I won't let him. Don't you dare chicken out because of some stupid guy!'

Oh. Total hypocrite alert.

Alana laughs and groans at the same time. 'Is this crazy? I mean, what are we even doing here?'

She doesn't need to say anymore because I feel it too. Pressure from every angle, squeezing us so tight we can barely breathe, paralysing us until we're too terrified to make a single move.

Enough is enough. It's time to start pushing back.

'Yes,' I answer. 'It is crazy. It's completely, totally, unquestionably crazy. But then maybe all the best moments in life are.'

A switch flips inside my head and I stand up, overcome by the need for action. Alana looks at me curiously then rummages in her handbag until she finds her sparkly compact mirror. She wipes the mascara smudges from under her eyes, re-applies her trademark red lipstick and pulls herself up off the floor.

'You're right. And let's face it, there's always going to be someone trying to stop us.'

'Exactly! As soon as we beat one obstacle, a new one springs up in its place. I'm so sick of it. Caspar, Dylan, Matty, the record companies, the online haters.' I pace up and down, past memories flooding my mind. 'And even before that ... the mean girls at school, my teachers, my parents, my brother.'

I've said Caspar twice. I guess he affects me twice as much as everyone else.

'I feel like I've wasted my whole life worrying about what people think of me – scared to make a single sound until my work is perfect. And then I met you, the girl who didn't care about that stuff and went out there and made her voice heard. When I saw you singing that night at open mic it was like watching freedom. Total freedom. Do you know how inspiring that was?'

Everything else is falling away from us – the business people waiting outside, the boys who have a hold on our hearts, and the ticking time bomb about to explode in a matter of minutes. Right now, it's me and her. Two girls who were meant to find each other.

Two girls who just want to make music together.

'The only time you've ever doubted yourself,' I say, 'is when you

**323**

stepped into my insane world. Up until then, you were fearless. You made *me* fearless. When we're writing songs, I don't think about anything else. Only the music.'

'Me too,' Alana replies. 'I can't actually believe everything that's happened since I met you. Let's get out there and tell our story the way we want to. With no filter.'

'Hell yeah! We need to strip away the crap and forget about what all those people out there think of us ... and forget about Dylan.'

Alana raises her chin, challenging me. '*And* forget about Matty?'

There is a tiny moment of hesitation before I nod in agreement. 'Yep, him too. Let's just play like we're in our room or at open mic. Let's play because we love what we've written, not for any other reason.'

'In that case,' Alana says, 'I want us to play "Second First Impression" instead of "Scripts".'

I did not see that curve-ball coming. 'What ... now?!'

'We have to, Meg. That song is so much more *us*. It's personal and emotional. It's your masterpiece. I love "Scripts", but we only get three songs. If we're going to show everyone who we really are then we have to change the set.'

'But ... but ...' *But I wrote that for Matty and he's out there and he's going to know, he's going to KNOW who I am and how I feel, and I'll never be able to take it back.* 'But we haven't practised it properly. We might mess it up.'

'I've got your back Meg, I know it as well as you do. And like you said, it's time to strip everything else away. We have to play this song. You know we do.'

She's absolutely right. I'm terrified, but if I'm ever going to be true to myself this is the moment. It's now or never.

'We might not get a record deal if we do this,' I say. 'Just putting that out there.'

Alana lifts the lid of the studio piano and gently plays the opening chords of 'Second First Impression'. 'We might not want a record deal.'

It's a bold statement. But as she stands at the piano, the music coming so naturally to her, I realise that this is a girl who will give it her all once she's made a decision.

'Well, I don't mind going the indie route. It would be harder, but we'd be in control of everything we do,' I reply.

'Exactly. Whatever happens, we should move forward on our own terms. Not with a company who wants to change everything about us.'

There is so much I could say in response. That it's a risk, but a risk worth taking. That I can't believe we ever thought about cutting this song in the first place. That we have so much to explore in our songwriting together and this showcase is just the first little square on a big old snakes and ladders board.

Only there are now two minutes and thirteen precious seconds before we have to perform and I can hear TJ announcing our names through the PA and calling for us to come to the stage.

Our eyes meet. It's showtime.

# CHAPTER FORTY-TWO

Everything feels totally removed from reality up here on stage. The audience has become a terrifying, dark blur just beyond the glare of the blinding lights. My throat has closed up as if I'm having an allergic reaction and my mind has erased all the witty stage banter I'd carefully prepared.

I hear Alana's confident voice beside me, introducing our first song. She starts playing the intro and OH. MY. GOD. I can't remember the first line. WHAT IS IT?! I've played 'Domino Effect' hundreds of times and yet the lyrics have been sucked into a black void'! I start to panic. My guts drop like I'm on *Detonator* at Thorpe Park. Nothing.

Wait. What? Who's that singing?

*I've been moving forward*
*No point in looking back*

*I've been pushin' on*
*Like a train on a track*

Someone's bailed me out and remembered the words ...

*It's getting everyone excited*
*But if you haven't bought a ticket ...*

Alana joins in.

*You're never gonna ride it ...*

It would seem I'm having an out-of-body experience because it's me. I'm doing it. I'm actually singing.

This is the thing I was most scared of. Performing in public. Putting myself out there. Exposing my real feelings through music. But suddenly I have no idea what I was so frightened of. My eyes adjust to the lights and I start to make out warm, familiar faces in the crowd.

Mum and Dad are right at the front, bursting with pride. Mum is filming us on her phone, but it doesn't bother me at all. There's something strangely comforting about seeing them here.

TJ is leaning against the side wall, arms folded. He gives me a *you-got-this* nod of encouragement that sweeps away the last of my nerves. He's right. We have got this. And as the song comes to an end, the room bursts into applause. I'm back in my body. I've found my voice.

'Thanks so much everyone! Our next song is called "And What?".

We had a lot of fun writing this one so we hope you like it.'

As I turn to count Alana in, I notice somebody who feels weirdly familiar. He's standing, alone, towards the back of the room, slightly removed from the rest of the crowd and staring with so much intensity that I'm surprised I missed him earlier.

It's Dylan. I've seen him in Alana's videos and it's definitely him. He's tall and pale with sunken eyes, wearing a worn leather jacket and hiding his good looks beneath an unkempt beard. He seems older in person – more haggard – and he gives me the same dark vibes that I got when I started watching *You* on Netflix.

I switch my attention back to Alana to check that she's ok, but of course she's carrying on like a pro despite Dylan's targeted glowering.

*It's easy when you can't see my face*
*To smack me with your rude opinion*
*Too terrified to stand in my place*
*Coz you can give it*
*But you cannot take it*
*So who cares what you got to say ...*

Alana's energy is contagious as she belts the chorus, directing every word at her uninvited guest. I'm right here singing it with her. I've forgotten that all these important people are watching us. It's like we're still doing our soundcheck and the gig hasn't started yet. It's only when the last chords ring out and the crowd starts cheering that I remember we've got an actual audience here, sharing this moment with us. This buzz beats a million likes on Instagram. This is real.

'So, as you all know, I've grown up in the spotlight. Or rather *next to* the spotlight.' I laugh and everyone else laughs with me – the sound warm and welcoming, encouraging me to keep going. 'But I guess it's my turn tonight and there's no one I'd rather be sharing the stage with than my new friend and fellow Lost Girl, Alana Howard.'

Alana gives a little salute to the crowd. She's in her element. I feel so proud of her. I feel so proud of *us*. I can't believe someone I've known for such a short amount of time has changed my life in such a huge way.

'We've got one more song for you.' The crowd cheers again. They're on our side, I can sense it, but here comes the sliding doors moment. Do we play it safe and stick to the original set list? Or do we take a risk and jump into the unknown? I lock eyes with Alana over the piano and we read each other's minds.

We're going to jump. Of course we are.

'This song is a Meg McCarthy original,' Alana announces into her mic. 'You probably don't know this, but she's been writing for years. So I'm going to let her take centre stage and share this beautiful ballad with you.'

The lights dim a little and Alana softly plays the intro chords.

Suddenly, I'm stripped bare. No guitar to hide behind. No vocal from Alana to blend with. Just me and the lyrics and all the emotions I've kept locked up tightly for years.

I scan the crowd, past Mum and Dad's surprised faces, past my over-excited boss, past TJ's furrowed brow, past the ghostly Dylan who is still lingering at the back ... until I see him at last.

He's been there the whole time, but I've been blocking him out. Matty Chester. LostGirl's best friend. The love of my life. He's holding his camera, twisting it sideways and taking photos, oblivious that I'm about to pour my heart out to him.

I miss my cue. I can't do this. I can't reveal the lie I've been living.

But Alana doesn't stop. She keeps playing the chords, round and round. I can hear her willing me on in her mind. I'm not alone. She's right here. Two Lost Girls together.

I take a deep breath and set the truth free.

♫

*Looks like I told too many lies*
*You've fallen for my disguise*
*If I knew how to tell the truth*
*You'd have seen it in my eyes*
*And the silence burns me*
*Too many words that I can't say*
*Wish you could see the better me*
*The girl behind the name*
*I'm the only one to blame*

The room has fallen silent. Everyone else has faded away and all I see is Matty.

*Will your heart wait*
*While my heart's breaking?*

*Is it too late*
*To make a second first impression?*
*Will your heart wait*
*While my heart's breaking?*
*Is it too late*
*To make a second first impression on you?*

He returns my gaze. Mesmerised. Puzzled. Slowly putting the pieces together.

Our whole relationship is unravelling like invisible thread between us: our list games, the years of confiding in each other online, all the secrets I shared without him ever realising who I was.

Until now.

*I kill each spark before it lights*
*Why do I do it every time?*
*It's hurting me that I'm hurting you*
*My thoughts and actions don't align*
*And the moment's frozen*
*A movie that I can't rewind*
*Stupid, guilty conversations echo in my mind*
*Now I'm running out of time*

He comes closer to the stage, but his camera is shielding him from the emotion which is pouring out of me. There's nothing I can do to stop it though. My head is a swirling mess of memories. All the times I've shouted and snarled at him and made him feel small.

I need him to know that I didn't mean it. I need every lyric to count.

*Will your heart wait*
*While my heart's breaking?*
*Is it too late*
*To make a second first impression on you?*

Alana joins me in an aching, lingering long note, rising and rising, holding the room hostage. She can feel my pain and my regret.

*The same old story*
*The one I always tell*
*Building these walls up*
*I sabotage myself*
*Trapped on the inside*
*Are feelings I don't show*
*Under my dark side*
*A love you'll never know*

My voice cracks the tiniest bit on the final line and that's when I see it.

Matty drops his camera to his side with a sharp intake of breath.

A thousand moments of realisation are simultaneously exploding in his mind. I feel the pulse of every one of them.

## Top 5 Words Running Through Matty's Head Right Now:

1. It
2. Was
3. You
4. All
5. Along

I close my eyes, blocking him out, blocking everyone out. A tear rolls down my cheek and all I feel is the song, this beautiful thing that I've created out of something so painful. Alana is there to catch me as I fall. Her harmony is my parachute, giving me the strength I need to finish singing.

*Will your heart wait*
*While my heart's breaking?*
*Is it too late to make*
*A second first impression on you?*

The stage is plunged into darkness. I'm surrounded by silence. The kind of silence you could fall into and never come out of. I can barely catch my breath.

'Are you OK?' Alana whispers to me.

The sound of her voice calms me down and almost makes me forget the enormity of what I've done. 'Yeah. Thanks Lan.'

Whatever happens next, I'm not alone. She's right here beside me.

And then I hear it. Clapping. Cheering. Rapturous applause. The lights come up and I can see the whole audience on their feet.

I've just faced my biggest fear in front of everyone I care about and they loved it. Then I realise one person is missing. I desperately scan the crowd of happy, supportive faces searching for that blonde hair or the glint of a camera lens. But he's not there.

Matty is gone.

# CHAPTER
# FORTY-THREE

We are mobbed the second we leave the stage. 'Where can I contact you?' *Handshake, handshake.* 'Do you have my email?' *Pat on the back.* 'Call me on Monday.' *Business card thrust in my face.* 'That was so Taylor meets Sia meets Larkin Poe.' *Embrace.* Woah, personal space boundary breach.

Being engulfed by such a huge cloud of admiration is a serious ego boost and I'm thoroughly enjoying the attention until I catch sight of TJ heading towards me, looking like a dog that's eaten a bee. With ultimate schmooze skills he removes me and Alana from the melee and hisses at us through gritted teeth. 'What the hell was that up there?'

'Erm,' I falter, 'we switched songs last minute.'

'So I heard ...' He ushers us further from the crowd. 'What on Earth were you two playing at? We agreed on the set list and those songs were chosen for a reason.'

'But "Second First Impression" is Meg's best song,' Alana interrupts. 'We couldn't *not* play it. And look at the reaction, everyone loved it.'

TJ stares her down. He's much taller than Alana and her sudden boldness wilts under his glare. 'They may have loved it, but that doesn't necessarily mean they'll want to sign you.'

Intense guilt shoots through me. TJ worked so hard to get everyone down here for our set and we've just thrown a ballad-shaped spanner into the works.

But do I regret our decision? No. Not at all.

'I'm so sorry TJ, but "Scripts" didn't feel right. We wanted to do something more emotional that we could really put our feeling into.'

'Girls, you've got to understand, people don't want to hear ballads as first singles. People want to hear hits. Maybe if it was a topline for a DJ it could work, but ...'

This is nuts. All these people came to see us because of our acoustic song going viral and now TJ is talking about DJ toplines?! How can people love what they hear then want to change everything about it? It's like jumping on bandwagons and following fads is more important than writing something heartfelt. No wonder making an album has driven Caspar crazy.

'OK, I get it. They only want hits and we messed up. I'm sorry if we wasted your time. If you've changed your mind about managing us then ...'

'Woah, woah, woah.' He crosses his arms into an X-shape. 'Stop right there. I never said I didn't want to manage you. Honestly, Meg I've got enough on my hands with Caspar's melodrama, I don't need you losing it on me as well.'

'Fair enough,' I smile with relief.

'And as there are two of you, you're only allowed a 50% melodrama quota each.'

'50%?!' Alana exclaims. 'Are you kidding? I use that up just deciding what to wear each morning.'

TJ groans. 'Look, I get that you want to do things your own way, but please talk to me next time. It's not good for my stress levels to get caught off guard by your risky stunts. I'm here to help you, you know.'

We both nod, and I know from the glint in his eyes that he's genuinely up to the challenge of making things work for us.

'Right, I'm off to introduce the next act. You two behave.' He winks and flashes a wide smile at us. 'You were both brilliant by the way. Absolutely brilliant.'

I feel myself blushing.

'DARLING! MY DARLING MEGGY! AND SWEET, BEAUTIFUL ALANA. COME HERE YOU FABULOUS GIRLS!'

Oh God. Mother incoming. Mother incoming. She barges through the crowd and throws her arms around both me and Alana at once, choking us with her perfume.

'You were so wonderful up there. I was in pieces the entire set! And I live-streamed the whole thing on Facebook, you had 215 viewers! And that's just my friend list so imagine how many people are going to get behind you when you have an official launch!'

I can already see the promotion cogs whirring in her head. It's slightly scary, but also, in a weird way, kind of sweet.

Dad and Laura are following in Mum's wake and if I'm not mistaken Dad actually has tears in his eyes. He squeezes me tightly then gives Alana an awkward Dad hug. 'That was really ... I mean, so ...' He tries to elaborate, fumbling for an appropriate compliment, but words fail him. Instead, he nods proudly. 'Just ... great job.'

'I can't get over it' Laura shrieks at Alana. 'How are you my Dodo Yoyo Alana? Your voice! It's incredible! And you Meg, and you. I'm completely blown away.'

'C-mon L-Dog,' Alana laughs, 'You hear me singing all the time. It's no big surprise.'

'I know, but it's so different with the lights and the microphones and everything. You didn't even get flustered by Dylan. I couldn't believe it when I saw him in the audience. Bloody cheek! Did you know he was going to be here?'

'No I didn't,' Alana replies. 'It's fine though. I guess his curiosity got the better of him.'

I've got to laugh at Alana's ever-optimistic way of framing things. Passive aggressive text message plus intimidating, ex-boyfriend death glare equals curiosity. It's not washing with me, though. I trust him less than a door-to-door salesman and I've got bad vibes about why he was here tonight. On the plus side, though, his weird, unwelcome gate-crashing has shown me how professional Alana is. Once she was on stage, nothing else mattered to her but the music.

Laura starts apologising for spreading the details of our showcase online. Poor Laura. She's got a torrid case of the cyber-runs and can't seem to hold anything in. Like, ever. Mum tries to help her by giving a long speech about media training. I start tuning out, scanning the room for a yellow T-shirt or a camera lens.

'Go find him,' Alana whispers in my ear. 'Before it's too late. I'll cover for you.'

Part of me wants to stay and enjoy the post-gig high and I really shouldn't abandon Alana with my chaotic family, but this could be my last chance. And he might still be here, somewhere.

A wave of sudden urgency hits me. I start excusing my way through the tide of people who are trying to get back into the live room for the next act. I knock someone's drink out of their hands, but I'm too frantic to stop and apologise. My instinct is telling me he's outside, but everyone seems to be blocking my way. Everything is conspiring against me. DAMN IT!

I finally make it down the staircase and throw myself at the heavy fire doors. The cool night air washes over me as I burst outside and try to catch my breath.

I see him. Leaning against the wall with his hands in his pockets. His head is tilted upwards as though he's searching for stars that can't be found in the smoggy night sky. That's the thing about him. No matter how dark it gets, he's always looking for the glimmers of hope.

I'm running on pure adrenaline. My legs are shaking, my heart is racing, and my voice is breaking.

'Matty,' I manage to call out. 'Matty, you're still here!'

He turns towards me, as if in a dream, and looks straight into my eyes. Time builds a suspension bridge between us and it feels like an eternity before he eventually speaks.

'I was so sure it was Alana.'

His words hang in the air like fog. I don't know how to find my way through them.

'I told you our voices don't sound the same,' I finally answer, followed by the most awkward of jittery, nervous laughs.

Why am I laughing? Oh God Meg. Get it together. Don't make this worse than it already is.

Matty takes off his glasses and rubs his eyes, dazed and confused. The silence is excruciating.

'All those conversations,' he mutters. 'All our chats and songs, and *everything*. It was you. This whole time it was you.'

I'm not sure if it's a question or a statement. Either way, I think it deserves an answer.

'I'm sorry.' My voice is barely more than a whisper, but I have to force out some kind of explanation. 'It was wrong of me to lie to you for so long. It's just, once we started talking, I didn't know how to tell you the truth. I thought that you'd see me differently and that everything would change if you knew who I was and who my brother is and all that bullshit that everybody has an opinion on. BandSnapper and LostGirl were perfect and I didn't want anything to ruin it ...'

A police siren is wailing somewhere in the distance. The kick drum thud of the next band is reverberating through the walls of the building. Cigarette smoke lingers in the still night air and my words pathetically float away like litter in the Thames.

'How did you even find me online?' Matty suddenly snaps. 'Did you know it was me?' His anger takes me by surprise and it's unbearable.

'I saw you on *Music Hunger* at school so I joined it to find you.'

'But you *hate* me!' he yells, throwing his arms up wildly. 'You're rude and awful to me all the time. I can't think of a single interaction we've had that hasn't ended in disaster. You literally *hate* me, Meg!'

'I don't hate you!' I cry out. 'I ... I ...' *I love you.* 'I don't hate you. OK?'

Matty rolls his eyes to the sky and starts stuffing his camera into the carry-case over his shoulder. 'Well, you sure could have fooled me.' He closes his bag with a pointed click. 'I can't get my head around any of this. I mean, how can it be you? We've been talking every single day for the past two years ... How can *you* be LostGirl?'

Before I can stop myself, I'm stepping closer and grabbing his arm.

'Why do you think our paths keep crossing? We've got a connection, Matty. I feel so close to you when we chat online and it kills me that I've ruined the chance of knowing you in real life. But I am LostGirl ... and I've been waiting for you to find me.'

Sparks crackle between us. Matty doesn't pull away. His face is so close to mine that I feel his breath on my cheek. I look at him and relive every perfect moment we've ever shared in our virtual world. I know he feels it too. It's undeniable. All the barriers I've built up come crashing down.

'Meg ...'

Matty whispers my name like an invitation. I lean into him and feel the solid warmth of his body. He pulls me in, his hand on the small of my back. My heart sends frantic messages around my bloodstream. I close my eyes desperate to feel his perfect lips on mine ...

And then he lets me go.

'I can't do this. I'm sorry. You lied to me. I don't know who you are. Meg and LostGirl are two totally different people ...'

'No, they're not! They're both me.'

'I feel so stupid. Like nothing we had together was even real.'

I hadn't anticipated how much of a disappointment the truth would be to Matty. What a disappointment *I* would be. But how can I blame him for reacting like this? He's had a story playing in his mind for years and I've completely ruined the ending.

'Look, I have to get back to Victoria. My train leaves in half an hour.'

Matty turns and picks up his camera bag, ready to walk away from me.

'Everything was real,' I say, my words breaking with emotion. 'You believed in me before anyone else did and you're the reason I never gave up.' I swallow hard then let the sentences keep rolling out. 'Matty, you're the kindest, smartest, most passionate boy I've ever met. You've been my anchor when everything around me has been a sea of phoney fakeness. I just couldn't tell you and risk losing everything. I'm so sorry I've been horrible to you. But I didn't mean any of it. You're my *muse*. The song I played tonight was about you. I wrote it for *you*.'

I'm shivering. Suddenly the night feels too cold. Matty gently touches the side of my face.

'Your song was beautiful,' he says. 'It's the best thing anyone has ever done for me.'

*So don't go,* I will in my mind. *Stay here and let's talk this out properly.*

342

'But I … I need some time to make sense of all of this. I'm sorry. I really have to go.'

'Come in the car with us,' I blurt out. 'We can fit you in. We're heading back soon and I'll answer anything you want to ask me. Or not. I'll sit there in total silence if you prefer. Anything.'

Matty laughs. It's so warm and so real. Like a star emerging in the dark above us.

'No, it's OK,' he says. 'I'd rather just …'

*Be literally anywhere other than with you.* Yeah, yeah I get it. No need to elaborate.

'You should enjoy this moment with Alana. You've earned it.'

'OK,' I reply. Because he's right. I shouldn't let this night end with a big heart-breaking drama, even though it's too late and my heart is already breaking.

'You know, I was kind of in awe of you when you first came to our school,' Matty adds, zipping up his jacket. 'You were so cool and intense and interesting. All I wanted was to get to know you. That's why I took that photo of you in the library, the one you freaked out about. I was trying to find a way to talk to you. Who would have guessed that I've actually been talking to you all along?'

I wince at the utter stupidity of my past self. 'But Matty, you know me better than anyone. You know the real me.'

'I don't think *you* know the real you, Meg,' he answers with a sad smile. 'So there's no way I can. Not yet.'

I'm winded. I can't breathe. I open my mouth to get air inside, to find something, anything, to make him stay. But by the time my lungs start working again, he's gone. I'm alone with nothing but the sirens and the pollution and the hidden stars.

*Will your heart wait while my heart's breaking?*
*Is it too late to make a second first impression?*

I guess maybe it is.

# CHAPTER
# FORTY-FOUR

A

Thanks for dropping me off. Can't believe we did it Meg. Was such an amazing night!

It really was. Sorry if I seemed a bit distant on the way home. I swear I'm super excited about where all this will take us.

M

A

Me too. And don't worry, nobody else noticed. You can tell me what happened with Matty at work tomorrow?

Thanks Lan. I'm super proud of you.

M

♫

'Meggy, let's watch your performance! Mum's got it recorded and we're dying to see it again.'

Dad hands me a late-night, celebratory hot chocolate. Wow. Apparently calories don't count tonight. No sign of He-Who-Must-Not-Be-Named. And even more shocking than the calories is that Mum and Dad don't mention him once. They're way too distracted by this evening's events.

'Can we watch it tomorrow?' I ask. 'I'm really tired ...'

'Of course, darling,' Mum replies patting my hand. 'You've worked so hard. Go and get your beauty sleep.'

'Yes, off you go, babygirl. It can wait 'til tomorrow,' says Dad, giving me a hug. 'Get Alana over after work and I'll order takeaway.'

Oh yeah, work. Talk about crashing back down to Earth with an almighty thud.

As I head upstairs I already know it's going be impossible to sleep tonight. My head is swimming with a thousand moments from this evening; singing live for the very first time, the knot of nerves in my stomach, Alana wiping her tears, Mum's ecstatic face in the crowd, TJ's shocked face in the crowd, Matty's confused face in the crowd, Matty putting the pieces together, Matty leaning in to kiss me, Matty turning away ...

*I don't think you know the real you, Meg.*

Yep. Hello insomnia.

Caspar's bedroom door is wide open across the hall. The lights are off, but there's a computer screen shining in the darkness. I guess he's still up. I take a step towards his room, then take a step back. I'm not sure I can deal with my brother right now.

'Meg? You back?' His voice comes out of the darkness.

I don't move. 'Yeah.'

A pause. I keep waiting.

'Hey, come in here a second.'

I hover in the doorway where I can just see him by the light of his computer, slouched at his desk in a black T-shirt and boxers. He turns to face me. 'How was it?'

'Is that a trick question?' I answer, instinctively bristling.

Caspar sighs. 'No. I'm genuinely interested.'

My fingers grip the doorframe as I hang half in, half out of the room. 'Truthfully? It was amazing. I don't know why I've never done it before. Even in front of all those people I got totally lost in the music.'

'I could kind of tell. Your voices worked pretty well together up there.'

I snap the light on, causing Caspar to tut and cover his eyes. 'Jeez, Meg. A little warning would be nice before you blind me, thanks.'

'What do you mean? Were you watching us or something?'

'Yeah,' Caspar mumbles. He won't meet my eye. 'I saw the whole thing on Mum's live-stream.'

So he was spying on us ... probably hoping we would mess the set up.

'It was good. Actually, it was better than good. Look, will you come in already? I'll make sure there are no guitars within smashing distance.'

'Yeah. About that ...' I say, perching on his bed. 'I get paid at the end of next week.'

'Don't worry about it, Meg. I don't need your money. Anyway, how come you didn't play "Scripts" tonight?'

'We changed our minds about it.' It feels beyond weird to be sitting here surrounded by all my brother's music gear talking about *my* songs. 'TJ was annoyed, but it didn't feel quite right for us.'

Caspar turns back to his computer, scrolling aimlessly through his Twitter account as he talks to me. 'Well, it's a good song.'

Typical. He can only give me a compliment when he's got his back to me. 'I didn't know you'd heard it properly.'

'I wasn't gonna *not* hear it after you stole my backing track.'

'You didn't want it! How can it be stealing when you literally threw it out, Cass? That's like binning one of Mum's Croquembouche attempts and then getting annoyed at me for eating it.'

'That's a horrible analogy.' Caspar turns to face me. 'Almost as horrible as that God-awful profiterole pile-up.'

'I know. Who the hell allowed her to watch Bake Off unsupervised anyway?'

Caspar laughs and the ice between us starts to thaw.

'Look, I was angry about the song at first. But then I really listened to it. TJ made me. Like I said, it's a good song.'

'Is that the most you can say about it, Caspar? It's a good song? It's a bloody great song and you know it. Why is it so hard for you to say anything nice to me?'

The smile drops from Caspar's face. 'Woah! Diva reaction

much? I thought we were having a laugh Meg. You don't need to get all frickin' heavy on me.'

'What do you expect, Cass?' I stand up to leave. 'You've been vile to me and Alana. You didn't even come and support us tonight. You have no idea how hard it is to be around you, so I'm sorry if I'm not feeling very receptive to your guilty Mr Nice Guy act.'

'It's not an act,' Caspar snaps back. 'I genuinely like your song, OK? And I ...' He pauses. 'I wondered if I could cut it on my album? I mean, if you guys don't want it.'

Of all the things I expected to come out of Caspar's mouth, a request for our song was not on the list. It wouldn't have even made my Top 5.

'You ...' My legs give out and I sit back on the bed. '*You* want to sing our song?'

Caspar shrugs. 'I like it. I think it could work. Maybe even for a single. You know, with some tweaks. If we make it a bit less girly and stuff.'

I personally know, more than anyone else, how intensely pedantic Caspar has been about his upcoming album. This is more than a big deal. This is a huge, enormous, galactic-sized deal that breaks through the stratosphere of my little world. Even though he's making out like it's nothing at all.

'Let me get this straight. You want "Scripts" to be your comeback single?'

He runs his hand through his hair. Playing it cool. 'Yeah, potentially. If you guys don't mind giving it away.'

'I'd have to talk to Alana. But ... I think she'd be open to it.'

Everything is falling into place in my mind. We loved 'Scripts', but something was holding us back from performing it. Now I can see it's because it was never *our* song. It was destined to be with someone else.

And that someone else might just be my brother.

'It would be a huge break for you,' Caspar adds. 'A single with me would basically launch you two as songwriters. TJ could make a big story out of it, you know, blow up the *McCarthyBrand*.'

Firstly, he's asking to sing my song. Secondly, he's actually laughing at himself the tiniest bit. What is going on here?

'Why are you doing this?' I ask. 'I thought you wanted to write all your own songs?'

Caspar glances at his notebooks of unfinished lyrics scattered on the floor. 'Yeah, well my own stuff is getting me nowhere fast. But this song ... Well, it makes sense to me. It feels like what I've been trying to say to my fans ... Only I haven't been able to get the words out right.'

*Scripts make every word*
*Sound beautiful*
*But I've got nothing to follow*
*Nothing to follow*

*And I will say the wrong thing*
*Every time, but now I know*
*The cliche you wanna hear*
*Is nothing but hollow*

I wrote those words for Matty. About how tongue-tied he makes me feel when we're face-to-face. About how I always get things so wrong. About wishing I could be a better version of myself for him.

It never once occurred to me that my brother could feel the same way. Only, he feels it about his thousands of fans. All the pressure and expectation has made him doubt his own voice just like I do. Suddenly I understand why Caspar wants to sing our song. He needs a script to follow as much as anyone.

For a while we sit there in awkward silence until Caspar turns back to Twitter, effectively ending our heart-to-heart.

'OK ... Let's talk about this more in the morning, yeah?' I say, shuffling off the bed awkwardly.

He nods. 'Yeah, OK.'

As I leave his room, wondering if this is all some cruel prank, Caspar calls after me. 'Meg, I know I've been difficult since I moved back home. It's just, there's such a lot riding on me, you know? I don't want to let my fans down. I don't want to let anyone down.'

I can't remember the last time my brother confided in me. However much of a pain Caspar is, his fans are important to him. He doesn't take them for granted. And all those cruel words floating around on the Internet hurt him just as much as they hurt anyone.

'You're not going to let them down,' I reply. 'Not if you love what you're writing.'

'That's the problem,' he answers with a humourless laugh. 'I don't. I'm so stuck in my own head that I don't even know what's good or bad anymore. It's all become a massive blur. I think your song reminded me of how music used to make me feel. That's why I loved it so much.'

He loved it. He just said he loved it. An unexpected thrill shoots through me. Of all the incredible moments that have happened in the last twenty-four hours, this one might mean the most to me.

'I shouldn't have said all that negative stuff ... I'll apologise properly to Alana. I went too far and she must think I'm a total douche.'

'No kidding ...'

'It's just that this industry is really tough, Meg, and I know how quickly it can swallow you up. TJ's been there for me since the beginning and I literally don't know what I'd do without him ...'

'I'm not trying to take him from you,' I interrupt. 'He's *your* manager and you come first. He offered to help us, that's all.'

'OK, I get it.'

'OK.'

There is so much more I want to talk about, but I don't know how.

'Can you switch the light back off?' Caspar says, dismissing me.

I hit the switch but something keeps me lingering in the doorway a moment longer. Before I can stop myself, I speak softly into the darkness.

'You know you're the reason I started writing, don't you? You were my idol when we were growing up. I loved watching all your YouTube videos. You inspired me to pick up the guitar and all I've ever wanted to do is write a song half as good as one of yours.'

Silence. Is he even listening to me?

'So, forget about everything else and write because you love it. You've got nothing to worry about, Cass. You're so bloody talented.'

There is still no answer. Sighing, I decide to give up and go back to my room.

'Thanks Meg,' he replies quietly as I'm walking away. Then so softly that I barely hear it, '... you are too.'

# CHAPTER FORTY-FIVE

**TWO WEEKS LATER**

As you know by now, I'm a huge fan of lists. When the rest of the world is spinning wildly off its axis, lists can make sense of the chaos. They're grounding.

So, in an effort to keep myself sane in the last two whirlwind weeks, I've written more lists than Santa gets in December. Because, as Alana and I have discovered, a lot can change in fourteen days. And in some cases, nothing changes at all.

**Top 5 Key Developments From the Last Two Weeks:**

1. We didn't sign a record deal

Yep. It turns out TJ was right about the set list choice.

Even though the audience at our showcase seemed to love 'Second First Impression', it wasn't quite enough to convince any companies to sign us. Maybe playing 'Scripts' would have made a difference. Or maybe it wouldn't. We'll never know now and there's no point dwelling on it.

It's not all bad news, though. We made good contacts that night, and loads of influential people are keeping us on their radar. So for now we're having fun being creative, finding our sound, and writing songs that we're proud of. When the time is right, I'm sure someone will want to back us – someone who loves our music for what it is not just because of that random viral video.

And in the meantime, we have the best person ever supporting us. Because ...

2. We did sign a management deal

It's officially in writing! Lost Girls are now managed by TJ of *Lonestar Management*.

Alana and her parents came over for an official celebration with my whole family (yes, even Caspar). Mum's cooking is sketchy to say the least so thankfully she decided not to risk a re-run of her famous pears-in-concrete dessert disaster and splashed out on a catered buffet instead.

We've signed a two-year contract and TJ's already making plans. His list looks something like this. *1. Build up our social media presence 2. Record an EP in his studio 3. Make a music video 4. Get a radio-plugger 5. Get support slots with his signed artists.* (Yes, this is a list within a list. It's list-ception. Deal with it.)

## 3. We kept working the day job

Reality bites and we're not playing the O2 yet. TJ's going to fund our studio time, but unfortunately nothing else comes for free so I'll be sporting the cross-eyed dodo cap for a while yet. Laura has asked me to keep working weekends and I reckon I can juggle it with sixth form. At least I've got my partner-in-crime working there with me.

## 4. The boys in our lives are keeping very quiet

Alana hasn't heard a thing from Dylan since he crashed our showcase. I have no idea what he was trying to achieve by showing up uninvited, but if his intention was to rattle her into messing up, he seriously underestimated her strength of character.

Cyber-fame can cause issues and I can't shake this horrible feeling that she hasn't seen the last of him. One sniff of success and all the cockroaches come crawling out of their dark, damp holes. I don't trust him. Not one little bit. He's got dark, damp cockroach written all over him. However, he'll have to get past me if he thinks he's scuttling back into Alana's life any time soon.

As for a certain blonde haired, blue-eyed photographer ... Silence. I've not had a single message or email from him since he left me standing alone on the pavement outside TJ's studios. I've tried to reach out. About a week into the silent treatment I couldn't stand it anymore and I sent him this list.

**LostGirl:** Top 5 Songs About Being Sorry:

1. Sorry – Halsey
2. I'm So Sorry – Kitty, Daisy & Lewis
3. Sorry – Nothing But Thieves
4. I miss you, I'm sorry – Gracie Abrams
5. Sorry – Justin Bieber

I've had no reply and there's not much I can do about it. He either accepts LostGirl and Meg are one and the same or he doesn't.

I keep telling myself that he needs some space to come to terms with all of my lies. But, then again, maybe the thought of *me* being his biggest confidant is so sickening that he'll never speak to me again.

Oh God. Going back to college in September is going to be fun. Not ... Anyway, moving on.

## 5. Caspar has found his inspiration

Who knows what triggered it, but last Wednesday morning Caspar woke up and instead of procrastinating for an entire day then going out partying, he locked himself in his room and actually wrote a song.

And then he wrote another. And another. He's been writing every day and quite often during the night too. Whenever I pass his bedroom I can hear him singing or playing piano or guitar.

Personally, I think taking 'Scripts' has freed him of whatever anxiety was holding him back. Maybe he thinks he can blame everything on us if the song flops. But hey. I'm just happy to see him being creative again rather than stomping around the house like a T-Rex with IBS.

And get this: he's back on stage too! This is why Alana and I are now in the very same live room where we played our showcase. Only this time, we're in the audience.

TJ has been so impressed with Caspar's new songs that he set up this special, live-streamed, acoustic performance. It's a way for him to test out the new material and reconnect with his most dedicated fans. It's also a way for TJ to reassure Caspar that he hasn't given up on him.

Seeing him sitting in the centre of the stage, acoustic guitar in hand, gives me a rush of pride. It's the same feeling I had when his first single came out and he would play these lovely, intimate gigs. He looks so natural up there and his voice is strong, deep, and resonant with a slight husk in the high notes. Hearing his hits stripped down in this setting is a treat for everyone and the new songs are met with whooping and cheering. I don't know why Caspar was worried about letting down his fans. They seem to love him more than ever.

'Thanks guys. I've really missed doing this.' More clapping, screaming, and hysteria. 'I'm going to play another new song for you now. This one might be my next single. Let's see how it goes.'

Caspar melts another few hearts with one of his trademark crooked smiles as he starts strumming the opening chords of 'Scripts'. Alana mouths the words 'He's playing our song!' at me, as if I don't know that he's playing our song. It's beyond surreal to hear our words coming out of his mouth, but it's as if they were always meant for him. He owns them.

I look around the room and take in the reaction of Caspar's fans. They're loving it. I feel weirdly emotional. This is a song that *we* wrote. The thought of so many strangers humming along, listening in their cars, adding it to their playlists, and learning our lyrics is overwhelming. This could be a song that really means something to them, like all the incredible, special songs that make up the soundtrack to my life.

Once again the audience erupts when Caspar finishes.

'Thanks so much,' Caspar says, visibly pleased with the reaction. 'That song was actually written by my sister Meg and her friend Alana.' He points over to our table and we wave self-consciously at the people surrounding us. 'They're working on some big things at the moment, so keep an eye on them.'

WOAH THERE! He just gave us a public thank you. A public endorsement. Is this for real?

'I'm gonna play another new one,' he continues, tuning up his guitar as he speaks. 'It's one of mine this time. Hope you guys like it.'

This is the first song of the set that I haven't actually heard yet. He starts strumming a rhythmic chord sequence that draws everyone in. I'm so curious about what he's been writing and I lean in closer as he starts to sing.

*She comes knocking at my door*
*Asking questions I don't answer*
*What did I do that for?*
*She comes looking for advice*
*Wish that I was open but I shut her out each time*

*And she's never gonna hear me say I'm sorry*
*For all the times I've taken up her light*
*And I know she's hurting*
*She thinks I haven't noticed*
*That I've got to move aside*
*Coz she's waiting to take flight ...*

It takes a moment for the lyrics to creep under my skin. For the words to be absorbed into my bloodstream. Alana shoves my arm, 'Meg, it's about you,' she whispers. 'You've inspired him!'

I shake my head in disbelief. Caspar keeps singing and suddenly I'm so moved that tears spill from my eyes and roll down my cheeks. This is everything he can't say to my face. He's far too proud to speak to me in uncomfortable, starchy words. So instead he's singing to me. It's the only way he knows how.

> *So she beats her wings*
> *Steps out of my shadow*
> *Ready to fly away*
> *She beats her wings*
> *Her own path to follow*
> *I won't stand in her way*
> *Coz everything changes, changes*
> *Nothing will stay the same*
> *She beats her wings*
> *Steps out of my shadow*

Our whole relationship flashes before my eyes, a lifetime of trying to catch up to my moody, difficult, brilliant brother. I am stunned at the honesty of his lyrics. Finally he's acknowledging my side of the story and how tough it has been living in his shadow. He sees me. For the first time in years I feel a weight lifting, floating away with the fading guitar chords.

Caspar catches my eye for the slightest fraction of a second. It's enough for an unspoken moment to flicker between us, unnoticed by the rest of the cheering crowd.

And then it's gone. The moment has passed and I realise I've probably got mascara running down my face. As I search in my handbag for some tissues, my phone flashes with a new message alert.

My heart stops.

It's from BandSnapper.

It's hardly the time or the place to read something that could very well break my heart, but I'm not sure I'll be able to focus on anything else if I don't look at it.

I'm a tearful, trembling mess as I open the message under the table. I was hoping for a long and detailed reply, but there's only one sentence.

> **BandSnapper:** I said I didn't know the real you, but I think this photo proves otherwise.
> Matty xx

Attached is a black and white photo and I immediately know it was taken at our showcase while I was singing 'Second First Impression'. My eyes are closed and my mouth is open as a lone tear streaks down my cheek. I look ethereal. Other-worldly. Like there's nothing separating my body from the passion flowing through me. Just behind my shoulder, Alana is a powerful presence silhouetted at the piano. We balance each other out, creating a strong and perfect picture of intense, strange beauty.

'Oh my God,' Alana gasps, grabbing my phone off me. 'Is this one of Matty's pictures?'

'Shh, Alana, we can't talk about it now.'

'But it's stunning!' she whispers. 'We should totally use this for our EP.'

It is stunning. Matty has caught something raw and honest and true. It's the kind of elusive, magic photo that becomes an iconic album cover. And it's of us.

Before I can say anything more Caspar's voice interrupts me, announcing the next song. 'So this is one me and Meg used to sing all the time. It was the first song I taught her on guitar, so she'd better remember it.'

Wait. Wait. What? Everyone is looking at me expectantly.

'I'd like to invite my sister to the stage ...'

Oh. My. God. No.

Alana pushes me. 'Go on Meg, get up there and show them what you're made of!'

Without further warning, Caspar starts strumming the old, familiar chords of 'Learn To Fly' by Foo Fighters.

The LostGirl of three weeks ago would have crawled under the nearest table, but today's Meg has no choice.

My cheeks are flushing and my pulse is racing as I pick my way through the crowd and take my place on the stage next to my brother. He plays the intro around one more time and then, with a cheeky wink, counts us in.

We're back in his bedroom. I'm eleven and he's fourteen. We're singing together on a Saturday morning just because we love the song so much. Just because we love music so much.

Alana is up out of her chair punching the air. Dad has his arm around Mum's shoulder and they are both beaming with delight. TJ has folded his arms in approval, nodding along with a satisfied smile on his face, and Caspar's fans are watching in wide-eyed wonder.

The future is a scary thing, but I'm not frightened to be myself anymore.

It feels like I've finally found the real me.

I take a deep breath, close my eyes, and let my voice soar.

# ABOUT THE AUTHORS

Becky Jerams is a singer-songwriter and YA author from the coastal town of Portsmouth, UK. She has written songs for films, Disney TV shows, adverts and international artists including the popular K-pop group, Red Velvet. Becky began writing fiction and sharing her stories on Wattpad, where she gained over 2 million reads. When she's not writing, Becky enjoys watching films and going to the theatre with her husband, playing gigs and meeting artists in her local community.

 @beckyjerams

Ellie Wyatt is a BAFTA-winning songwriter and musician from Brighton, UK. She has written music for a wide range of films, TV shows and adverts. Her musical journey first began with touring in a band, session work and teaching music. She then went on to become a professional composer, creating numerous scores and themes tunes for CBeebies, Sesame Street and other children's TV. Ellie is passionate about the arts and is a committed environmental campaigner. She lives with her husband and daughter by the sea.

 @elliewyattmusic

## Our Top 5 Thank Yous:

1. Huge thanks to our agent, the lovely Gill McLay at Bath Literary Agency, for believing in the concept of a 'Booksical' and sticking with it through the ups and lockdowns. We've finally made it a reality!

2. Thanks to the music-loving team at Sweet Cherry: Cecilia, for totally getting it and making editing fun; Divia, for your belief and hard work; Ashley, for your perspective; Sophie for the beautiful cover art.

3. A special thank you to our fantastic producers Jonathan Owusu-Yianomah, Jack Ruston, Jussi Nikula and Jonas Wallin, and the incredible voices of Megan Tuck and Cathal Murphy, for bringing our songs to life.

4. Massive thanks from Becky to: Mum for being my biggest fan and for always talking through plot holes with me; Dad for always supporting my dreams; Paul Lees for book club and real true talk; St. John Crabtree for early feedback;

Katie Paxton for being my beta reader and YALC-buddy; Sazzie Mcintosh, Hannah Knox, Corinna Jane, and Sophie Dewing for all your kindness and support; my real-life Matty for absolutely everything.

A great big thank you from Ellie to: Mum, Dad, Chloe and Alicia for always cheering me on; Rosie Flint and Jasper Gibson for the early encouragement; our first enthusiastic readers at Burgess Hill Girls;  David Burkman for helping me out of the shadows and encouraging me to write; my own BandSnapper, Andy, for inspiring so many songs and always wanting to listen; Alice for being my most treasured reader, and for making my heart sing.

5. Finally, thank you to pop music ...
You've always been there for us.

For support and advice for your mental wellbeing, please contact your local healthcare provider or:

**United Kingdom:**

**Calm (Campaign Against Living Miserably)**
Phone: +44 (0)800 58 58 58
www.thecalmzone.net

**Mind**
Phone: +44 (0)300 123 3393
www.mind.org.uk

**Samaritans**
Phone: 116 123
www.samaritans.org

**Young Minds**
Phone: +44 (0)808 802 5544
www.youngminds.org.uk

**Worldwide:**

**Befrienders**
www.befrienders.org

**Crisis Textline**
www.crisistextline.org